Dead Birds

By the same author

Dead Birds

John Milne

HAMISH HAMILTON LONDON

First published in Great Britain 1986
by Hamish Hamilton Ltd
27 Wrights Lane London W8 5TZ

Copyright © 1986 by John Milne

British Library Cataloguing in Publication Data

Milne, John, *1952–*
    Dead birds.
    I. Title
    823'.914[F]   PR6063.I3787

ISBN 0–241–11921–9

Filmset by Input Typesetting Ltd, London
Printed in Great Britain by
St Edmundsbury Press Ltd, Bury St Edmunds, Suffolk

To Pierre Hodgson and
Virginia Bonham Carter,
who both encouraged me
when I first began to write

Preface

Sometimes I have this nightmare, only it doesn't go away because it's true.

I'm sitting in the wheelman's chair of a small boat, the kind of fishing boat that's built for pleasure-fishing, not work. It's a modern, white-painted boat and there's a blue canvas canopy over my head. The canvas stretches over all the stern part of my boat. It looks like a rich, blue-shaded sky. A sky that protects, not burns. Not like the one outside. The sun in the real sky outside is fierce, even though it's well after noon. Outside the canopy is brilliant white light from the afternoon sky. Outside the canopy is white-painted decking reflecting the light.

I shift out of the wheelman's chair and squeeze my eyes up so I can look along the decking. I can see a seagull. The seagull is my friend.

We're on the Mediterranean Sea, about twenty miles south of Malaga; I don't exactly know where and it doesn't matter much. I can't be bothered to work out where I am. Twenty miles off Malaga will do. I reckon we should have another three hours before we reach our destination. By then it'll be dark. I'm very tired for no real reason and finding it hard to concentrate, so I decide to tell the seagull a little about myself.

'I'm going to tell you about myself, Mr Seagull, whether you're talking to me or not. I'm going to tell you a little of my story.'

The seagull didn't move. He didn't leap up and down and applaud me or anything . . . well, I didn't expect him to. He said nothing. I said nothing for a long time after that

1

too. The only sounds were of the engines throbbing and the splash of the swell against our bows. Sometimes a glass bottle rolled back and forth in the cabin. I could hear the hollow sound. The bottle never seemed to roll in time with the boat's motions.

I tied up the wheel with rope, so that I shouldn't have to steer, and turned my attention to the seagull again. I said, 'My story's a detective story. I never dreamed how I'd get it, just like I never dreamed how I'd become a detective.'

I stared at the seagull. I waited, unreasonably, for a response. I got none. Maybe I was mistaken. Maybe he wasn't my friend. Suddenly I wanted to walk up the narrow gangway and kick the seagull over the side. I couldn't manage it, though, and I couldn't reach him from the steering-well.

'I always wanted to be a detective. When I was at school I dreamed of being a detective. When I left school I became a policeman. First a cadet, then a constable. Always wanting to be a detective. That was me . . . always wanting to be a detective.'

I rubbed my face and thought of my early days as a copper. All 'where's your road fund licence, sir?' and seeing old ladies across the road. To become a detective in the real world you needed an alarmingly high arrest-rate on real criminals or you needed to look like a prospect to your governor. I had had no chance on either count. The seagull didn't know that. I didn't tell him either. There's no point in making excuses to a seagull.

'I transferred to the West End of London. I thought it'd be more exciting. In the West End there's vice and drugs and all sorts of big-time thievery. There's embassies and royals and I suppose I thought, "If this isn't a bit more exciting I'll knock the whole business on the head." That's what I thought. If I didn't get any joy in the West End I'd give up wanting to be a detective and I'd give up being a copper. I'd become a television repair man or something. That was a laugh.'

We were both quiet for a long time. No one laughed. I said, 'I had a career in the West End, okay. I'll tell you.'

Again I was silent, again the bird made no comment. I told him anyway.

2

'My brief and spectacular career as a copper in the West End lasted three days only. My companion, my shower-round during these three days was a youngster, a flash-Harry called Willy. What a big head he was!

' "I can't show you who the villains are, James," he said, "because they could all be villains. That's how this place is. Don't think just because some Henry's in a Roller he's not a prospect . . . he may well be. Same goes for the old IC3s . . . just because a bloke's a darkie it doesn't mean he's necessarily a prospect round here. He might be a senior diplomat. He could be anyone. It'll work out well if you don't pull any diplomats on sus or something." '

'I said I knew.

' "You don't know," he said. "This isn't Romford." He took off his helmet, wiped his forefinger along his brow, looked at the sweat on his finger, then waved the hand at the street. He said no more on the subject of geography, just marched off and began talking to a copper in a flat hat at the corner of the street.

' "This is big Andy, Diplomatic Protection. Andrew Tyson . . . James Jenner." '

'Big Andy nodded. He was built like a barn door and you could see his gun, even under his loose-fitting tunic. Willy said, "Andy here is charged with making sure the bloody Ay-rabs don't wander up and down Regent Street, shooting each other. As they are wont to do, I might warn you. Andy's specific job is. . . ." '

I broke off. I'm not such a barmy as to go round explaining myself to seagulls. I just needed to talk. I was tired. The image of Andrew Tyson, the Diplomatic Protection Group policeman I'd met all those years ago in Regent Street, stayed with me. I leaned back in the wheelman's chair and closed my eyes. I'd only met him for a few minutes but his face had stayed with me. The sun beat down on my boat's canopy and I was thousands of miles and some ten years away from it but still that man's image was in my mind. I was so tired. I slept in the chair and I dreamed of Tyson's face and Willy's tough guy talk. I dreamed of Regent Street. Regent Street is my nightmare.

*

I awoke with a jolt. I'd only meant to doze, to 'rest my eyes'. I must have slept for some time though. The sun was descending in the west. By luck – or someone else's good seamanship – I hadn't bumped into any other boats. The sea had become heavy while I'd dozed and it was the force of the bows smacking into one of these waves which had woken me. My neck hurt and I was shivering. I couldn't go into the cabin for a sweater. I sat back in the wheelman's chair and thought about Regent Street and Willy and all that stuff again. I'd gone to sleep thinking of it and I'd woken thinking of it.

I was thinking of Andrew Tyson's face, then I was thinking about a grey BMW with a couple of fellows sitting in it. They didn't look like tourists. Tyson saw the car as I did. The passenger jumped out and did a runner, I could see the driver leaning forward under the dash. I could see a wire in his hand, too. The man I was chasing turned suddenly and faced me. I stopped dead. He held a pistol in his hand. Suddenly I went deaf and did a somersault all at once. I never saw my Arab again. I found out later he'd gone through a shop window. Just as I found out later Big Andy had gone through some railings. I was on the floor. Bits of BMW, Willy and Arab-two rained all around me. I turned and saw the smouldering bottom panel of the BMW. Its tyres were on fire. A big black column of smoke was going into the air.

Women began to scream, a man came running. He shouted. 'This one's hurt, this one's hurt!' and I thought, 'Poor bastard, who's that?'

The man shouted, 'Oh, he's lost his foot. Oh God, he's lost his foot.'

I tried to stand and help but I fell over immediately. It was me who'd lost the foot. I kept blacking out but I remember the man crying and saying I was going to die and whispering Catholic prayers to me. I remember twisting my head and looking at the burning car.

Newly woken, shivering and tired, I rubbed my face on my coat and wondered which BMW image I'd really woken with, the grey car or the smouldering wreck. There was no way of knowing. Five minutes out of a dream and it seems impossible to grasp it at all. The story in Regent Street was

4

true, though. My true story. Not a dream at all. It was a memory.

That's my story. It's my true story and that's how I told it to a dead seagull lying on the decking of my borrowed fishing-boat. The bird was on its side on the decking and blood had run from its head, smearing red-brown on the brilliant white decking. Talking to a dead bird is crazy, but I don't think I was that afternoon. Just tired and lonely and tense.

The heavy seas broke over our bows a little now. Spume and salt-spray flew past the sides of the hull. One wave washed the seagull over the side. So much for telling stories to dead birds. The sun was dropping quickly, like a piece of red steel from a forge, liquid and angry. The white glare of the sea around me had transformed to orange and red fragments, the sun's rays shattered between the black shadows of the waves. I switched the marine radio on and clicked from channel to channel, searching for an English voice; I mean an *English*-English voice, not just the language. Somewhere out there would be an English voice.

I untied the rope from the steering wheel, turned up the motors a little and peered into the setting sun for some sign of land. The hint of a shoreline came as darkness fell, then electric lights showed, became bolder and bolder and I left off the navigation lights and let the boat bob towards the shore. I picked up the microphone to the marine radio, clicked over to coastguard calling frequency and said, 'This is A-Alpha A-Alpha C-Charlie Eight, fishing vessel from Malaga. Are you receiving me? Over.'

No reply.

'This is A-Alpha A-Alpha C-Charlie Eight, fishing vessel from Malaga. Are you receiving me, coastguard? Over.'

Still no reply. I tried several more times but all I got for an answer was a squawk from the loudspeaker. I clicked the send button again and shouted into the mike, 'This is A-Alpha A-Alpha C-Charlie Eight, fishing vessel. Are you receiving me, coastguard? Over!'

No reply. I was close enough to the electric strip to see the navigation lights of a fast-moving craft separating from it. I was about eight miles from the shore then, I guessed. I had only the strip of electric light with which to guide the guess. No moon had risen and I seemed suddenly surrounded by inky darkness. I guessed the fast-moving craft was a coastguard craft and that it was about four miles from the shore and the same again from me. Sometimes its lights would merge with those on the shoreline and I'd think it wasn't there, but then I'd see the navigation lights again. I decided to let the craft come close before I would switch my lights on. In case it wasn't coming for me.

The lights kept coming and I kept chugging towards the shore. I cut the engines and turned my lights on. My fishing boat bobbed around in the waves as if it was a dinghy. I could see the outline of the approach craft now. It was a big, fast military boat. It looked to be travelling three times as fast as my fishing boat ever could and it was coming straight for me. I sat in the wheelman's chair and shivered against the cold and waited. I didn't have to wait long.

·One

It started in London, as things do. I was working for myself as a private detective and enquiry agent. I had a writ to deliver for a woman on her ex-husband. I think it was about money, I'm not sure. I didn't care and I didn't read the writ or even bother to ask the solicitor who gave me the job what it was for. They're usually for money owed or children sought. My part in the business was to make sure I had the right guy, slap the writ on him, pick up my pay cheque and be prepared to stand in court to swear that I'd done just that. In fact I never swear in court, I always affirm . . . it comes to the same.

The serving of such a writ should be a routine matter, can even be done by post in more usual circumstances. These were not usual circumstances. The man I was delivering the writ to was a boxer called Tommy Lynch . . . or as the writ had it 'Thomas Edward Charles Lynch'. He was a little cockney lad and he boxed as little cockney lads do, with fire and gusto and not a little street sense. What made him different to the others was that he was a world championship prospect, the first for many years at his weight, and I was given the writ to serve just a day before his world title eliminator fight with a man called Diaz.

I took the writ to Tommy's home. He wasn't there. His girlfriend said he wasn't there, he wasn't coming back and she didn't know where he could be found.

'He trained in Yorkshire for the last fight,' she said.

'All of it or any particular part?'

She frowned and said, 'Or was it Scotland?' She meant it, too.

I tried his manager's office. The manager was called George Duncan and he had a gym in Smithfield and an office there. I phoned the office and they said they were setting up a special press bureau for the Lynch/Diaz fight.

'I'm not a pressman.' I said.

'All Lynch enquiries will be dealt with there. Mr Duncan says this fight mustn't disturb the other boxers. I'll give you the number.'

'I said I'm not a. . . .'

But she read me the number and gave me the address anyway and then put the phone down. I should have just such a middle-aged female dragon working for me, overseeing the credentials of every nutter who comes knocking on my door. I should be so lucky. I went to the place in Shoreditch where the office was supposed to be, but I met with another stone-walling secretary. She was younger than the one I'd met on the phone, about twenty-five with hennaed hair and a smocked dress but she wasn't as much of a drip as she looked and she gave me the class 'A' runaround. No, I could not have the address of Mr Lynch's training ground; no, she could not even tell me whether it was in Scotland, Ireland, Wales or England. Is it in America? I asked. She looked sternly over a pair of glasses big enough to grow cucumbers under and said she wasn't prepared to give any indication.

'Where's Mr Duncan, then?' I asked.

'I can't say.'

'What *can* you say?' I said.

'Here.' She gave me a sheet with PRESS RELEASE splashed in red across the top. 'I can tell you any of that.'

'Thanks. Thanks a lot.'

I went and sat in my car. After twenty minutes or so a green Jaguar XJ6 pulled up. I'd seen George Duncan a few times before – I used to use a gym he owned – and I recognised him as he got out. He was a big, grey-haired man in a blue chalk-stripe suit. He was aged about fifty with big, floppy jowls, grey eyes and burst red blood vessels on the upper part of his cheeks and the end of his nose. He had a cigar like a log and as he left the car he tapped the ash from his cigar into the gutter, as if he didn't care to have the Jag filled with cigar ash. The driver of the Jag was obviously a minder as well as a driver. Six feet two, about seventeen stone with a suit he seemed to be bursting out of and a big red neck that really did burst out of the suit to support his bullet head and ugly face. I recognised him, too. Harry Whitlock, former British heavyweight prospect. Hard as nails and always led with his chin. He had looked good until he'd met the champion, Bugner, back in the mid-seventies and Bugner had had a big enough punch to hit him right on the chin and draw the curtains on Harry Whitlock's short career as a British title prospect. Driving cars was what Harry had been reduced to . . . so much for the big time.

Duncan was in the office for ten minutes, then he and Harry came out to the Jag and set off north. I followed.

Seven a.m. the next morning found me parked in a layby in Chigwell. There are some big houses in Chigwell and Lynch was in one of them, about fifty yards from my layby. I'd followed George Duncan and Harry Whitlock here the day before from Shoreditch. I had tailed them carefully but I needn't have bothered. Harry Whitlock was no better as a minder than he was as a boxer. His driving was a bit irregular, too, swerving between the kerb and the white line. Duncan would've been better off if Harry had only been charged with polishing the Jag. It had a nice coat of polish.

Today was the day of the big fight. It was a grey May day and I sat in the layby sipping Thermos tea and waiting for something to happen. Rain splashed around me and I kept the windows nearly closed. I had a *Daily Mail* on my lap, a newspaper I don't often buy, but they'd just done a piece on me and the journalist said it would be in today. It was. Under the headline 'HOPALONG COPALONG' and the byline 'By Eric Brand' it said, '*James Jenner is a retired policeman running a private detection business. Nothing wrong with that . . . except Jenner has only one foot and is deaf in one ear, the result of the horrific injuries inflicted on him in the Regent Street Embassy Bombing. After seven years as one of our boys in blue and a further two recovering from his injuries it looked like Jenner's cherished ambition, to be a detective,*

9

had slipped from his grasp. I can reveal now, though, that not only has Jenner established his own detective agency, but his super-sleuth skills were responsible for the return of Nati Saud, a distant member of the Saudi royal family and the girl at the centre of the "Drugs in Rolls Royce scandal" . . .'

And so it went on. There was a picture of me, too, looking as gormless as only newspaper photographs could make a man look. The technique is to get five hundred quid's worth of Minolta or Nikon, put a wide-angle lens on it, shove it into the face of some hapless interviewee and take a picture a two-year-old shaking with ague could have got from a Box Brownie. The article stank; well, they all do. I'd been forced into it by Brand, the journalist, simply because I *had* to explain what he already knew.

The girl had done a runner from her family in London. The little I know about Saudi families makes that reasonable. What no one could have considered reasonable was the information, given to me by the police when I became involved, that the girl had a drug problem and had been using the family's diplomatic corps Roller to import the stuff. Import, I should add, in quantities large enough to supply a small town. Hence the family row, hence the girl doing a runner. She was pretty easy to find, but finding her was a diplomatic problem . . . she was a diplomat's daughter, the father was important somehow to us, no one wanted to drag them through the legal system. The answer for the drug squad, who'd located the girl, was to get her father to hire a private detective to 'find' her, then have the private detective advise the girl and her father that they'd be better off in Riyadh than Reading, and wouldn't they like to take the Roller for one last drive to Heathrow?

All that meant using a private detective the police involved in the case could trust. After all, not only did they not want a Saudi in a British prison, they also didn't want anyone to know that that was the way things were. Since several of the coppers in the case knew me and knew I could be trusted to keep my mouth shut I was 'volunteered'. It all went as sweet as a nut. I went to Keighley (that's right *Keighley*) 'found' the girl, flushed the suspicious white powder down the loo, drove her back to London. The family headed off to Heathrow. I was given a pat on the back and

10

a fat fee by the father, and for all I know the girl was buried alive in the Arabian sands. She was a nasty piece of work and I really didn't care.

Then Brand turned up. He's a freelancer, a pasty-faced little Fleet Street porker, with washed-out blue eyes, a permanently half-shaven chin and a greasy headful of sandy hair. He was making a living in Fleet Street on the strength of his wits and his contacts. His wits were no good. His contacts were formidable. Eventually he broke the 'Princess and Drugs' scandal (though the girl was not a princess), then started pressuring me for an angle. I blanked him, but he must have had a contact either in the drugs squad or Whitehall, because he had the story better than I did. After four weeks of fobbing him off I'd given him the highly edited version that was in the *Daily Mail*: that I'd found the girl at her father's request, that I knew nothing about the alleged existence of a bag of cocaine, that I'd driven her back to London and passed her on to Daddy and they'd paid me off and headed for Saudi. As Brand had put it, '*This brave young man had been duped into becoming an agent for a foreign power while our own police had been left completely in the dark. Jenner was blameless in the affair, of course, while a spokesman from Scotland Yard told me, "We have no information on this matter, and so I can't comment." '*

In other words a politician, a diplomat, a senior policeman, the Customs and Excise service, maybe even the Saudis themselves, someone was settling a score through Brand. I suppose I should have been grateful to come out of it with two grand and not completely stinking as far as my name went. Brand certainly considered I owed him a favour . . . but then *he* would. I felt as if no copper would ever trust me again.

Trying to look on the bright side, I supposed that the *Mail* article would drum up some work. It doesn't hurt to have your name in the papers. But then you always know the kind of work you'd get from that sort of publicity would all be rubbish. I've had it all before, scrawly written letters with, 'Dear Mr Jenner Esq. I no you are a good detective and wonder if you wood be so kind as to help find my beloved Tiddles, who I have lost by leveing the back door

11

a jar last week. We have serched high and low for him and are gettin desperate. Enclosed I have put five pounds as a fee. Plese rite and tell me if there is change . . . yrs kindest, Dorothy Perkins (ps I am a poor old lady of 75).'

I know *all* about newspaper publicity. It costs me a fortune in stamps to send their wrinkled-up fivers back. I folded the paper angrily and slapped the steering wheel with it. A headline on the back page said, '*Will Lynch do it again?*' Good question. Diaz obviously thought Lynch would not. I stared down the rainy road for what seemed like a week but was in fact forty minutes, then a green Jaguar nosed out of the hedgerow and was quickly over-taken by a very small man wearing a grey tracksuit with the hood up. The Jag crawled along the kerb following the little man. I reached into the dash for the writ. When he passed me I'd jump out, whack it on his chest and bobs-your-uncle, mission achieved. All I needed was the writ. My hand flapped around in the empty dashbox, then I had a sparklingly clear vision of the writ, all safe and sound and snuggled up tight against my mantlepiece clock – at home. So much for organisation. Maybe I should employ Harry Whitlock as my secretary. He couldn't be worse at it than me.

I walked along the road. I expected they'd be gone for half an hour or so; I mean, anything less is hardly worth putting your togs on for.

I thought I'd mooch around, find out if this was where Lynch was living permanently. I stood at the edge of the road in the gap in the hedge, looking at a big nineteen-thirties house. I didn't move forward because I didn't get a chance. Tommy Lynch was back as soon as he'd gone, almost; running right up to me. A fine drizzle brushed his face, and close-to I could see that his hood was a towel tucked into his running suit. Fine droplets of water hung on his clothes. He ran on the spot, legs lifting, hips swinging, fists punching the air before him in short, sharp jabs. The Jag's horn sounded and we both moved out of the way to let it in. I started to step back onto the slick grey tarmac of the street but Harry Whitlock leaped out and grabbed me.

12

'Hang on you,' he said under his breath. With his big fist grabbing my collar I never even thought of doing anything else.

George Duncan meanwhile climbed out of the car and threw his arms around the boxer. Cigar ash fell onto the tracksuit, darkened as it met the water. Duncan said, 'A hot shower and a rest for you, my son, then down to the weigh-in. Don't drink nothing.'

Tommy Lynch stood still, shoulders hunched a little. George hugged him again and said, '*Enjoy* yourself, son. It's your day. Try to enjoy it. Let it sink in.'

Duncan leaned in the car, reached for a towel and gave it to Lynch.

'You're gonna do it, Tommy. All the way. You're gonna do it, you know that.'

Tommy said nothing. He wiped his face with the towel, still jogging lightly. They went in, crunching the gravel of the drive underfoot. Harry banged my shoulder. It felt like the nudge you'd get from a bus.

'What's your game? Spying?'

I pulled at my tie and said fiercely, 'I *beg* your pardon, my man? I'm house hunting . . . I was sent here by the estate agents.'

'What estate agents?' His brow curled up like a lettuce leaf. I could almost hear his brain ticking under the crew-cut hair.

'Regis Partners. This is Cholmondeley Street, isn't it?'

He pushed me roughly. I didn't take it so well because of my bad leg. I nearly fell.

'Hey. Don't cut up rough because a chap's come to look at a house,' I said.

'*House!*' spat Harry. 'You press boys make me sick. I can smell you a mile off. Get out of here and don't come back.'

He's a very big man and just because he couldn't turn Joe Bugner over didn't mean he couldn't eat me alive. I got out of there and I didn't come back. Just as he asked.

By eleven thirty the same morning I was outside a big new sports hall in Shoreditch. I was using my office landlord's car, a Toyota with rust latticing the wings and doors. I'd changed my clothes, too, from a cheap suit and a plain tie to a windcheater and golfer's slacks. I always reckon people don't see you as well if you've changed your clothes. That's my theory. Above the sports hall door was a painted canvas sign hung on red ropes '*Lynch v. Diaz here tonite*'. A gaggle of pressmen were waiting in the entrance hall, a couple of BBC outside broadcast lorries were blocking-up the car park. I parked the Toyota next to the BBC, then I went over to the foyer of the sports hall, flashed my 'disabled' bus pass at the uniformed council official there, dragged a notebook from my pocket and joined the gaggle of pressmen.

Diaz turned up a few minutes later. He was a good-looking boy in the way that Latins often are: jet-black hair, olive skin and dark brown eyes, sad eyes. They went in. Lynch came, bouncing out of Duncan's car and minded by Duncan himself and a couple of big fellows I hadn't seen before. Harry stood by the car. All the pressmen yelled questions at once. Outside two old ladies were standing by Duncan's car. They yelled loudest of all, so their voices followed through the open doors. Duncan held an impromptu press conference in the foyer while Lynch went inside to strip off. Still the old ladies' voices came over loudest.

'It's 'im, innit? I said to her it's 'im. I said to Elsie "ain't that 'im?" and it *was* 'im.'

The other one yelled at Harry.

'It *was* him wasn't it?'

Harry muttered something and began wiping the car with a chamois leather. George Duncan carried on his press conference, raising his voice to compete with the old ladies.

'I bet you're a boxer, too,' yelled one of the old ladies.

Harry looked grim and nodded. The woman was small and grey-faced and stunted. She wore a coat thirty years out of date. All she'd have needed was a flower-pot hat to make her into a pre-war Hoxton cleaning-lady. The shoulders of her coat were faded a lighter shade of dun than the rest.

'I was,' said Harry, as she repeated her question. I could see Duncan glancing out towards him. Harry took the hint and got in the Jag, prepared to drive away. The woman in the dun coat called after him, 'Who d'you fancy tonight, then?'

The pressmen all burst out laughing.

One said, 'She must be a spy for Harry Carpenter.'

She looked in at us and laughed, her false teeth clacking. 'Who are you backin', mate?' she called at us.

The journalist who'd spoken shouted, 'It's not a bleeding horse race, missus.'

Her friend took her arm. They looked like a couple of witches.

'Who?' she insisted.

George Duncan held his arms above his head. '*Tommy Lynch!*' He yelled. All the pressmen laughed again. '*Tommy Lynch! Tommy Lynch!*'

We began to move into the sports hall. Cameramen checked their cameras. A young man was balancing above his head some Heath Robinson device with an intense white light in a box and a lot of tissue paper stuck around it. The old women tried to come in too, but the uniformed man wouldn't let them.

' 'asn't it got a bar?' the one in the dun coat said.

'Not for you,' said the official.

'Rude git!' she yelled into his face, but he still wouldn't let them in.

The weighing-in was in a room off the main hall. It wasn't a very big room and didn't seem to be ventilated at all, but it was packed with pressmen, officials, managers, aides, fighters and me. Flashguns fired all the time. Tommy Lynch and Diaz squared up for the cameras. The Panamanian had a beetle brow and thick lips. He spoke almost no English, and when he tried to speak it came out comic-book English. He had a Spanish interpreter with him but no one could understand what the interpreter was saying. The interpreter understood the questions but the pressmen didn't understand the answers. He was like a one-way valve for language. It went in but it didn't come out. The reporters gave up and spent all their time talking to Tommy.

'Is it true you'll go for the world after this, Tommy?'

'Are you feeling good, Tommy?'

'Hold your fist up will you, Tommy?'

'Are you going to beat him, Tommy?'

'Which round, Tommy?'

'Square up to him again, will you?'

Lynch smiled politely and answered all their questions and complied with all their requests except the last because the Panamanian had gone. I wandered out into the auditorium and there he was, arguing furiously with his interpreter in Spanish. His English manager sat beside them and stared at the ceiling. The gaggle of pressmen rushed over and the argument got even louder. TV technicians were setting up. They tested their lights for a second. The Panamanian was under the lights screaming at his interpreter. The English manager was sitting now with his head in his hands. George Duncan came out the side room with his arms around Tommy's shoulders. The aides followed them, turning every now and then to shoo a reporter who'd come over.

'Enough now . . . you'll see it all this evening.'

The English manager looked across at Duncan, who waved his cigar in reply. He said to Tommy, 'Look at this. Look at it all. It's your doing.' He waved his hand at the hall, the rows of seats, the ring. 'All this is yours. *You* can fill it. *I* can't and I'm sure that bloody dago can't. *You* can drag people away from their TVs. The next fight will be America, then you'll bring the championship back to the Albert Hall and take the Frenchman on there . . . eh? They'll come for *you*, Tommy. They love *you*.'

Tommy said nothing. I approached them. One of the aides jumped forward and said, 'No press now, I'm afraid. You've had your chance, watch the fight tonight.'

I ignored him and pulled the writ from my pocket and slapped it on Lynch's bare chest.

'Are you Thomas Edward Charles Lynch?'

'Yes,' said Lynch. The aide grabbed me, the same one who'd tried to shoo me off. His grip was in the same class as Harry Whitlock's. I managed to keep the writ held out, though.

'Then I serve you with this writ on behalf of the Sheriff of the High Court.'

He took the piece of paper.

'What's all this about?' he said. 'Let him go.'

'I don't know, sir', I said. 'Would you sign me a receipt?'

Lynch looked at me for a long time, then signalled to the aides with the flat of his hand. He said to Duncan, 'Wait here,' and crooked his finger at me. I followed him.

In the dressing room we were alone. There were dozens of lockers along the walls and a massage table in the middle of the room. Cool white light filtered through a fanlight.

'My wife thinks I've got a load of dough,' he said, and heaved himself up to sit on the massage table. 'But I'm skint, see. She thinks I'm going to America and not coming back . . . but I will. I'll pay her out.'

'I don't know anything about it,' I said. I held out my receipt, 'But if you'd be kind enough. . . .'

'Course,' he said. Close to, Tommy Lynch seemed very gentle. He was a small, almost frail man with short black curly hair and a handsome, unmarked face. 'Got a pen?'

I gave him the receipt and my biro.

'You're Jenner,' he said as he signed. 'I remember you. I thought I recognised you outside the house this morning.'

I nodded and took the pen and paper from him. A man stuck his head round the door.

'Give us a few minutes, Bill,' Lynch said, then to me, apologetically. 'It's my brother. He worries.' He wiped his face with a towel and stood. 'I remembered you from the newspaper stories a few years ago, I was only a kid but I remembered it. It made me want to become a copper.'

'Why didn't you?'

He laughed and held his hand flat and horizontal about four inches above his head.

'That's why.' We both laughed. 'Can't you say anything to my wife?' he said. 'I'm not going to dump her and the kids with no money . . . but I've got to earn some.'

'I don't even know your wife', I said. 'I got that from a solicitor.'

'Couldn't I hire you to talk her round?' he said. 'You could talk her round, I'm sure.'

'Sorry.' I walked towards the door.

He went to a locker.

'Here. Do you like the fight game?'

'It's okay,' I said.

'Come and cheer me,' said Tommy, 'I could use some good luck from you. I'm sorry it's only for a single seat.'

'You don't need good luck.' I held the ticket in my hand. It was printed *Row B seat 4* and had a big £75 stamped across the wavy lines that were on it to stop counterfeiting.

'This is worth a fortune,' I said.

'I could use the luck.' He slapped me on the back and led me to the door.

I said, 'You don't need luck.' But he shook his head and held his hand out.

'Nobody turns good luck down, Jimmy. Have a nice time this evening, and say hello to that stinking wife of mine.'

Then the grey door closed on him.

Two

The fight was top billing, starting at ten. I took a taxi because there was no chance of parking, and I arranged to be picked up at eleven fifteen.

The seat Lynch had given me was in the second row, right behind some radio and TV commentators' tables. I was among the press boys again – I felt as if I was getting used to it. Instead of the empty, echoing hall of the morning there was a full house, passing hip-flasks and beer cans between themselves. The rough boys at the back were chanting.

'Here we go here we go here we go, here we go here we go here we go-o.'

The TV lights made a stark and blinding space, an arena where the contest should be acted out. The lights looked natural, part of a pre-ordained way the thing should be. Behind the lights would be millions of television viewers. I saw it but I couldn't believe it.

The Panamanian, Diaz, came on to cheering, whistling and jeering, all at once. He seemed to flinch even from the cheers. He came into the ring in a cold sweat, danced a few steps but he never looked convincing. He looked as if his feet would go at the first punch. He was like a jumpy amateur.

'HERE WE GO, here we go, here we go here we go here we go-o, here we go here we go here we go, here we go-oh, here we go,' sang the crowd. The Panamanian kept his hooded dressing gown on and stared at his feet.

A fanfare introduced Tommy. Four burly men in dinner suits surrounded him, marched him to the ring. Tommy

19

kept his head down, avoided everyone's eyes. His gloved hands were on the shoulders of the dinner-suited man before him. Tommy's trainer and his second followed behind the group of five, wearing blue silk shirts with *Tommy 'Banger' Lynch* emblazoned on the back. They looked like the tail of a comet, a flash of light in the darkness.

'Here we *go*,' sang the crowd.

The fanfare went on, then a recording of 'Rule Britannia', which the crowd sang along with, la-ing most of the words.

'Ladies and gennermen, innerducing a worl title e-limi-nater, on my lef, inner blue corner . . . Tommy "Banger" Lynch.'

The crowd around me went wild. Tommy held his arms up, still careful to look at no one. He danced around the ring. The Panamanian's introduction was lost in the cheering for Tommy, but he danced around and held his arms up anyway, for the sake of form.

The fight lasted two rounds. If the Panamanian hadn't been so brave it wouldn't have gone outside the first. He took a big right from Tommy halfway through the first. It caught him on the jaw, he ran backwards into the ropes, then bounced off to meet a straight left. His nose broke. Blood poured onto Tommy's shoulder and chest.

The crowd bayed for more. A radio commentator in the seat in front of me was screaming above the noise, 'Some-one's cut, someone's cut . . . I think it may be Lynch. He's ab-so-lutely *covered* in blood. He steps back . . . no, it's Diaz, cut on the face is it? . . . and this-is-war, *out*-and-*out*-war. These two men are really going hell for leather.'

They stood toe to toe, swapping punches. Diaz knew he'd never go twelve rounds so he tried to punch it out with Lynch there and then. Tommy Lynch was the bigger puncher. He hit Diaz two more big punches to the body, on the lower ribcage. The Panamanian's arm dropped. Then Tommy hit him in the head again. Diaz reeled. An arc of blood sprayed the canvas, the ringside seats. Diaz's eyes rolled, his legs buckled. The bell went.

His corner cleaned him up, but twenty seconds of the next round was enough for the referee. He led Diaz to his corner. The Panamanian spat his gumshield out and swore in Spanish, he waved his arms furiously.

'Is okay!' He yelled. 'Is *okay*' Blood bubbled across his nose and mouth. 'Is okay . . . I go!' He looked round frantically for his translator. Diaz's brow furrowed and his big lips twisted and he began to howl in anguish at being beaten. He put his arms around the Board of Control doctor and blubbered tears and snot and blood onto the man's dinner suit.

Across the ring, Tommy's seconds were sponging him off. Reporters scrambled into the ring. The bouncers pushed over-excited supporters back from the ropes.

'And will he go for the world, Mr Duncan . . . *George Duncan*! BBC here. Will you be fixing a fight in New York or London next?'

Tommy's seconds rubbed him down with towels. He was sweating like a racehorse, all over. One second knelt and rubbed his legs. Reporters mobbed him. A TV camera was pushed into his face.

'How does it feel, Tommy?' a reporter asked. I squeezed into the aisle and George Duncan was standing there with the BBC reporter. The reporter said, 'And surely the world next, George?' George Duncan took a pull at his big cigar and said, 'We'll have to see.'

He looked across at Tommy and seemed satisifed. Tommy was enjoying it at last and Duncan had a world title challenger on his hands. That's how it looked to me in the aisle, anyway. Later in the street is looked different. But then that *was* different.

Three

Everyone expected Tommy 'Banger' Lynch to beat Diaz. I'd seen Lynch fight a few times on the TV and I've never seen a more obvious prospect than him. What took everyone by surprise was the speed of the victory. It took me by surprise. I limped up the gangway towards the exit as the fight finished, then flashed my 'disabled' bus pass again to gain entrance to the bar. I don't know how well it works on buses – I've never used it – but the old 'disabled' bus pass gets you past all kinds of officials.

The bar was empty. For tonight it was doubling as an entertainment area for the booze firm that was sponsoring the fight. One corner was partitioned off for press telephones and a nice young girl from BT dressed like an airline hostess was giving instructions on how to use a phone to some drunken lout from Grub Street. I ordered a couple of beers and took them into a corner and settled in a big chair. I ordered two beers because I didn't want to queue for a second, and when the mob hit the bar five minutes later I was congratulating myself on my foresight. I sat back and drank my beers while less prudent souls were forced to queue.

I was outside waiting for my cab at eleven. I could hear car doors slamming and the metallic clunks of the TV boys clearing up. Every now and then a yell would carry across to me. The weather was warming up; it wasn't raining any more and the night had become muggy and thick, like the tropics. The TV technician's yells cut through the air with

22

a blunt edge, and the sounds of cars starting were half-muffled and distant. My street was deserted. I could hear some drunks singing a couple of streets away, 'Here we go, here we go here we go . . . well we *done* it, didn't we, eh?'

Thinking back on Diaz's nervous face I began to wonder if they actually *had* done it. Lynch was just the channel for their desire. I checked my watch. Eleven-oh-five. There was plenty of time for the cab to come yet. Then a big car engine came, smooth and burbling. It stopped a hundred yards or so from me. Two men tipped out and scrambled across the pavement, arguing furiously and sometimes squaring up to each other. One was a big man wearing a suit, the other was a little slim fellow in casual clothes. They swung round and round in the yellow street light and swore loudly at each other. Then the driver got out, too, and a young woman who even at that distance was well-dressed and handsome and carried herself well. The shifting attitude of the yellow street light as she followed the men along the pavement shaded her face, but I recognised the driver. It was big Harry Whitlock, and then I could hear the voice of the little man.

'No . . . No! . . . I'm not interested . . . Stuff "up west". Stuff the press . . . no!'

Tommy Lynch was having his second fight of the night. This time it was with George Duncan. I could hear Duncan's voice too, fierce and low.

'No!' cried Tommy again. 'Our contract finished tonight and you're not coming to America with me . . . you're greedy, George Duncan. You want too much.'

A white Rover cruised slowly past me. There were four men in it and they were big enough to fill the car up as if it would burst.

'You want me to provide for you as if you were my father or something. You think I should foot the bill for your lifestyle . . . well I won't. Find someone else. You make me sick.'

The Rover stopped by them. Three men got out.

Duncan didn't appear to see them. He took a swing at Tommy. He couldn't have been surprised to miss. Then Duncan turned on one of the three men and fell on him, arms flailing, mouth spitting abuse. The man hit him hard

23

in the face. Harry stepped forward but there were still the other two and they were both as big as himself. Duncan was on the floor. Harry did nothing.

A car stopped by me.

'Mr Jenner for Stoke Newington?'

I nodded.

'That's me, sport. Sit tight a minute and put your meter on.'

Duncan got up and threw himself at the man again and the man hit him hard again. I heard a definite 'smack' as the fist connected, then another as Duncan fell to his knees and the man hit him again.

'Stone me!' said my cabby. 'I'd better radio for the coppers.'

'Leave it,' I said. I couldn't see how having the police there would help Tommy Lynch, tonight of all nights. And whatever was happening to Duncan he seemed to be bringing on himself. The cabbie picked up his radio mike but I said, 'Leave it,' again and he did.

Tommy Lynch climbed in the Rover with the other men and they drove away.

George Duncan lay on the floor, sobbing. Harry, his minder, sat back in their Jag. I asked my cabbie to drive slowly past. When we reached them George Duncan was on his feet and the woman was slapping him hard, slowly, first one side of the face then the other. I asked my cabbie to stop, then I pulled down my window. The woman was slapping George and yelling at him at the same time.

'You (slap) stupid big pig (slap). You've ballsed it up once and (slap) for all (slap) now. You stinking (slap). . . . .' A lighter one. She'd seen us and turned. I couldn't see her face still. She wore a forties-style outfit with a wasp waist and a broad-brimmed hat.

'What are you staring at?' she called across to me.

'Nothing,' I said from the safety and darkness of the cab. 'You okay?'

'Of course I am, you stupid swine. Sod off.'

Charming. They looked like they'd live through it, so I asked the cab driver to go on. It was a funny way to celebrate a big fight win, that's for sure, but then it wasn't any of my business and I put the affair out of my mind.

Four

'My name's Jenner. James Jenner. I'm a detective.'

I went through my teens practising speeches, entrances like that. I could picture myself wearing a gabby mack and a pork-pie hat.

'Detective Inspector Jenner, Flying Squad. Keep your hand away from that gun, Smithers.'

The reality was different. As soon as I joined I was identified as the sort of material that's good for thirty years of School Crossing Patrol, wearing a big hat and doling out informal 'evenin' all'-type salutes from the peak of my helmet. Maybe they were right. Maybe that was all I was good for, after all, someone has to be good for it. We can't all be in charge, and most of us aren't even able to be little actors in a great big drama. We're the audience. Take a seat.

If the scheme for life had worked I would eventually have saved enough money for a semi in the suburbs and a Ford Escort to go with it. If I could only have passed the Sergeant's Examination I could have swapped the Ford Escort for a Vauxhall Cavalier. It's not much of an ambition but it was the game-plan I was offered. I even began to believe in it. I had a girlfriend, a WPC called Judy. Nowadays Judy's in the Criminal Intelligence Section in New Scotland Yard. Then she was a WPC whose main job was wiping the noses of lost kids and being present when male policemen interviewed women prisoners. Now she's a star, but then she was my little fiancée and she was all in favour both of the semi and the Ford Escort. We wanted to be man and wife. She's gone off the idea since; well, so have I. She reckons she can't stand being part of an alliterative marriage – Jimmy and Judy Jenner. I looked 'alliterative' up. She reads too many books.

There's always the chance that she'd prefer a man who's complete, who has all his parts still. I have no evidence to offer on this one and Judy has never been anything other than kind to me about the results of my 'incident'.

That happened a long time ago now, and Judy has always been very helpful. Very soothing. It took two-and-a-half years before I was in any shape to do anything. I have a false leg from just below my right knee and have to use a stick if I'm going to walk for more than a couple of minutes and stay comfortable. Judy, who was by that time a Sergeant, stayed very close, still talking about marriage and all that. I didn't want to marry, of course. They kept slicing lumps off my leg because it never worked for months and months, right up until six months, I suppose, before I went down to Roehampton and got my plastic one. I was still nervous they'd call me back and operate again . . . I know it's unreasonable but they'd done it three times and I just thought they might do it a fourth. Sometimes I felt like a ham on a slicing machine. I felt it would never end. I could imagine Judy getting just a head on a plate, like Salome. I'd be great at foreplay but things would peter out pretty quickly from there on in. Not much use as a husband.

When I said I was going to leave the job she backed off, as if I was leaving a close family. In a way I was. NSY had offered me a post in the Commissioner's Office, on the end of a phone. It was more than they had to do, I wasn't fit for duty, but I didn't want the job. I still had a little bit of that teenage ambition left in me, and I thought the promotion prospects of a one-legged telephone answerer in New Scotland Yard were even worse than for a well-meaning but stupid beat-plodder in Romford. I had a bit of dough, insurance pay-outs, Criminal Injuries Compensation, all that, so I didn't have to worry about getting it wrong. I would never starve. Anyway I told Judy I was leaving and she stopped mentioning the marriage. Just as well, really.

I was encouraged in my decision by a certain Detective Inspector of my acquaintance, a man called Denis O'Keefe.

O'Keefe is about six years off retiring, and is hell-bent on feathering his nest in Southend first. I suppose he's so active now because he knows no one'll ever put him in a position of trust again. He'd be right, too. O'Keefe is a clever dick and nasty with it. He's mobbed-up, though, with every insurance assessor in London. He's also mobbed-up with every villain. He's a very important contact for the tyro private detective to have . . . and that's what I'd decided to be. If the State wouldn't have me as a secret squirrel, I'd make myself one. I rented a room and called myself 'Jenner's', as if I were 'Pinkerton's'.

Even before I'd left the job, O'Keefe had arranged, for me to organise a payout to recover some gear for an insurance company. He would cop ten per cent, of course. So would I. I did it, the day after I put my papers in to leave. I hobbled down to a railway arch in Coldblow Lane, Bermondsey, and swapped a big packet of money for a medium-sized packet of gold trinkets. Bermondsey isn't my manor and I was a bit nervous. I mean I could hardly have run from trouble with my stick, could I? It earned O'Keefe and me £1600 each in the process; his unofficial, like. I put mine in the restoration fund of a Catholic church in the Old Kent Road. It's more than I can bear to see a church in need of re-pointing and I got a warm glow from the thought of all the bricklayers and roofers people like me can take off the dole by a small gesture. I believe O'Keefe spent his on sending a maiden aunt to Lourdes to get her cystitis cured.

I kept up my contact with O'Keefe after I left the job. Discreetly of course. I did quite a few little jobs for him and with him, the sort of thing it's not illegal for me to do but it would be indisciplined for him to do. He could get on a fizzer for it, but as a civilian, I couldn't.

I found my own work as well, made my own contacts. Most of my work is brain, not brawn. Cunning brain, too . . . you don't need a university degree to do it. I flatter myself I have a cunning brain. I'm nobody's idea of an intellectual.

I've found people. People that have gone missing from

their families. I don't do any debt collecting. I'll never be that hard up. I went into an insurance broker's and worked out a scam one of their branch managers had going on cash premiums. I liked doing that one. I worked out where a load of cakes were going for a bakery (all, I swear *all* of their delivery drivers were at it with their branch managers). The drivers would take, say, nine trays of bath buns into a shop and bring three out again. Very nice. Since the bakery couldn't sack all its drivers and all its managers they simply sent them all nasty letters and paid me a twelve-hundred-quid fee. When I pointed out they were employing criminals they sent me a cheque for another eight hundred with a note '*re. underpayment of fee, please sign receipt and return*'. I sent them a bill for three hundred quid VAT and they paid that too. So much for the murky waters of industrial relations). I found husbands who'd done runners leaving the wife and kids with the bills – it's surprising how many of these there are. I've served writs for solicitors, recovered 'tom' – booty, jewellery-style – for insurance companies, accompanied the son of a rich man to school in Dorset (the boy was under no threat, he just wouldn't go to school and his old man couldn't be bothered to take him), sat up all night looking after a load of designer clobber in Oxford Street . . . in fact I've done everything the ace private eye of my dreams should do except two. I've never been asked to offer physical protection to anyone and I've never been asked to uncover some dastardly murder. The first is easily explained . . . no one wants an enforcer who's only got one leg and a walking stick. The second only happens when people like me are played by people like Eliot Gould on the movie screen, or James Garner on the TV. You'd have to be an American to even think of it. English coppers, should they get a whiff of cadavers and dirty deeds, throw everybody who's in the slightest bit connected with the matter into the chokee until they've sorted out what's what. This is the voice of experience speaking. More than once I served the unfortunate suspects their breakfast. *Habeas corpus?* Do hop off, John. You watch too much telly. Eat your bacon and try to relax.

No one wants an enforcer with one leg . . . that's what I said. Well, you never know.

I've got an office in Canning Town, above a newsagent's, confectioner's, stationer's, small post-office and we-sell-anything shop run by Mr Chardray, a mate of mine. I've known Chardray since our days in Romford. He's a proper English Indian, comes to work in a tie and dons a brown dust-jacket to serve in. His nephew runs the shop in Romford now.

I haven't been busy lately, and though I've got my own front door old Chardray (he's particular about how you spell it) notices everything.

'Busy?' He came out of his door and watched me as I fumbled with the key to mine. He knew I wasn't busy. He knew I hadn't been busy for weeks. That's how my game seems to go . . . all rush rush rush, then quiet for a couple of months.

'I'm all right. You?' I said. I wasn't all right. I'd been knocking back gin and Italian vermouth with some mates in Hackney. Now, at four o'clock, I was just about all in. I've got an old horsehair sofa in my office. It would do me a treat. I've got some gin and a telly, too.

'I'm all right. You had a visitor.' He smiled. He loves to be one in front all the time.

I opened the door and looked onto the mat. There was an envelope.

'He left a note,' Chardray called.

'Thanks. Thanks for telling me.'

'I recognised him from the old days.'

'Good. Indian, is he?'

Chardray laughed and tidied the papers on the stand beside his front door. Week-old, yellowing *Guardians* were shuffled to the top, a new City Prices *Standard* went into pole position, at eye-level.

'No. I recognise him from the Romford days. You knew him then, I'm sure . . . *I* did, but I can't put his name on him.'

I looked at the envelope. I didn't recognise the writing. Chardray was still hanging around. I said, 'Nor can I', went upstairs, threw the papers off my desk and poured a gin. I don't like gin. I was introduced to it by a lady whose husband I was supposed to be finding. She got me drunk on gin and then I behaved in a thoroughly unprofessional

29

way with her, so much so that I sub-contracted the finding of the husband and concentrated my own resources on comforting the client. *That* worked so well the husband came round and said if I wasn't a cripple he'd beat my head in, but for now just a sock on the jaw would do. She was as pleased as hell to get the husband back, I got two hundred quid, a sore jaw and the remains of a gin bottle. I have a *taste* for the stuff, but I don't *like* it. It makes my jaw sore.

The note in the envelope read '*Urgent I speak with you soonest. Would you please ring my hotel a.s.a.p. George Duncan*'. It was written on paper headed 'Hotel Bonaventura, Knightsbridge'.

It was ten days since the fight in Shoreditch. Tommy Lynch had been in the papers both for the prospect of a world title fight and for the fact that he'd gone over to the managership of Lenny Grant, a retired boxer in his mid-thirties. Judging by the photographs I'd seen in the papers of Grant with his new signing, Grant was the man I'd seen thumping George Duncan outside the boxing hall in Shore-ditch. So the fight game was getting a little rough. I rang Duncan anyway, though if he was looking for protection he was on to the wrong man.

'James! Good to hear from you, James! God when I came to that fly-blown dump in Canning Town I thought I must've been in the wrong place. It was only the sign and that darkie from the shop that convinced me you were the James Jenner I used to know in Romford. How've you been doing?'

'I'm fine. I'm doing fine.'

'Listen. I should have recognised you when you came out to that place in Chigwell, but you know how it is . . . I was busy and I had a lot on my mind.'

'That's okay. No reason why you should've.'

'Good . . . good. I always knew you were the kind of fellow who could take it okay. I knew you wouldn't hold a grudge just because I never recognised you.'

'Right. We've got that clear . . . well, what can I do for you?'

'It was my wife that recognised you, and she'd never met you,' he went on. 'She saw your picture in the paper and

30

she said, "That's the chap who served the writ on Tommy"
. . . that's what she said and my God she was right. The
Daily Mail, it was.'

'I know.'

'Well of course I should've recognised you from the very
beginning, I know. Have you changed your hair?'

'No.'

'Well, I just don't know what it was, but I couldn't see
you for the young man who used to come to the old gym
in Romford until . . . until. . . .'

'Yeah yeah. I've got it. What can I do for you?'

'Well, Jimmy old friend. When I realised who you were
I realised that you were just the man to do a job of work
for me in your new trade. I realised I could trust you and
I could talk to you honestly . . . . know what I mean?'

'Go on.'

'That's all. Let me talk to you, Jimmy.'

'What about?'

'I've got a proposition I'd like to put to you. I'd like you
to do a piece of work for me. All very simple stuff, but a
bit private.'

'What is it?'

'It's a bit private, like I said. Could you come down here
for an hour and have a drink?'

'When?'

'Now?'

'It's rush hour, Mr Duncan. I won't be able to park my
car there. I have to use my car. Can't we make it nine
o'clock?'

'Nine's fine. Look forward to seeing you then. *Bye.*'

He put the phone down. I drank my gin and went down
the creaky wooden stairs to the street-door. Traffic roared
past. I fumbled the keys again. Chardray was positioned by
the papers again. The *Guardian* was on the move again,
back to the centre of the stack. Maybe he was expecting an
SDP voter to pass.

'I just can't place him,' Chardray said.

'Who?' I hung my stick round my neck while I buttoned
my coat. Even during May I feel the cold nowadays. I don't
know why. My central heating bill's a cricket score.

'Your visitor. I just couldn't place his face from my

memory. But I know who he is, somehow. Didn't it say on the message?'

Nosy swine. I just turned my back on him and walked away. I knew it would drive him crazy for days.

I've got a couple of lads that do odd jobs for me. One's called Gary or Gal for short, the other Zorba. Zorba's a miserable, stunted, ex-pat Greek. I think he may be a Cypriot. I don't know whether he picked up his nickname because he's the absolute A1 opposite of the Anthony Quinn character in the movie or because his real name is just a load of consonants jumbled up. That's how Greek names all look to me. For whatever reason he's come by the name, Zorba is Zorba. Five feet six and two-twenty pounds of unrestrained out-and-out nastiness. He's so swarthy the hair seems to grow straight out of his collar, as if it's bursting to get somewhere. His eyes are so shifty they've turned into permanent slits, no eyeball revealed, between his stubbly chubby cheek and his hairy chubby brow. I'm glad he's on my side, because, as my grandad would say, he'd skin a turd for a tanner.

I use Zorba to look after me if I've got a dodgy bit of work going on. If I had to do that payout in Coldblow Lane nowadays I'd have Zorba backing me up. I'm getting too old for nervous afternoons and evenings, and I've always been nervous of dark places.

I had to walk a bit to find Zorba. He's not the kind of bloke you open up the phone book at 'Z' for and give a bell . . . he's dodgy. First of all you have to find Gal. And finding Gal means walking. I worked my way up the coffee bars, greasy spoons and various dives of Barking Road. No Gal. I took a cab (my leg was giving me gyp) to Roman Road, Bow, had a pie-and-mash and jellied eels because I can't walk past one, then found my boy Gary in the first amusement arcade I came to. He's a big skinny kid; nineteen, faded denims, on the dole, mucky brown hair and a washed-out face. He carries a scruffed-up copy of the *New Musical Express* permanently in the back pocket of his jeans, and as often as not he's wearing a faded denim Bob Dylan pillbox cap. I told him once and he said, 'Bob who?'

That's how life goes forward, by leaps and amnesia. Gal knows everyone who's anyone in the . . . shall we say the seedy end of London life? He knows all the deals that are doing and all the dealers that are doing them. He has also sworn to defend the world against Pacman, or whatever the latest Japanese electronic invasion is called. When I found him he was bending over an electronic screen, green flashes racing past his ears, his body jerking spasmodically. His back twitched all the time. I only recognised him because of the *NME* sticking out of his pocket. I snapped the main electric switch to the machine with my walking stick, then held my hands up as he turned angrily.

'*What* the . . . oh, hello Jimmy.'

'Where's Zorba?'

'I dunno. He was drinking down the road until an hour ago . . . I don't know where he might have gone since then.'

I drew him outside to the street.

'I want you two to do a little job for me. Discreet enquiries about a man called Duncan, George Duncan. He's a boxing manager. Here's the key to my office. I should be back by eleven, say. Get all you can, then dump your body on my sofa and wait there till I come. Wait till half eleven.'

'Zorba too?'

'No. Only one of you need come. But I want all the dirt on him, anything and everything . . . and Gal.'

'What?'

'I've marked the gin. Bring your own booze.'

Five

I took a cab across to Knightsbridge. I'm lazy about driving. All the way across the cabbie treated me to his family history. A very interesting family they were too, *if* you were a family member. His uncle had the Burma Star and his Dad had been to Germany. Well, not *to* it so much as *over* it. In a Lancaster. He'd got a sister who'd married a wally, his own wife was an 'absolute dear, a darling' and he'd got a two-year old son. He got all that out between Cambridge Heath Road and Knightsbridge. If I'd been going to Heathrow I've no doubt he'd have told me when his mother lost her cherry and he'd have been recommending psycho-analysts to me.

The Hotel Bonaventura was between Knightsbridge and the Brompton Road. It had obviously been a family house once, perhaps before the war. Now it was shabby. The building had suffered generations of kids doing *Europe on Six Dollars a Day* or whatever the lastest incarnation of that book is. Outside there was a bunch of North American girls and boys helping each other strap on rucksacks and an angry coach driver trying to gee them all up.

I went inside and stopped one of the preppy North American kids.

'Where's reception?'

He laughed and went on. There was no reception. I yelled up the stairs, 'Duncan, hey! George Duncan.'

'Hello. Wait!' echoed back.

Right place, anyway. I waited. Kids smiled, stared or frowned at me, as it took their fancy. Then George came down the stairs wearing a blue chalk-stripe suit, a grey fedora hat and a bowtie.

'I've got to stay here on the quiet,' he confided. 'I don't want no one to know where I am.'

We wandered down to a pub in Knightsbridge, looking like George Melly and Hopalong Cassidy. The idea that no one would notice us, that we'd be here on the quiet, was a non-starter.

He took the hat off, grinned, drank half an enormous measure of scotch and sat at a table out of the crowd before he apologised.

'I expect you're thinking it's not my thing, eh? I expect you're wondering why's a big fight manager like me staying in a dump like that, eh?'

He sucked at a flame through an enormous cigar.

'I didn't think about it really. I suppose you have a reason,' I said. Of course I was wondering.

'I'm trying to fix up a fight . . . no no. I can't say *what* fight. Just a fight. It's got to be *well* on the quiet, so I've got the geezer from stateside visiting here rather than somewhere that could be staked out by a load of mateys from the press. Know what I mean?'

'Uhuh.' I nodded. George fluttered his eyelashes, sucked his cigar and picked at some fluff on his lapel.

'I need some looking after . . . no, no,' he held his hand up, 'not heavy minding. Gawd knows I've got enough hooligans if I just want someone on the door. More?'

I said yes, he went to the bar and refilled our glasses. I tapped my walking stick on the floor. It had better not be heavy minding. George eased himself back into the seat and went on.

'I've had some threats. I can't go into them, and there's no good asking me who from because I don't know. Some fruity-pie shot a twelve-bore into my front door the other day, I've had a lot of nasty phone calls. All that sort of thing.'

'Letters?'

'One. I've got one. What it's all about doesn't concern you.' He pulled a big handkerchief from his pocket and mopped his brow. 'Well, it's all about a fighter. Let's just say that. The point is that I'm well tied up over the next couple of weeks and I want someone to look after my missus.'

'How "look after"?'

'She don't know it's going on. I can lay on no end of brawny yobbos to take care of her, but I want someone with a little savvy. Whoever's having a go at me is doing just that, having a go at *me*. She's under no threat and I don't expect she will be . . . I just want someone to be an eyes and ears for me, make sure she doesn't walk into any stupid trouble.'

'Who's threatening you?' I asked.

'Not your business. I pay a ton a day and you make sure my missus doesn't fall under any buses, that sort of thing, for the next two weeks. Then I'll have finished all my deals and all that crap and I'll take back responsibility.' He put an envelope on the table. 'There's the first two days' worth. You shape out how I think you will and I'll be able to pay you a bonus, three days' pay, say, at the end. That'll mean seventeen hundred greenies for swanning round in my Jag for a fortnight. Not bad work, eh?' He pushed the money towards me. 'My address is in there. It's in Saffron Walden. Get the train up tomorrow, then a cab from the station. I'll pick up the expenses. I've got a chauffeur, Harry . . . do you know him?'

I shook my head.

'I think he was around the gym in Romford when you were. He's a good bloke but thick as a plank. No use for this at all. I've sent him on holiday, and you're his replacement for the holiday . . . that's what she thinks.'

'Why not tell her the truth?' I asked.

He shook his big, silvery-haired head.

'It'll get her all lathered-up. She'll stick to me like a limpet and I don't need that now. I can't do with having me missus cracking up right at the moment. Know what I mean?'

'No,' I said. I didn't, either. The woman I'd seen slapping him around in Shoreditch didn't look like she'd stick like a limpet to anything except herself.

He pushed the money again.

'Count it. Take the job. Turn up at my drum in Saffron in one day's time. What d'yer say?'

'What time?'

'Same as now. Get there for eight or nine. You get the train up from Liverpool Street. Leave your car in London because I think you'll finish with us in London. It'll save you coming back out to fetch your motor.'

'Your car an auto?' I slapped my leg.

'Yeah. I already thought about that.'

I stood up. He leaned forward and shook my hand. I couldn't believe him: chalk-stripe suit, big yellow bowtie (*lemon* yellow at that), comes in wearing a fedora and then goes to a quiet corner of the pub 'so we won't be noticed'.

'Deal?'

'I'd prefer to know what you're worried about. It's hard to see it coming if you don't know what you're looking for.'

He ignored me.

'Deal?'

'Call my office in the morning and I'll let you know.'

I went outside. It was a stormy, muggy night. All wrong for May. I walked as far as Hyde Park Corner, then went down to the tube. A man was drunk, sick-drunk on the stairs. He was on his knees and wobbling about. I would have picked him up if I could have. I was frightened he'd fall down the steps and split his skull. If I tried to pick him up we'd both go down the stairs head first, I knew that for sure, so I had to leave him.

I'm a strange man to hire for muscle, for protection. *I* wouldn't hire me as a minder . . . why should Duncan want to? As the train came in I heard a wail from the drunk on the stairs, then a dull thud. Either the muggers or the forces of gravity had got him. Whichever, he was beyond my help. The doors shushed open and I stepped aboard.

Six

I was surprised to find myself at the Lynch-Diaz fight in Shoreditch again. They weren't in the ring. Two soppy-joes were beating each other's heads in for a warm-up. I could feel it and smell it and hear it, and even though it was all wrong it was exactly as it should be, with all the sweat and leather in glorious three-D before my very eyes. I was in the front row and the two soppy-joes were trying to kill each other above my very head. The timekeeper's table was just along from me a way and he rang the bell and the joes kept fighting and he rang the bell more and they still kept fighting and he was ringing and ringing and ringing.

Then I was sitting up, sweating in my bedclothes. On the floor there was a trail of abandoned female underwear, plus the wrapper for a new pair of tights, plus the normal debris Judy leaves as she gets up late for work . . . one shoe, a hairbrush, a crumpled skirt she'd stepped out of last night. Last night! I didn't even remember her coming, didn't even know she was here. The bell kept ringing. I yelled, 'All right!' and strapped up my leg before pulling my dressing gown on and staggering down the corridor to the door.

'Gal. What are you . . . oh, last night, eh?'

'You should open a window,' he said. 'Also you shouldn't get up so late. It's after ten. You'll waste your life.'

'I had a few bevvys in Soho, then I . . . er. . . .'

'Forgot,' Gary said. 'You forgot your ace assistant was waiting faithfully in your office, all primed up with info just as you asked. You meanwhile. . . .'

'Was being a bar prop in Greek Street. I know. What did you get?'

'What's it worth?'

I struggled with an expresso machine, a very expensive birthday present from Judy. I can't work it though. I spilled ground coffee all over the worktop, then gave up and put a kettle on.

'Tea do? Good. Don't muck about, Gal. How am I supposed to know what it's worth before you've told me?'

'It's good. Very good.'

I went to the living room and fetched my wallet. Pulled out two fivers and put them on the table. With no coffee in it and no hint from me that it should the coffee machine started pouring out steam. Why do machines feel entitled to be so unreasonable? I switched it off and pushed the fivers at the kid.

'Come on, Gal. I haven't got all morning.'

'Okay.' He took his cap off and sat up straight. 'George Duncan had a boxer called Lynch, Tommy Lynch. Tommy Lynch left him, you must have seen all that in the paper.'

I shook my head.

'I didn't see it in the paper. I was *there*. Tell me something I don't know, Gal.'

'And Lynch went to a geezer called Grant, Leonard Grant. He's an up and coming manager . . . *as* they say in the papers you don't read.' He paused and smiled. Gal was pleased with himself. 'And Grant is a front man – and *only* a front man – for a mob of villains led by a guy called Wilkins. Very nasty piece of work, Wilkins. It seems Duncan and Grant had a barney in the street on account of Duncan not being entirely over the moon about his man being poached just when he's ready to go for a big one.'

'I know . . .' I said.

'Don't tell me,' he broke in, 'you were there when the barney took place. Why ask me to find out things you already know?'

'Because I'm an organiser, Gal, and you're an operative. You do what you're good at and let me do the thinking. Tell me what else you've got.'

'All right.' He stood and poured boiling water over the tea bags in our mugs, then swizzled the bags around with the wrong end of a fork. 'I don't suppose it matters. I only wore me feet out, lied me head off and almost got a kicking

39

getting this information for you. Why should it worry me you can't be bothered to open the paper and find out the basics of who's who and what's what in the fight game?' He gave me a mug of tea. 'I'll give it to you from the top. . . .'

'Don't bother. I've got it. Where did you go other than the public library?'

'Ha ha.' He slurped at his tea, set the mug on the table and leaned back in his chair. 'You don't want to know the rest, then.' A pause. 'I thought you would. People have been leaving Duncan in droves, and word is that Grant is using the Wilkins muscle to fix venues and contracts if not actual fights. George Duncan is up against it. Rumour has it he's getting out of the fight game altogether . . . either that or the game's getting out of him, since he don't have no boxers.'

'What else do you have on him?'

'Lot of rubbish. He's on his third marriage. A South African bird called Alison. Pretty tasty by all accounts. He's got a flat in the Barbican and a house in Cambridgeshire. He lives well, plenty of dough. He's reckoned to be mouthy but not much bottle . . . oh, and he's disappeared for the last week. No one's seen him or his wife. A guy that knows his chauffeur reckons he's pissed off to some little hotel to do some deal. If he's going to run up against Wilkins' lot his best deal would be if he got himself measured up for a cheap wooden overcoat.'

I laughed so much that tea ran up my nose. Wooden overcoat! This boy, when he isn't playing Pacman, watches nineteen-forties gangster movies. I could imagine him lying on my horsehair sofa thinking that one up.

'Wasser matter?' Gal pouted.

'Nothing. Remind me not to let you make the tea any more. What did Zorba get?'

'Nothing. I couldn't find him. I brought your car round. The keys were on the desk.'

'Cheers. Where does Wilkins run out of?'

'Walthamstow.'

I pushed him another fiver.

'Not bad for one evening, eh? I've done well, I mean . . . only for a couple of hours' work. I don't s'pose you want

40

to make a small contrib to the time I wasted in your office, eh?'

'No,' I said, 'but I won't charge you rent either, nor for the cup of tea I've just donated. I won't deduct anything for telling me he had a house in Cambridgeshire when it's in Essex, either, dummy.'

Gal was hurt he'd got that wrong. He's half-man, half-boy still. Sometimes hard and clever, sometimes very vulnerable. I like him. If I really liked him, I'd buy him a cheap home computer and then he could save his money in the arcades. But then he'd never see daylight, never meet anyone and never be any use to me. He'd never make any vitamin D, either . . . or is it vitamin E? Who cares, unless you're short of it? That's true for everything. It's too early in the morning for philosophy, I thought, and took my tea back to bed.

I have one of those funny phone-answering things, a tape machine in the office and then I have a little gadget I keep in my pocket so that I can 'collect important messages *all* over the world'. I don't know about all over the world, but sometimes it works around London and sometimes it don't.

'*You are through to Jenner's. James Jenner speaking. If you'd like to leave a message wait till the tone, then leave your name, number and message if you wish and I'll get back to you as soon as I can.*'

Beep.

'Hullo, Sjimmy. Zorba here. I'm no goina be round for a few days, so I'll be here in touch as soon as I can.'

Beep.

'O'Keefe here. I'd like you to phone me on my home number as soon as.'

Beep.

Beep.

'James. It's Judy. Where the hell are you? It's ten thirty and you were going to meet me here at nine thirty. *Here*, in case you've forgotten is The Marquess of Anglesey, Bow Street. Do you remember where Bow Street is? I'm stuck here with a couple of lemons from the Serious Crimes Squad

41

and if you don't come and rescue me soon I'm going to be *really* angry.'

Beep.

'Duncan here. I take it you're not in your office yet. I'll call back later, Jimmy.'

Beep.

Beep.

There followed half a dozen beeps, then a long, rambling message from a guy I'd found his wife for. He'd gone off the beam, I don't know why she wanted him back. I suppose she loves him or something. He's small, in his thirties, balding and he smokes so much he smells of it all the time. He smells terrible. I read a survey once that said that women who smoke too much conceive less than women who don't smoke. The reporter suggested nicotine as the cause. But it's not true. They don't conceive because they smell bad and then no one wants to sleep with them. Sleeping with someone is a vital part in the conception process, *I* know. I think that woman must have really loved her nutty husband, who was called Bernard something. I forget the whole name. As soon as I hear Bernard's voice on my telephone I put my right ear to the phone. My right ear doesn't work very well.

I called Judy and arranged to take her out to lunch. I also asked what the name Wilkins from Walthamstow meant to her. Then I called Duncan's hotel in Knightsbridge and told him I'd see him in Saffron Waldon that evening. Then I went back into the kitchen to do battle with the expresso machine. I'm not being beaten by a mere lump of metal . . . oh no.

'What's wrong with your hand?' Judy said. We were in a big boozer in Horseferry Road.

'I scalded it. It's nothing.'

'Looks sore.'

'It's okay. Come here.' I put my arm round her. She's lovely. Good skin, better figure and wide blue eyes, pools of cobalt. There, I'm a poet, too. She's so clever it makes me weep. Top ten in her Sergeant's Exam, looks like she's passed her Inspector's, too. She's a uniformed officer, though she works in Criminal Intelligence. Her thing is computers. Sometimes she brings home great piles of green-lined computer paper, all gobbledegook to me but she understands it. I don't know what she's doing with me . . . I've told her too: 'You should find some brilliant young barrister and marry him.' Then she gets angry.

Judy was wearing a nondescript beige mackintosh. It more or less covered the uniform underneath. I pulled at her collar and apologised about last night.

'Good Jimmy,' she sipped her orange juice. 'I'm glad you remember where you were getting drunk. It's a good thing not to lose control completely. For myself, I ended up being bored to death by a couple of louts all evening, then I had to fight one off all the way home in the taxi while his mate sat in the other seat, laughing. I had a really good time.'

'I'm sorry. I did come all this way to apologise.'

She shook her head, then brought her lips to my ear and said, 'No you didn't. You came all this way to find out about Albert Wilkins, you bastard. Don't lie to me.'

She kissed my ear. I felt like fainting. I've known her for years and years and it always drives me mad when she kisses my ear. Who cares about Wilkins?

'I've got my car outside,' I said. 'We could go off.'

'I've got fifteen minutes of lunch left. Time for another orange juice and a walk back.'

We walked close to each other on the way back. I like that. I like it when it's rainy and you can smell her perfume and she's close but not close. I like walking with her, nearly touching.

'Albert Wilkins,' she said, 'was born in Leytonstone in 1928. He's the son of a labourer, one of seven children. Here's a photograph of him. Don't look at it now, but tear it up and throw it away when you have looked at it. It's one of ours, taken on obbo. Wilkins has only two bits of form; one, believe it or not, for handling forged petrol coupons. That was in 1947. The other is for GBH in 1958.'

'What GBH?'

'He cut a bloke's ear off outside a dance hall in front of witnesses.'

'Charming.'

'He did time for that. He was nicked for attempted

43

murder in 1960 too, but that didn't stick. Something to do with the witnesses to the 1958 case all falling down stairs once a month while Wilkins was doing his bird for the GBH. The word got round, I suppose.'

It wasn't raining yet but it looked like it would. The sky hung dark and heavy over Victoria Street. Buses passed, lamps aglow. The traffic lights seemed unnaturally bright. Above us, in the New Scotland Yard building, neon lamps flickered on. I tucked the hooked part of my walking stick into my rainmac pocket, then took her in my arms.

'Thanks,' I said. 'I don't like to ask.' I kissed her. She smiled.

'It's okay. The things I've told you are matters of public record. You could have spent days finding them out, but it's not breaking any rules to tell you about it. It's a bit of a cheek to kiss your lover outside your boss's office, I think.'

I let her go and took my walking stick out of my pocket again.

'But ten floors below,' I said.

'Okay. Ten floors below. Jim, it definitely would be against the rules to tell you that Wilkins has run his own organisation for the past twenty years and that he's very high on the league table of target criminals. A lot of people inside that building are absolutely dying to get his scalp on their belt. Well, that's the sort of thing I wouldn't tell you.'

The rain started. Dollops of water splattered on the pavement. There was a flash in the distance, miles away, and a low rumble. The rain audibly splashed around us. I pulled a floppy, showerproof canvas trilby from my pocket and belted my mackintosh. Judy put up her umbrella and we crossed the road together. We parted in the entrance hall of NSY. The guard on the door recognised me and nodded. I think it's the stick as much as anything. I nodded back.

'What wouldn't you tell *me*?' Judy asked.

'I'm going away, probably for a few days. I've got a client who feels he's under threat from Wilkins, or at least from one of his drones, a man called Grant. Lenny Grant. That dodgy bugger Denis O'Keefe wants to get hold of me. I don't want to see him. I've decided I don't need him any more.'

'Good move.'

'Thanks. A solicitor in Clapton, Menke, is having trouble getting the money to pay me out of one of his clients. That's his story, anyway. Apart from that my entire life is hunky-dory and there's nothing I wouldn't tell you.'

'He's not asking you to offer physical protection, this client?'

'No. Don't be silly. I'll phone you at your flat when I get back.'

'Do,' she said and touched my lapel. We didn't kiss goodbye. It's not the sort of place you do.

Seven

I drove straight from NSY to Saffron Walden. I wasn't having any of that 'just get the train' nonsense from Duncan. I wanted to give his place a good look over and I wanted to be able to put his money through his letter-box and buzz off home under my own steam if I felt like it. All the way there I listened to a radio phone-in about when the Task Force was going to kick the Argies out of Port Stanley. I'd only heard of the Falklands a couple of months ago. Now it looked like people would die for it. I hoped not. I certainly wouldn't have volunteered to face any guns I didn't have to and I could do without losing any legs I didn't have to lose. I wished I could've told those boys that.

If I'd had the sense I'd have put Duncan's money through his letter-box there and then. I already knew he was lying to me. His wife, who he'd reckoned had recognised me in the paper, had never clapped eyes on me before. She hadn't been in the hall in Shoreditch when I went for the weigh-in before Lynch's fight, later in the street she hadn't seen me any better than I'd seen her, and she hadn't been George Duncan's wife when I used to use his gym in Romford all those years ago . . . no, I didn't believe a word of that. All the buddy-buddy crap from Duncan himself was hard to take, too. I mean, he'd owned the gym, I'd worked out in it. So had a couple of hundred other fellows in the course of a week. Duncan didn't know me from Adam. He'd seen my face in the papers – *maybe*, as an outside chance – and he'd seen me for two minutes maximum when I'd tried to serve the writ on his fighter. Someone may have reminded him that I'd used his gym in Romford, and he'd needed a private detective and just lit upon me because I'd come to his attention. As for Alison Duncan needing protection . . . that was a joke, as far as I could see.

My trouble is I've got an over-developed sense of humour. Also, it beat finding lost spouses and serving writs. Unwittingly, George Duncan had offered me a piece of real detective work, and I was hooked. The way things worked out later, I came to wish I hadn't been. Curiosity killed the catfish.

I'd never been to Saffron Walden before. It's not very remarkable. It's just about commutable from London, full of picture-postcard Essex houses, all coloured plasterwork, pargeting and revealed oak beams. It's the kind of place that makes me sick. Like Disneyland . . . though I haven't been to Disneyland. Chocolate-box-top England. Syrupy.

I put my car in the station car park at Audley End. That's where you go for Saffron Walden on the train. Then I pulled my gumboots on – not as easy as it sounds – and took a cab into town.

We went past a big house, no doubt the home of the Duke of Audley or some such robber baron made good. The cab driver pointed it out; very proud, as if he lived there.

He dropped me off in the main street. It's a pretty rich street, plenty of Range Rovers and all that stuff. Lots of middle-aged women in Home Counties uniform, pleated blue skirts and fluffy dogs. If Saffron Walden has any council estates they're well tucked away.

I bought a map of the area, located Duncan's house on it, then took a taxi to a road I reckoned was two fields away. The rain had started to fall pretty heavily here, too, and the cabbie clearly thought I was barmy for getting out of his car in a deserted country lane in the middle of a storm. I waited till he'd rounded a bend and then struck up the bank into a field. The field was full of green stuff and mud. The mud I recognised but the green stuff has to be in a sealed plastic Sainsbury's bag and clearly marked 'Broccoli' or 'Brussels Sprouts' or 'Bobby Beans' before I know what it is. I plodded through the green stuff and the rain fell on me and the mud stuck to my gumboots.

I got to a ditch and a hedge about a hundred yards from Duncan's house. I had to lie on the bank of the ditch, rain or no rain. I'd overestimated my walking ability – or underestimated the fact that ten minutes' downpour can turn a dry field into a quagmire. I was all in. I lay there with the rain splashing on my face for some minutes. The ditch smelled terrible. My back was soaked by the grass on the bank, my front by the rain. My hair was getting wet from rain soaking through the showerproof material of my hat. I turned over and watched the house through a hole in the hedge. I could see Duncan moving around inside. All the lights were on and I could see him moving back and forth in front of the window. If he was scared he wasn't acting like it. The house was lonely and exposed, a big red-brick job from the middle of the nineteenth century. There were a couple of outbuildings and I saw him go out to them once, scurrying with a coat thrown over his shoulders and a hat on his head. He didn't see me. He wasn't looking.

I didn't see his wife. I only saw George moving around and some laundry van delivering. The wife didn't even go out to that. Maybe they *were* scared. There was no wall around or in front of the house and you could see into it for miles around. The rain kept falling and I was tired and wet and cold now, cold as if I were catching a chill. It wasn't the weather. George Duncan made himself a cup of tea and settled down in his chintzy sitting room with a newspaper. Lucky old George. A rabbit sat on the lawn and stared at me. I left care of George to the rabbit and walked back into town. It's a long walk. It's even further to the station, which is where my dry clothes were in a bag in the boot of my car. What would the cab drivers of England do without me? I wondered.

By eight o'clock I was in a comfortable chair in a pub. I could still hear rain outside and I was reading previews of cricket matches from the morning's *Times*. I had three large scotches inside me, a fourth on the table in front of me, dry clothes on my back and a cab on the way to pick me up. It beat lying in a field. There's something nice about reading journalism when you've got the drop on the journalist, like

48

knowing the matches he'd previewed couldn't be played and hadn't been.

'Taxi for you sir,' called the barman. The driver was the same one who'd driven me out to my rendezvous with the rabbit, but if he recognised me he said nothing. I made him carry my bag. I don't tip for nothing.

Eight

'*Jimmy! Jimmy!* Come in, Jimmy.' George Duncan greeted me as if I were a long-lost brother and the suitcase at my side were full of pound notes instead of shirts, socks and underpants. 'Alison, c'm 'ere. This is the guy I was telling you about. Harry's short-term replacement.' His accent hovered in mid-Atlantic. I wondered which side it would land.

A woman came down the stairs. Mid-to-late twenties, blonde but natural – not-too-blonde. Beautifully dressed in an emerald green long thing, all off the shoulder and clinging where it should. She looked a cracker. I was in love until she opened her mouth.

'*So* pleased to meet you, Mr Jimmy. My husband has told me much about you.' She was reciting lines she'd learned and she wasn't very good at it. I took the hand she offered. It was cold and damp. She was apprehensive, I could see that from her face. I didn't know what of; not the threats against Duncan. He'd said he hadn't told her.

'*Jenner*,' I said. 'Jimmy, or more precisely James, is my first name.'

'Oh.' She let her hand drop. 'How stoopid of me, Mr Jenner. I'm so sorry.'

It was me. *I* was making her nervous. She turned half away. She had her hair up, pinned loosely behind her head, and as she turned she showed a long, cool, naked neck, downy and handsome. I smiled to let her know she wasn't 'stoopid' but she wouldn't look into my face.

'Why don't you run upstairs and fix your bag or something while I give Jimmy a drink and have a chat with him?'

50

She went up. Slim ankles slid in and out of a vent at the back of the green clingy dress. Looking after Mrs Duncan would be the nicest job I ever had – as long as she didn't open her mouth again. No . . . who cares? For a hundred quid a day I'd even listen to the mouth.

Duncan steered me into a study off the hall. It was lined with photographs of boxers and books about boxers. There was a big mahogany desk with a leather inlay. On top of the desk was a tray with a whisky bottle and glasses.

'I'll only give you a small one. You won't be staying long, I'm afraid. Your first job is to take Mrs Duncan back to London tonight. See her to our flat, but you can just leave her there and go back in the morning.' He handed me a huge glass with a very lonely bead of whisky in the bottom.

'Ice?'

'No. I don't want to smother it.' I put my hand over the top of my glass. He didn't even laugh.

'Trouble?' I said.

'Nothing to concern you.'

I drank my whisky before it evaporated.

'Nothing to do with your "dispute"?' I asked.

He sat in a mock-antique captain's chair on the other side of the desk, rocked back in it and took a good gulp of his whisky.

'I told you all I'm telling you. I'm paying you good money to make sure my wife's okay. Don't fill your head with a load of stuff that's not your business.'

'I need to know what's going on, though,' I said. I sat on the edge of the desk. He frowned. This obviously wasn't a desk that was sat on a lot. 'For instance, is your wife going to a party?'

'Party?' He frowned again. He was not a pretty man and his muscles must've been practising that frown for well over forty years. It made him look like he'd been eating a lemon when the elephant sat on his face. 'Oh . . . you mean the dress.'

I nodded. I could've been rude and sarcastic but he was paying for the interview. I'm only ever rude and sarcastic for free.

'She likes to dress up when she's meeting people,' he said.

51

'Who's she meeting?'

He stood, drained the glass and set it on the leather. I noticed there was a space on the wall, pride of place in the middle of the photographs. I'd have laid a pound to a penny that's where Tommy Lynch's photograph had been until recently.

'*You*, dummy. Come on, I'll show you the car.'

We went back into the hallway. Alison Duncan was heaving a large suitcase down the stairs. She was wearing a three-quarter length pale blue rainmac over the emerald green evening dress. Some of her hair had fallen down from the clasp behind her head.

'Will this do?' she called down. She meant the mac, I guessed. George Duncan looked at her for a second.

'You'll do.'

'I've got another bag upstairs,' she said.

George waved his hand magnanimously.

'Plenty of time, doll. Bring them out in your own time.'

He opened the door and pointed at a shed.

'The car's over there. Have you driven a Jag before?'

I nodded that I had. I wondered why he hadn't put the mortise lock on if he was so frightened. The door was held by a rim latch alone.

George Duncan showed me all the controls of the Jaguar as if it were Concorde 002. He insisted. By the time he'd finished his wife had dragged the bags down and across the yard to our shed. George lifted them easily and dumped them in the boot. He said goodbye to her and pulled the shed doors wide to let me get the car out. I flicked the headlamp switch and the beams fell on old rusted farm implements, a hayrake, a pitchfork and some big metal flail thing that goes on the back of tractors. Alison Duncan sat in the front passenger seat and I nodded at the rusty farm gear.

'I didn't realise this was a whole farm you had here.'

'Oh it's not, Mr Jenner.'

I nodded again.

'What's all that stuff for then?'

She stared through the windscreen, blinking.

'What stuff?'

She sounded like a speak-your-weight machine. I backed

the car out. I hung around so he could come over and say goodbye properly to her. He never did though. Now it was time to go, Duncan seemed nervous and anxious to get on. He never even waved goodbye to her. He just stood in front of his house, watching in the rain till we turned the first bend and we lost sight of him. Mrs Duncan didn't look back, either. I thought perhaps they'd rowed before I got there. What was it to do with me, eh? Duncan was right – it was no concern of mine. The fact that she was nervous, didn't want to speak, had no South African accent and sat next to the hired hand in the front of the car; all this was no concern of mine also. Nothing was my concern. A man has an ugly villain making threats against him – and, I presume, his wife – he has bird-shot fired at his door, a threatening letter delivered to his house, and then he hires a crippled detective to protect his wife; a wife who's a rotten actress and has clearly never been chauffeured around before, a wife who's supposed to come from Cape Town but whose accent wandered between Stafford and South London. It stank.

We'd been set up, I was sure. I drove north to Cambridge. Even Alison knew we weren't in London.

'This isn't London,' she said.

'I'm missing the motorway,' I said. 'I saw a sign in Saffron saying the motorway was closed.'

'I didn't see a sign.'

'Don't worry, Mrs Duncan. I saw it.'

She leaned forward and switched the radio on, pushing the buttons until she got some pop music. What sounded like a cat being strangled swore everlasting love and loyalty to his Ramona, then plucked his guitar with his brothers. A husky, late-night lady DJ assured us she was filling in for someone else. I knew how she felt. I took the road for Baldock and London. I kept looking in the rear-view mirror for car headlamps. It was rainy and night-time, though. What should I expect to see but headlamps in my rear-view mirror? I saw hundreds. By the time I was on the A1 all the headlamps were keeping pace with me. That's the point of a motorway. Things are never the way they're made out in films. My back was soaked with sweat from fear, my hands gripped the wheel too hard, I flinched every time a car moving too fast went past, I was dying for a pee but I wasn't stopping the car in the service area. Who wants to die in South Mimms? It's not very prepossessing. They don't put that in the films, either.

We reached the Barbican around midnight. It's surprising how empty the streets of the City can be. The rain had stopped at last. The water squelched between the big tyres of the Jag and the tarmac. We drove down Chiswell Street, then under the arch and down Aldersgate Street. We went round and round the Barbican, with her peering out of the window.

'Haven't you lived here long?' I said.

'Oh, ages. I just get confused by it all. I always get confused.' She said all this without looking at me.

We found her block. A copper showed us, one of those pantomime City of London coppers with a big hat, rolled up rain-cape and a red-and-white duty-band on his arm like nothing had changed in the City of London police for fifty years. Like they'll never be short of time to give you directions. I followed his directions, with the woman I was now convinced was not Mrs Duncan avoiding my eyes and not speaking and me trying to drive and follow the street signs all at the same time. When we got there I locked her in the car, walked upstairs and had a good poke around the flat and the landing outside. It was an expensive flat, expensive to rent and expensively furnished. All brash and bad taste but very clean and very tidy and smelling of lavender polish. There were more pictures of boxers on the wall and another gap where I suppose Tommy Lynch had rested till recently. He must feel like Stalin's ghost. I sat on the sofa and listened to the silence. Nothing. A tap was dripping in the bathroom. I went out on the balcony. All clear, no muggers or murderers or bashers-up on the balcony. So far so good. A hundred feet below me I could see the shape of the Jaguar. I'd left the sidelights on. I knew the woman would be sitting in there waiting for me. I wondered what would be going through her mind . . . did she know Duncan had set the two of us up? I doubted it. Had he? I thought so. Should I tell her? I supposed I should. I didn't know. I went inside, poured myself a big measure of Duncan's whisky and went to the fridge for ginger ale and ice. I went back onto the balcony and drank the whisky from Duncan's big expensive tumbler. I looked at his big expensive living room through the french windows. I turned and looked over London. Yellow strips of street-lighting ran towards me. Some lights were on in an office block in Wood Street. I could see matchstick figures moving about in it. I looked down at Duncan's expensive car again, drank my whisky and then threw his expensive cut-glass whisky tumbler over the top of the balcony. I heard it tinkle as it hit the ground, but by that time I was inside again and on my way to the lift.

'Where have *you* been?' "Mrs Duncan" had decided to go on the attack.

'Get out,' I said. 'Is the stuff in the bags yours or hers?'

'I don't know. . . .'

'Cut that rubbish out. I'm not in the mood.' I went to the boot and pulled the bags out. I nearly fell over. '*Are these yours*?'

'I'm sorry, I don't know what you mean.'

She was either very stupid or Duncan had promised her something.

'Look, whoever-you-are. I think Duncan's been having me on. Either he's been having you on too, or you're in it with him. What's it to be?'

She hung her head and looked at the bags and said again, 'I don't know what you mean.'

'Suit yourself,' I said. 'The lift's over there. I've been upstairs and there are no bogey men. I won't offer to carry your bags,' I picked up my stick from where it had been lying, against the side of the Jaguar. 'You can see why.'

'I don't think my husband's going to be very pleased about this,' she said. I couldn't see her face properly in the gloom. I wanted to help her but I needed a shove, some push towards it. I thought if Duncan was using us as targets for Wilkins then 'Mrs Duncan' would be able to use any help she could get. The best help I could give her would be to put her in a taxi back to wherever she come from. She picked up the bags.

'I don't know your husband, Missus. But I think you may be right. Why don't you go home?'

But she carried the bags over to the lift. It took her several goes. She had to keep stopping because the bags were too heavy. I locked up Duncan's car and took her the car keys.

'You'll need these, too,' I said.

The lift door was open. I took a long look at her face in the light of the lift compartment. I smelled her perfume, looked into her eyes. They were brown and soft and stupid, like a milch cow. I had a nasty feeling that's what she was to Duncan, and it's what I was meant to be. I turned and walked away as quick as I could.

I walked to Finsbury Circus, went in and sat on a bench for half an hour. I was really angry with Duncan. I could hear some tramps drinking and arguing on the other side of the little park. A copper came and threw them out. I left before he came over to me. I splashed through the puddles to Liverpool Street Station, bought a coffee and drank it watching trains that didn't move. A policeman was moving people on here too, but I obviously looked like a bona fide traveller because he ignored me. Other bona fide travellers embraced over the ticket gates, holding each other desperately, kissing passionately. A loud but muffled announcement came over the public address. A black man passed me pushing a broom and a pile of rubbish. He waited patiently for me to lift my legs without asking me to do it. I ignored him and after a while he went away, still pushing the rubbish. I couldn't go home. I'd presumed I was staying in Saffron Walden and left my flat keys in the car. Judy had a set, but I didn't feel like waking her at one a.m. to ask for my flat keys. I went to a phone and called Zorba's number. No answer. He could've put me up. I rang Gal.

'Were you already awake?' I said.

'Yeah. It's okay.'

'Have you got a motor?'

'Me brother's.'

'Come and pick us up in Liverpool Street, will you, Gal? And bring my office key too.'

'Whereabouts?'

'In front of Bishopsgate nick.'

Nine

Canning Town had been washed clean by the rain. As clean as it was ever going to be, anyway. Gary drove me there in his brother's Rover three-and-a-half litre. I don't believe a kid like Gal could be insured to drive it. Come to that, I'd be surprised if his brother's insured to drive it.

I felt better with Gal. Being with Duncan and the woman had left a nasty taste in my mouth. I washed it away with two cans of Special Brew Gal had in the back of the car and a take-away doner kebab we picked up in Whitechapel. The nice thing about doner is that if you have enough raw onion and chilli sauce on it you never know what harm it's doing you. Wash it down with two cans of Special Brew and you'd think nothing could do you any harm. That's how I felt when Gary dropped me off. I gave him some of Duncan's money, told him to go to Audley End and get my car in the morning and to dump the stolen Rover now and walk home so he didn't get arrested.

'What stolen Rover?' He grinned.

'Just dump it, Gal, and give me the office keys.'

He gave me the keys and drove away like a man possessed. One day the police'll catch him. I could see one of their Transits from my doorstep, cruising slowly on the Canning Town flyover. I went upstairs, noticed that Gal had brought his own wax crayon for the gin bottle last night, pulled an old army blanket from a cupboard and curled up on the sofa. I felt dead. I'd picked some letters up on the way in. They could wait. I just needed to sleep. I slept in my jacket and trousers under the old army blanket and I went off as if I'd been drugged.

I woke at dawn, whenever that is. I don't see it often. Maybe the chilli woke me, maybe sleeping in an unfamiliar place (for sleeping), or maybe it was the sun. There wasn't much traffic on the flyover so it was pretty early, I knew. I made some Camp coffee in a cup and opened my letters. They were all rubbish, including a request from the solicitor, Menke, that I find the disappeared owner of the house a client of his wanted to buy. Menke's jobs were money for old rope as long as you didn't ever expect to *get* the money. I wrote 'no' on the bottom of the letter he'd sent me, then sealed the envelope with sticky tape and wrote 'return to sender, not known at this address' on the front and drew an arrow pointing to Menke's address on the back. I don't mind earning easy money but I like to get paid for what I do.

I phoned directory enquiries for Duncan's number. I thought I'd give him a good morning call, some obscene message like what he could do with his rotten job. He wasn't in the book. Then I rang Zorba's flat again. No Zorba. How come I'd woken at dawn for the first time in my life and no one wanted to be awake with me? I rang Gal's flat and his young lady answered and said she didn't know where he was, she thought he was with me, and did I know what the time was? I said no and hung up. I played my tape machine.

'You are through to Jenner's. James Jenner speaking. If you'd like to leave a message wait till the tone, then leave your name, number and message if you wish and I'll get back to you as soon as I can.'

Beep.

'Where've you been, Jimmy? Didn't you get my message? I've been looking all over town for you, but I can't find you. I've been looking all over for your crazy Greek pal, too. Phone me at home, whenever. Any time.'

O'Keefe again. He's persistent. I wondered what he wanted with Zorba. Even if I were in a mood to talk to O'Keefe, which I wasn't, I couldn't help him find Zorba. I didn't know where he'd gone, either. All I'd had was the tape message: 'Hullo, Sjimmy, Zorba here. I'm no goina be round for a few days.' If O'Keefe wanted him, Zorba had better make it a few months.

I lay back on the sofa. I could feel a lump by my spine.

58

I pulled the blanket over my head. I remember thinking I should get the sofa restuffed if I was going to keep using it as a bed, then I was asleep.

I woke up when the door caved in. It only came part the way at first and then a big meaty fist came through the smashed panel and turned the key on my side of the mortise lock. What seemed to be ten but were in fact three men burst into the room. They were ugly and large and unshaven and they looked angry. They were also carrying pistols and the pistols were pointing at me.

'Hi,' I said.

'Shuddup,' said the one in the middle. He was over six feet and as wide as he was tall. He holstered his pistol under his arm and it was then I knew they were policemen, not maniacs in the service of Duncan or Wilkins. The policeman in the middle advanced on me while his fellows covered him. Maybe they'd been told I had a sten gun built into my leg.

'Hands in the air,' said the one who'd advanced on me. He was a dark-haired fellow with a bushy beard and gleaming brown eyes; deep brown, almost black. I held my hands up. Who wouldn't, having been asked so nicely at the point of two guns? He pulled me upright.

'We haven't been introduced,' I said.

'Shuddup,' he said again. 'Lie face first on the floor.'

My office is just that, an office. It has two chairs, a sofa, a desk, a built-in cupboard, two filing cabinets, a telephone, an answering machine, a desk lamp and me in it, as a rule. I can easily accommodate one other person in it, two extra's a squeeze and three a definite crush. All that's presuming no one tries to lie down. We compromised on the matter by having me lie on the stairs. They handcuffed me behind my back and then searched me. The big bearded fellow stopped when he got to my leg and said, 'What's this?' meaning the harness for the false part. I'm afraid I lied and told him it was something I'm sure my mother would be shocked to discover I even knew such a word for. Maybe she wouldn't. I had noticed a marked absence of Judge's Rules, even *Christie versus Leachinsky* and all that in these boys' techniques, but when I pointed it out to the bearded guy he kicked me in the side. I can take a hint. Meanwhile the other two detectives were ripping my office apart. Through the doorway it looked like a snowstorm, only made of paper. Glass broke, drawers slammed.

'Just tell me what you want,' I said, 'I'll bring it to you.' The bearded man came down to me again.

'Okay, okay . . . I'll shut up. Stop kicking me,' I said. But he kicked me again anyway. I had the distinct impression that the three detectives had taken against me. I'd been in on arrests and searches before, but I don't think I'd ever seen it done so roughly, or unfeelingly. I didn't stay to see the end of the search. Two uniform men came and half-pulled, half-carried me down the stairs. I said I needed my stick but they wouldn't speak, and then when I got to the street they were surprised by my wobbly walk. I'd have been okay if the big ape hadn't kicked me in the side. The uniform men stuffed me in the back of a traffic car – strawberry stripe, blue light, the lot – then they sat either side of me. There was a sergeant in the driver's seat. I didn't say anything more, my brain had woken up by now. I didn't know what they were all so upset about but I'd worked out they'd tell me sooner or later. I could wait, at least till my hands went numb. Then I'd have to say something.

The sergeant put the blue light and the two-tones on and we drove down to the Blackwall Tunnel Approach, then along the motorway to Hackney and finally Shoreditch via Old Ford, Old Ford Road, Cambridge Heath Road and the Old Bethnal Green Road. I guessed the time for about ten a.m.. The traffic was heavy. The driver didn't rush. Wherever we were going didn't need the fire brigade. We just kept the horns on and drove at a regular pace, he didn't make the tyres screech. We crossed Hackney Road and went into a maze of little streets, then stopped next to a railway arch.

They pulled me out of the car. The sun was warming up. Little white clouds moved slowly across the sky. The railway arch looked dark and uninviting, and there was red-and-white tape across the road to stop people straying into the arch. At the far end I could hear a generator going and an arc lamp cast a little pool of light on two men bending over a bundle. Out of the other side of the arch I could see a group of people milling around and more of the red-and-white tape. The people were lit by daylight there. Then I could see cars and vans and I could hear police radios. A middle-aged man separated from the crowd and ducked under the tape at the far end of the arch. He walked towards me.

'All right, sergeant. Thanks very much. Can you release the cuffs and come down here with us, please?' It was framed as a question but it was an order. The sergeant called one of the uniform boys over from their Rover to uncuff me. I took a long look at the middle-aged man. He was about fifty, dressed in a smart but not flashy blue suit. Neat tie, neat haircut, sharp blue eyes, almost white hair. His face had that repose, that confident look of a man used to giving orders and having people follow them. I thought he's the sort of man who'd never yell, and that would make him all the more dangerous and difficult. The uniform policeman released the cuffs and the detective held up the tape for me to bend under.

'I can't,' I said. 'My leg.' I could, but I wanted to give nothing away. I didn't even want to bend under a tape. 'I can't walk far. They wouldn't let me bring my stick.'

The detective unpeeled the tape from the two-sided sticky stuff holding it to the wall.

'I'm Chief Superintendent Maher. You are Mr Jenner. Sergeant, would you be so kind as to let this gentleman lean on your arm? He's disabled.'

We walked through the arch to the arc lamp like this. When we got there the Chief Superintendent waved the two men away from the bundle, then indicated I should draw near and keep out of the cast of the light. A train went over. The arch shook. Maher waited until the rumbling had quite died away and then said, 'You used to be a policeman, I believe, Mr Jenner.'

I wanted to say, 'I've got a police pension, a Commendation from the Commissioner himself and the Queen's Police Medal, now what's the idea of having me roughed up?' It came out as a silent nod.

'Well?' he said. 'I'm right in that presumption, yes?'

'Yes.'

61

'I wonder if you'd give me the benefit, then, Mr Jenner, of your considered opinion about this.'

He leaned over the bundle. It was covered by a plastic sheet, dull, green plastic the colour of shooting boots. Maher pulled the sheet back. Under it was a bundle of clothes. Some of the clothes had arms and legs pointing out of them. Some of the clothes were a pale blue ladies' rainmac. The others were a green emerald evening dress. It was a long dress but it was all twisted up around the shins of the body inside it. I could see a little vent at the front that was originally meant to be at the back and let the slim ankles slide in and out as the lady wearer walked upstairs.

'It's a body,' I said.

Maher nodded.

'Good, good.' He held me by the lapel and dragged my face down close to the body. 'Dead, you think, eh?'

'Huh.' I nodded.

He pulled me down closer yet, leading me sideways so as not to lose the light from the arc lamp.

'And what do you make of this?'

I was inches away from the head of the corpse. It wasn't like a head I'd ever seen. There was no skin from the mandible up to the crown of the cranium. No scalp, no hair, no flesh on the cheeks and there appeared to be no tongue within them. Several teeth appeared to have been torn out, but most were there. The eyes had gone, too. So had the ears.

'It's had the flesh stripped off,' I said.

'Good. What else do you see?' said Maher. He whispered the words close by my side. His face was near to mine, his hot breath on my cheek. Another train went over.

I waited until it had gone this time and then I said, 'There's no blood. It didn't happen here.'

'Good. Good.' He let me go and I wavered for a second, about to topple into the corpse, my face into its 'face'. The uniformed sergeant pulled me back. I breathed heavily. I was sweating.

'You could've been a detective,' said Maher. 'Anything else you want to tell me? No little bells being rung?'

'No.'

Maher wiped his brow with his palm, then turned his hand to the light so he could see what had come off.

'It could be quite a long journey you and I are setting out on, Mr Jenner, I can see.'

I shrugged. He said, 'Would you take this gentleman down to Peter Street, sergeant?' The sergeant took me back to the Rover. I could see flashguns going off under the arch, official photographers, not press, I knew. I wanted my walking stick and a cup of coffee and a roll. I wanted a newspaper to read while I sorted my thoughts out. Most of all I wanted to get out of the Rover and walk away. They handcuffed me again, only this time with my hands in front of my body. It's against regulations (Force Orders, policemen call them) to handcuff a man behind his back. The two uniformed constables piled in on either side of me and the sergeant drove us away from the arch.

Ten

They kept me in for twenty-four hours. It seemed like a month. During the day nobody spoke to me hardly. They noted who I was, took my tie, belt and shoelaces away, then took me down to a cell. When I asked for something to read, a pink-faced young constable brought me a week-old copy of the *Guardian*. I don't even like fresh copies of the *Guardian*, but I took it anyway. They gave me three meals I'd have had to have been starving to eat. I ate the supper because I was starving by then and I drank some watery cocoa at about ten. I remembered that when I was a probationer a fat desk sergeant locked us new boys in a cell, one to a cell, for about an hour one night. He said it was to make sure we knew how it felt. It was a fine idea but I could have told him now that it doesn't compare to when someone locks the door and means it. I didn't like that night locked in. I still had ground-in ink on my skin from where they'd taken my dabs during the afternoon. I lay all night in the brightly lit cell looking at my dirty fingers, then reading every page of the newspaper, then looking at my fingers, then reading every page of the newspaper. I finally fell asleep around dawn and was immediately awoken by another pink-faced young constable and offered two slices of old, unsmoked bacon with the rind on and a half-cooked, still-watery egg. I gave it back but drank the tea that came with it. The young constable took the stuff away and came back with my shoelaces and belt. Not my tie, though, and not my jacket.

'I hope you've got my jacket hung up neat somewhere,

constable. It's a very important jacket. Very good-quality stuff.'

He stood in the doorway and swung the keys on the big gaoler's ring but he said nothing.

'I don't know why you took my shoelaces, anyway. I mean, I'd understand it if a man could commit suicide by hanging from his wrist or his ankle but he can't. It absolutely *has* to be the neck, and unless you pick up a man in mountaineering boots there just ain't enough material in a shoelace to go round even *my* neck. Know what I mean?'

He still wouldn't talk. We walked along the corridor to a door then through the door and into a little yard.

'Exercise,' he said.

I heard someone locking the door behind us. I said, 'Walking stick, Tonto.'

But he just turned and began to pace the little yard. Above us a patch of morning blue sky stared down. The young constable walked round the little yard, about ten paces in each direction, as if to show me how it was done. I hobbled along behind him. After ten minutes of this the door to the yard opened and a nose peeped out.

'Bring him in.'

It's very strange to be talked about in the third person while you're there. Only parents and schoolteachers do it, hospital consultants with their students, lawyers in court. That more or less exhausts the list. Now I have to add policeman, though I was a policeman for years and never noticed.

I was taken in, through the charge room and upstairs to the CID offices. I was shoved into a room there full of typewriters, phones and desks. That's all – no people. Chief Superintendent Maher followed me in and then came a young detective I'd never seen before, with mid-brown hair, a five-ten, inconspicuous young man; more or less the perfect detective, I should think. He had a plain, ordinary face with mid-brown eyes and the most ordinary mouth I'd ever seen. A lip on the top and one on the bottom. He didn't even have a broken nose. If I had seen him five minutes later in the street I'd never have noticed him.

'Sit down, please,' said Maher. 'This is Detective Sergeant

Robson. He'll make notes.' The door opened again. 'Not now!' called Maher. And it closed.

I sat.

'Give me your version of it, Mr Jenner.'

'Of what?' If they hadn't taken me into the detention cell or an interview room it must mean the place is full of 'suspects'.

Maher sighed. He looked at the plain-faced detective who sighed too. I sighed . . . why not?

'Let's go from Tuesday. Where were you on Tuesday?'

'On Tuesday I was in Essex. On Wednesday I was beaten up by men in your employ, then shown a body and brought here. This is Thursday. I've been here continuously over Wednesday and Thursday.'

'Fill it out.'

'No . . . you.'

Maher sighed again and sat in a chair by my side, very close. He looked in front of himself while he spoke and at first he was wringing his hands, as if he was very agitated. He soon calmed down, though.

'Mr Jenner. You are something of a hero to the Metropolitan Police, to the public at large and, most importantly, to the press. I don't know why you did it but you left the job and you've spent the years since consorting with the scum of the earth, muggers, pimps. . . .'

'Coppers, lawyers?' I offered. He ignored me.

'Every type of social undesirable. You were seen in the company of a woman. Her husband claims he employed you to protect her. You do not appear to have made a very good job of the protecting. She is dead. When I look at the hire car her husband had, I find your dabs all over it. When I go to her flat, I find your dabs all over it. Did you kill her?'

'No.'

'Make a note of that, Sergeant Robson.' Robson made a note. Maher turned and clapped his hand on my shoulder. '*Now* fill it out. Tell me why I shouldn't believe this man's wife was killed by you.'

I shook my head.

'Why should *I* kill her?'

'Tell me,' he said, 'tell me.'

I gave Maher the story of my couple of days in the employ of George Duncan, how he'd contacted me, how he'd asked me round to the Bonaventura. I didn't tell him about my recce in Saffron Walden. I told him about meeting 'Mrs Duncan' and how I'd been led to believe she would be South African.

'She wasn't,' I said.

'How do you know?'

'Her accent. It was all wrong. It wandered.'

'She'd lived here a long time,' Maher said. 'She was even born here.'

'She'd have had to have spent her life on the M1 motorway to get *her* accent.'

He smiled to show he had a sense of humour. I went on.

'I'd seen her before, anyway, after the Lynch fight in Shoreditch.'

'Yes?' He sat forward. I had him hooked. This was something new.

'I delivered a writ on Tommy Lynch the morning of the fight. We got chatting, very friendly like, and he ended up giving me a ticket. Afterwards I waited outside for a cab. Duncan and Lynch argued. A car full of heavies drove up and took Lynch away, then Duncan's wife started yelling at him and whacking him round the head.'

'Did you get a good look at her?'

'No. It was dark and I was some distance away.'

'Did you hear her speak clearly? You're the only one who's mentioned a South African accent.'

I shook my head.

'No. The bit about the accent was supposition. She was yelling and you know how it distorts someone's voice.' I cracked my knuckles and leaned back in my chair. 'I don't have any evidence that the woman I picked up at George Duncan's house wasn't his wife. . . . I just felt it. She was the right shape for the woman I saw outside the boxing hall, she was the right age too, I guess. The accent bit I just don't know about. It just *felt* wrong, you know? It just felt like a set-up.'

'You're claiming that the woman you picked up from Duncan's house wasn't his wife?' Maher said.

I nodded.

67

'Yes.'

'And you don't have any evidence to offer. It was just a feeling.'

'Yes.'

'And you're claiming that you thought the whole thing was some sort of set-up, and that you didn't like the look of it so you got out . . . am I right?'

'That's what I thought. I still do.'

'If you were right and this woman wasn't Duncan's wife, didn't it occur to you you were putting her in danger?'

A phone rang. D. S. Robson picked it up and said, 'No.'

I said no too. I said I'd made her a perfectly good offer of an 'out' and she'd chosen not to take it. What could I do? Move in with her?

'As a matter of fact,' I said, 'I don't even know that that cadaver you showed me *was* even the woman I dropped off. She was wearing a similar dress and coat, but I guess you could get those anywhere. Maybe there were three women. Or maybe it was her. I don't know. I just had a gut feeling.'

Maher didn't look very sympathetic to my 'gut feeling'.

'It was her. We printed her, of course. Her dabs were in the car, plus yours and Duncan's and a couple of thousand others. We're working our way through the others. For now all we have is you and Duncan.'

'What about him?'

'He spent that night at the house of a close friend in Saffron Walden. He went over there after you and his wife left, drank rather more than was good for him and stayed the night.'

'Maybe the friend was lying,' I said.

Maher shook his head and stood up. 'Coffee,' he said to the DS, who duly left. 'The friend is the head of a Regional Crime Squad. I don't think he's lying. He's been in the job for twenty-seven years and he's never been caught lying. I don't see why he should now and I'm going ahead on that basis. You might be, though, Jenner. Someone might have got at you to take the Duncan woman somewhere quiet and do her in. The characters who took Duncan's boxer away, for example. Maybe they got you to do it. Maybe they only got you to deliver the woman . . . I don't know. You look like a good suspect and all you're giving me by way of alibi or excuse is some nonsense about the body not being Mrs Duncan. You're the only person who thinks that.' He sighed. He didn't believe I'd killed her. He was just trying the story on me.

Suddenly Maher said, 'Do you know who drove Lynch away that night?'

'I think it could have been a bloke called Grant, a rival manager.'

'And he never hired you to kill the woman?' There was a twinkle in his eye as he spoke. He was asking the question for the sake of form, I knew. He was asking so he could write, 'I asked Jenner. . . .'

'And why should I do it?' I said.

'Money?'

I shook my head. Robson brought the coffee back. It was good coffee, not the stuff they gave me downstairs. In the cells they give you the cheapest instant brown stuff they can lay hands on. I drank the coffee and asked for another. Robson scowled but Maher sent him off for it.

'You'll find a cheque book in my belongings downstairs. Prepare a letter of authorisation and I'll sign it and you can find out for yourself how my bank account is. I don't need money and I don't need to kill for it.'

He nodded. 'I'll do that.'

'You do. I'll sign.'

'Something else?'

'What? *I* had no reason to kill her. I've never killed anybody and I don't have any reason to start now. You find someone who did have a reason and there's your killer. But it ain't me.'

Maher took my arm and pulled me towards the window. Outside ordinary people rushed past on their daily business. Lucky them.

'What do you see?' he asked. It was obviously a favourite trick of his.

I said, 'I don't know.' I was tired of the trick. Maher pulled my arm more and held me close to himself and to the window.

'I see people,' he said. 'Hundreds of people. Bus-loads of people. Pavements full of people, shops full of people. I see people walking and people waiting. People standing . . .

69

look, I even see one sitting.' He pointed to a child who'd obviously gone off this walking lark and sat on the pavement's edge, refusing all exhortations from his mother to abandon his kerb and come home. 'What do *you* see, Jimmy Jenner? Tell me what you see.' He let me go. I pulled back the anti-blast net to see better.

'I see people too,' I said.

'But what's the difference between those people and you, Jimmy Jenner?'

I stared a little longer. Robson came back and put a fresh cup of coffee on the window-sill between us. Maher put his hand on the cup.

'Answer me.'

'They're out there and I'm in here.'

He pursed his lips.

'Not bad. Not bad, Sergeant Robson, eh?'

'Not bad, sir.'

'We think that's quite a good answer. What other differences, Jimmy Jenner?'

I was really fed up by now, I said, 'They've all got two legs and I've got one.'

Maher nodded, letting his brow touch the window where I'd pulled the net back. A film of grease stayed on the glass. I looked closely at his face. He was tired, he seemed to have aged ten years since our meeting in the street yesterday. We were getting on towards lunch on Thursday and I'd have been willing to bet this man had hardly slept since early Wednesday. Whenever they'd found the corpse.

'Shall I tell you what I see, Jimmy Jenner?'

I didn't answer. He said, 'I see hundreds of people who *weren't* the last person to be seen with Mrs Duncan. I see hundreds of people who *weren't* hired to look after her. That's what I see. That's why they're out there and you're in here.'

'Do you believe I killed her?'

'No. Though I'm willing to have it proved to me. You're our only real suspect. You know how it is.'

I took Maher's hand off my coffee and lifted the cup to my lips. It was nearly cold but I drank it anyway.

'I know you've got nothing on me. I haven't gone in for all that "Where's my lawyer" caper up till now because I

70

thought you'd ignore it, but I have to say now I've heard it that you don't appear to have a whole lot of stuff to hold me on. I'd like you to charge me with her murder or let me go because I'm getting a bit fed-up in the glossy green steel barred paradise I have for a home at the moment. I want out.'

Maher nodded. 'I'll let you out.' He opened the door.

'I'd like you to call off your hounds, too. I'd like you to tell your colleagues on this investigation that you don't believe I did it. I don't want to be followed round London by coachloads of flatfeet. It'll ruin my business. I don't want any early-morning alarm calls like yesterday's.'

He smiled.

'Come with me and I'll do it now. I'm sorry about yesterday. The men who came weren't from here. They just got the message you were a murder suspect, then they went to get you with the kind of firmness a murder suspect might need. As for your business,' he held his hands out, palms up, 'I couldn't harm that the way you have. I don't suppose there'll be much call for your services once the word gets around that your clients' wives die. Come this way, anyway.'

I followed him along a corridor. We went into a large room through a door marked 'Incident Room'. There were telephones, typewriters and *people* in this one. It was crowded and noisy and busy. The noises subsided as people saw Maher. He held his arms up for silence, like a football star.

'For those who aren't familiar with him, this is Mister James Jenner, formerly of the Metropolitan Police. I'm sure you will remember the unfortunate series of events that overtook him a few years ago in the West End. Some of you probably know he's been mixed up in this business we have to hand, and he's anxious that you should all know I don't believe he murdered the Duncan woman.'

People nodded and carried on working. I had to admire him, it was much better than showing my photograph round 'this is one of our suspects, keep your eye on him'. They'd never forget me now. Maher bent into a cupboard and came out with my walking stick and a set of keys. My flat keys.

'We borrowed these from a young lady friend of yours so you could get home okay. You can pick up the rest of your property at the desk. Show Mr Jenner out, will you, sergeant?'

The sergeant touched my elbow. I moved away. My attention was fixed on a poster-sized photograph on the far side of the room.

'Who's that?'

'Alison Duncan.'

'No it's not,' I said. 'That's not the woman that I brought to London. That's someone else completely.'

The room stopped again. Men and women looked at me. A young WDC speaking into a phone dropped her voice to a whisper.

'It *looks* like her but it's someone else. Definitely. That's not the woman I dropped off at the Barbican,' I said.

Maher walked me downstairs himself.

'Photographs make a difference,' he said. 'You may have trouble just with the photograph. It wouldn't be the first time a man or woman didn't look like his or her photograph.'

'It's not her.'

'Who is it then?' he asked.

'That's your job.'

He waited while the desk sergeant counted out my belongings from a plastic bag and I signed for them. He looked over my shoulder while I loaded my pockets with the kind of rubbish you need in your pockets. Then he opened the frosted glass door and led me to the street door.

'Goodbye,' said Maher, ' . . . by the way, a youngster was picked up yesterday in a stolen Rover. Barking police reckon there are three sets of dabs inside it. One's the kid's. One of the others appears to match the owner. They reckon the third matches the ones we took off you.'

'Oh yes.'

'That's right. I told them they were wrong. They must have been. What do you think?'

I pretended to consider it.

'Looks like a mistake to me.'

'Mm. That's what I told them.'

'Good. What happened to the kid?'

'What kid?'

'The one in the car.'

'I should think he's on remand in Ashford. Why do you want to know? I could find out for you if you'd like to step back in.'

I shook my head and walked away quickly. 'It's okay, don't worry!' I called over my shoulder. 'I don't care!'

There's a word for people like Detective Chief Superintendent Maher. Let's see if I can think of it. . . .

Eleven

When Maher let me go I wandered the streets aimlessly for a while. I wanted to think. I stopped and looked in the shop windows, any windows. Travel shops, re-upholsterers, a railway modelling centre (as it proclaimed itself). I wanted to look at anything, hear the traffic around me, let the light fall on me. If you're like that after twenty-four hours, God knows that you'd be like after twenty years. I wondered if you'd get used to confinement. There's no reason why you should. I meandered along for half an hour. Fat black ladies pushed past me with their shopping, pretty girls stared at clothes in shops, or told each other jokes or lit cigarettes, workmen paused to let me and my stick past. When I got tired I hopped on a bus (haha). I left it in Islington, on Upper Street. I knew I was being followed. I expected it. As I pushed my way along the lower deck of the bus to get off I saw a big, black-haired and black-bearded man stuff his face into the women's page of the *Guardian*. I'd never seen such an obvious *Daily Express* reader in my life. It was the copper who'd kicked me all round my office yesterday. 'Right,' I thought, 'I'll have you.' I'd lose him. There's a cinema that does matinees in Upper Street. It'd be just the job. They've got a lav with two doors. He'd never know. Then he'd have to go back and tell Maher he'd lost me.

That was the plan.

I walked along the kerbside, looking for a place to cross. The traffic was heavy and there was dust and noise in the air. I turned and saw the black-bearded man about twenty yards behind me. He made no attempt to conceal himself. I saw the plain-faced DS Robson too. He looked surprised

74

that I saw him, then he followed my gaze to the bearded man and looked even more surprised. Robson opened his mouth to say something but was pushed to one side by the bearded man, who ran at me, grabbed me and began to shove me in the back of a Ford Cortina that had stopped by my side. He was much too big for me to resist, you need a lot of strength and a lot of balance before you start to take on a man that big. I managed to get the handle of my walking stick into his crutch, though, and I gave it a good shove. He yelled but kept shoving me into the Cortina. The stick broke as he knelt on it. Then we were accelerating away with the rear door swinging and Robson clutching at it. The bearded man pushed him away, closed the door and then turned back to me. I butted him very hard between the eyes. He put his hands to his face and when he took them away the hands and his beard were full of blood.

'Bravo, Jimmy my son!' cried the driver. 'Nobody's drawn blood on that big ape for years. Bravo!'

He slowed the car, turned left into the City Road and turned his head half-sideways.

'Brian Borden, James Jenner . . . I believe you two have met but never been introduced.'

'Denis', I said, 'this is not very funny. This is the second time Lizzie Borden here has attacked me in two days. One more time and I'm going to get *really* angry.'

'He's sorry about yesterday, aren't you, Brian?'

Brian Borden said, 'Yuff,' through his bloody hands.

'Is he sure?' I said.

Brian's black eyes glared at me over the tops of his fingertips.

'Well?' said Denis O'Keefe.

'Yuff,' said Brian. 'Ayer thorry.'

I could have asked him to kiss me better (one of the places he'd kicked me was my bum) but I thought I wouldn't push it too far . . . today.

'Brian knew you were my friend but he thought he'd better act as if he didn't yesterday morning.'

'Perhaps you'd ask him not to be so convincing next time, Denis.'

He laughed and drove us down to Old Street, then through Clerkenwell. At Lamb's Conduit Denis got out.

'My friend and I are going to have lunch, Brian. You drive this back and I'll see you in the office later.'

Brian nodded. I shook my head.

'I'm not going anywhere, Denis. You wait here, Brian and me are just going round the block.'

'Why?'

'We're only running down to Bloomsbury Way. Brian's offered to buy another stick for me, to replace the one he's just broken.'

Denis O'Keefe thought that was very funny. Brian Borden didn't. He bought the stick, though.

Denis O'Keefe looks more like a gangster than a copper. He wears flashy, smooth-cut suits, he appears to have his hair cut three times a week, he wears a gold ring with a large diamond in it on his left little finger and he always has a silk tie on. He's not a handsome man but he makes what he thinks is the 'best of himself'. Brian Borden dropped me off outside Holborn Police Station and Denis was on the far side of the road. He looked older than when I'd last seen him, some six months before. Maybe he'd put on weight or something. He had fine, crinkly brown hair that he fiddled around the front of his head to hide his receding hairline and he had calm, sure brown eyes that made you trust him more than his clothes or his manner would suggest you should; more than prudence would normally allow anyone to trust a Detective Inspector of the Metropolitan Police that everyone *knew* was bent. I suppose I had trusted him in the past because I knew what form his bentness took – he liked money too much. With other people it might be power or promotion or choirboys or all three. I'd trusted Denis in the past because I'd known what he was. Also because he'd given me a lot of introductions in the insurance and security worlds. I'd stopped trusting him some time ago because he was about to retire on twenty-five years' service and he seemed to be getting a bit frantic and a bit chancy in his rush to put his 'nest egg' together. I didn't want to take part in any chancy deals.

He took my arm and we walked south, down Red Lion Street and into a pub. The pub was full of lawyers and nineteenth-century frosted glass. I couldn't say which century the lawyers were from. There didn't appear to be any policemen.

'The best place to talk business, James, is surrounded by lawyers. They don't want to know. They don't want to get involved, so they don't overhear. What'll you have to drink?'

'Orange.'

He raised an eyebrow but ordered me the orange. He had a glass of something clear with lemon in it. I didn't catch what but if I know Denis it was 'slimline' something or other because he's always worrying about his weight. If you own as many clothes as Denis does growing out of them could be a financial disaster.

'What were the amateur dramatics in aid of?' I said.

'Maher had a man following you. I didn't want him to notice us meeting.'

'*Denis!*'

He patted my hand and shoved my glass of orange into it.

'Don't worry, they won't trace us through the motor. I've fixed that.'

'How?'

'Er . . . we borrowed it from a police station yard.'

'Your police station?'

'No. Don't *worry*. You worry too much.'

I shook my head.

'I'm not worried. I'm not drinking any more bloody orange juice with you either. You're crackers.'

I went outside. The air was fresh and warm and really summery. A line of office workers had formed outside a sandwich shop. A traffic warden was arguing with a cab driver. This was a normal world, the one we all know about. There were no bodies with their heads stripped of flesh here, no nights in the cells, no DCS Maher, no Brian Borden and DS Robson. No dawn raids. There were no Denis O'Keefes here, either.

'Come on James. Let's take a walk.'

'I'm not walking anywhere with you, Denis.'

We walked south towards Holborn.

'I was disappointed you didn't ring me. You should get

that machine of yours fixed. It's no good if you don't get anyone's messages.'

'I get all the messages I want. I'm not walking with you, Denis, and I'm not talking to you either.'

We continued south to Lincoln's Inn Fields, through Great Turnstile and into the calm of the park on the Fields. Old buildings looked down on old trees which in turn looked down on old men sitting on benches and making a plastic cupful of tea last for hours. O'Keefe and I found a bench of our own. It faced the tennis courts and pretty young girls bobbed about in front of us wearing miniature dresses and waving racquets. There are worse places to sit.

'I'll tell you straight,' said Denis.

'It would be the first time ever.'

'Come *on*. Stop talking tough and listen to what I have to say. I need desperately to find your pal, Zorba.'

'Why?'

Denis rubbed his face with his hands, nodded appreciatively at a failed overhead shot which left a tennis player upside-down against the wire netting.

'He was doing a job for me. A payout. The payout seems never to have got made and now I can't find your Greek pal nor the insurance company's money.'

'How much?' I asked.

'Quite a lot.'

'How much?'

'Er . . . my bit of it was three-five.'

'And Zorba's?'

'Five hundred.'

'So he was carrying forty thousand?'

O'Keefe nodded.

'I know it wasn't a very shrewd move but I had to get it done quick and you seemed to have lost interest in it. I thought we'd known him for long enough.'

'What you should have done, Denis, was paid him out properly or just given him a tenner. For two grand he wouldn't have looked and for ten quid he wouldn't have bothered. For five hundred it's worth having a peek . . . it doesn't matter, anyway. I'm sure we've seen the last of him. His wife took their kids off home a couple of months ago because they'd fallen out. No doubt he's popped off there with your forty grand to buy a big house and keep all seven of them in comfort and style for the rest of their naturals. You've been stuffed, Denis.'

He shook his head again, stood up and walked around in a little agitated circle. He wasn't even noticing the girl tennis players now, though he wasn't so distracted by his problem as to forget to smooth down his jacket and make sure there was the right amount of shirt cuff sticking out.

'More than you think. I was on a cert for a consultancy place with this firm when I finished in the job. That's gone down the tube.' He sat next to me again. 'Find him for me, Jimmy. I'll pay you, I'll cover your expenses too but find him and get the dough back, otherwise my name'll be mud.'

'Have you got forty grand?'

'No. They'd never be able to sue me for it anyway. . . .'

'But they could get you dismissed from the job, eh? And that'll put the kibosh on your pension and any chance of you getting another job. And you might go inside for it . . . right?'

'Yes.'

'I wish I could help, Denis. I like you in a funny way.' I stood. 'I can't though. I'm up to my ears with your mate Maher. I don't even know where to begin with Zorba. I don't know his proper name. All I've got is his phone number and the address of the council flat where he lives. I'll give you those.'

'Done it. Been all round there. Tried his mates, too, but they just clam up when they see me. I look too much like the copper. You don't, though, Jimmy. Have a go for me . . . see what you can find for me.'

He swallowed and walked away.

'Hang on,' I called. 'I can't go that fast.' He waited till I caught him up. 'I'll do what I can. Let's go and have our drink, Denis . . . and let's have a proper one. There's something I want from you in return; several things, in fact.'

I had several drinks with Denis while I explained to him what I wanted. Then I went via Liverpool Street to Audley End to pick up my car. I didn't chance my luck by driving over to look at Duncan's place . . . there would be nothing

79

to see, anyway. Any leverage I'd get on him I wouldn't get face to face. I drove straight home. At that time I was living in a flat in Stoke Newington. It was a purpose-built block from the nineteen-sixties with a car park in front of it. As I leaned under the bonnet of my old Humber auto (to disconnect the ignition – I'd had to 'steal' it at Audley End because Gal had my car keys and he was still in the nick) I saw a young man in casual clothes across the road kicking the tyres of his Ford. The tyres looked okay to me and they seemed to have his entire attention. So much for undercover surveillance.

I went upstairs. The German lady who lives next door with her teenage son said there were some men in my flat yesterday and that when the son went to find out who they were they were very rude to him. I thought, 'I bet they were', but I said, 'I'm sorry to hear that and would you please thank your son for his diligence,' or some such rubbish. A visit was exactly what I'd expected. I went in, picked my way through the mess – though to be fair I'd seen worse messes – and lifted the phone. Two clicks and a dialling tone.

'Hullo Mr Maher. Jimmy Jenner here, reporting in. How are you doing? Any news? I hope you'll get back to me.'

The dailling tone went on. I put the phone down, poured myself a glass of whisky and sat on top of a load of broken-spined paperbacks that had taken up residence on the settee. I had to think.

I had to think that either George Duncan had had his 'wife' killed or that Lenny Grant and Wilkins had had it done. None of the three had any particular gripe against me, so they hadn't done it to fix me. They'd done it to fix the woman or each other. If they'd done it to fix the woman the body wouldn't have been found . . . she'd be off Shoeburyness wearing what my boy Gal would describe with loving care as a 'cement overcoat'. I could hear him say it. No. Whoever had caused that mess under the railway arch had done it so the mess would be found . . . and the only reason for that would be so that it put the frighteners on someone. Why else? – so someone could get something out of possession of a corpse, maybe. Like an insurance claim, or property, or both.

I went downstairs and walked a couple of streets to a phone box. I wanted one of those blue pay-phone affairs, so I didn't get any pips. The undercover man with the Ford did the best he could, following me fifty yards behind and staring at hedges.

I phoned Judy first at work.

'How are you? I've been worried,' she said as soon as she heard my voice.

'I'm okay. I took it you knew where I was.'

'Yes. We have to talk, James.'

'I know. I'm going to stay with my auntie in Southend. You know where it is. Come down for the weekend.'

'Thanks.'

'Come alone, Judy.'

'I will. . . . . Jimmy. . . . .'

'Yes.'

'Oh . . . nothing. Take care.'

She is never going to get to the top of her particular tree like that. She should have just made out she didn't know me. I rang Peter Street nick.

'Hopkins here, from the *Argus*,' I said. 'Is Chief Superintendent Maher there still?'

'He's in conference, sir,' said the boy on the desk, 'can I help?'

It's gratifying when people show initiative.

'Yes, you may be able to. When he briefed me earlier I wrote down some wretched scrawl for the name of the Home Office doctor who's doing the post mortem.'

'*Done*, Mr Hopkins. He's done it. His name is Sir Mark White . . . okay?'

'Thanks a lot, constable. It's stupid of me.'

'We're here to help, sir,' he said cheerily. I couldn't believe he was serious. I rang Shoreditch Mortuary and got an assistant clerical officer.

'Detective Sergeant Robson here, Peter Street CID' I said, 'look, I've got a nearly unreadable copy of Sir Mark White's p.m. report here, and I can't raise his secretary on the blower. What *exactly* is the knife used on the Duncan woman?'

'A flat-bladed knife, sergeant. Something like a carving knife only with a point on it.'

81

'And the cause of death was?'

'A thirty-two calibre pistol shot in the chest. Lodged in the right atrium.'

'Thanks.'

I put the phone down. My babysitter was tying his shoelaces. By the amount of times he swapped legs I reckon he'd done them good and tight – all three. I didn't ask the morturary desk for the time of death because it didn't matter. There were a lot of other questions I wanted to ask him but one of the things I had asked O'Keefe for was a copy of the report. It would all be there. If I were just to be patient for a few days I'd have all my answers about the demise of Mrs Duncan. Except who did it, of course. Maybe I'd even get that.

Something else I'd asked O'Keefe for was waiting for me when I got home. The phone was ringing. I opened the door quickly and rushed to it. I hate that minute when you're jiggling your key in the lock and knowing, absolutely *knowing* that it's going to stop ringing by the time you reach it. This time I knew wrong.

'Watcher cock, I've been bailed.'

'Good. I can't talk now I'm in a rush, Gal. Meet me in the old place at eight, eh?'

'Okay, what's the time now?'

'Ah . . . I don't know. I haven't got a watch and the clock's in the kitchen. It's about four, I think. What's the time, constable?'

'Constable?' said Gal.

'Yeah. Don't forget my car keys.'

'Haven't you got any spares?'

'Zorba's got them. He's got my spare flat keys too. As a matter of fact Zorba seems to have everything at the moment.'

'Oh . . . oh. Oh! *Constable . . . I* get it. Meet me in the *old* place. *Yeah*.'

'Bye, Gary.'

Perhaps I won't buy him the home computer. I padded round the flat picking up torn books and papers and stuffing them in a black plastic bag. I don't like a lot of my books anyway. Perhaps I should get the CID to pay me a visit more often. I shoved the drawers back in my tallboy. It's the only decent piece of furniture I have and I wished they hadn't treated it so rough. Then I got fed up with the whole business and left the drawers as they were, half-open, half-closed, and went to shave and shower and change.

By five I was chugging up Leytonstone High Road looking for the Canary Club. I had a whole convoy of coppers in tow, the Ford and a Bedford van that I could see. They obviously thought I knew something. I thought I knew something too, I just didn't know what it was. All the facts of a particular case are always there, it's just a question of seeing them and then putting them in the right order. What I knew for sure was that *I* hadn't done it. I don't know how Maher and his boys felt about that, so my list of suspects was minus one compared with theirs. I also had no idea of any other extra suspects they had, no extra information. All I had was Wilkins, Grant, Duncan and me. I was on my way to see Wilkins.

The Canary Club was above a bookshop. It wasn't the kind of bookshop you'd find in competition with W. H. Smith. There was a plastic fly-curtain on the bookshop door and a fat guy dressed-up-to-look-tough to catch any flies the curtain didn't. The Canary Club was entered through a mock-Georgian door at the side of the bookshop. The door had one of those 'speak-here' boxes, a brass spy-hole and peeling yacht varnish. I can never work the 'speak-here' boxes. You push the button and the box squawks and you lean over to talk to it and a buzzer goes in the door and by the time you've pushed the door it stops going. Then you push the button again and talk over the top of the squawk and you step back in frustration and the buzzer in the door goes while you're stepping back so you miss it again. Then you push the button again and the squawk says 'stop messing around with the button' and you say 'sorry, it's Jenner, can't you just open the door?' and then you're not sure whether you should be pushing the buzzer to speak or not so you push it anyway and hold it there. Eventually they come down and let you in. People always come down and let you in in the end so I don't know why they didn't just stick with the old system of having a doorbell and their own eyes, ears and legs.

There was a plastic multi-coloured fly-curtain behind this door too, but the man who let me in wasn't just a fat guy dressed up to look tough. He was small and wiry. He had dark eyes and a pinched mouth, a turtle-neck shirt and a dark blazer. He searched me in the little space behind the fly-screen and he laughed when he found my leg.

'What's that?' he said.

'It's my leg.'

He laughed again and led me upstairs.

Wilkins was holding court in a back room of the club. The front of the club was opening soon and a smooth, oily-looking young man was polishing glasses. He let us past his bar counter to a rear door which led into the back room with Wilkins on a sofa and a racing print above his head and two men and two women in there with him. There were two lamps on a sideboard – that's all the light there was. Wilkins stood and waved the four out of the room, then motioned that I should sit on the sofa.

'It's a little low for me,' I said. 'My leg.'

'He's got a false leg, Wilkie,' said the little fellow.

Wilkins laughed. It was a sharp laugh and not the sort you were expected to join in with. You were expected to smile politely and shyly for the big man's joke.

'A policeman with one leg,' he laughed. 'Now I've heard everything.' He gurgled the words out between laughs. It sounded like a crow being strangled. He pointed at a tall stool. 'Sit on that then.'

'I'm not a policeman,' I said, 'I'm a private detective.'

'I thought they only had those in America now that you can get divorced so easily here. What keeps you in work?'

'Insurance claims, mostly. A little company theft, a little company fraud. A few missing persons.'

'He works for insurance companies,' he said to the little fellow. 'And the Salvation Army.' They both laughed this time. Suddenly Wilkins grew serious. He pointed at my leg.

'Take it off,' he said, 'and Charlie'll take it outside. I don't want to find out you've got an electronic leg with a *real* copper on the other end of it.'

Wilkins and Charlie were almost crying, the whole thing

seemed so funny to them. Just when they'd both subsided to chuckles again he poked little Charlie in the ribs and said, 'I can't do business with a man who's got a bugged leg.' And they both started all over again, slapping their thighs with their palms and dabbing at their eyes with paper tissues from a box on a coffee table in front of his sofa.

'We don't get many people around here as funny as you, Jenner.'

The barman put his head in from next door.

'Bring us a drink. Bring us all a drink, Bill. Charlie and me're having a drink with a one-legged tough guy.'

Bill brought two drinks, ice cold beers for Wilkins and me. Little Charlie had nothing – a thimbleful would have got him drunk. The beers were foreign lagers and beads of water dripped down the sides of the bottle as the barman poured them. Wilkins shoved a lot of used glasses to the end of the coffee table.

'Put 'em on here Bill.'

Bill brought the drinks from the sideboard to the coffee table.

'Clear up later. I want to talk to this one-legged tough guy.' He laughed again. 'Pull back the curtains on your way out. I want to get a good long look at him.'

The barman pulled back some mock-velvet curtains that ran all along one wall of the room. Light flooded in, rushed round the room like a happy child, touching things, examining the dust, passing the used and greasy glasses on the coffee table, then brushing Wilkins' face. He looked heavy, thick-jowled. He was close-shaven and his hair was cut short; black, spiky hair that had clearly been dyed to keep it black. The face was sad. Wilkins had thick lips and washed-out grey eyes; busby black-dyed eyebrows above the eyes, red lines of burst capillaries on the fat cheeks below the eyes. He wore a mohair suit with a broad chequer-board design on the cloth, one soft grey square laid on another, all the grey squares darkening then lightening, shimmering as he leaned forward to pick up his beer.

'Why do you need me, Jenner?'

'Sorry?'

'Why d'you come here?'

'You know about George Duncan's wife?'

He nodded.

'Terrible business. My heart goes out to him . . . what about it?'

'I've just spent two days in the chokee. The police seem to think I had something to do with it.'

'*No*.'

'I'm afraid so.'

He smiled into his beer.

'And you claim you didn't.'

'No. Not quite that. I had plenty to do with it. I was hired by Duncan to look after her and as far as the whole world is concerned I ballsed-up. As far as the police are concerned that's the very least I have done.'

'What else do they think you've done?'

'Well . . . they know I can't account for myself for the night it happened. They're not pushing me on that one yet but they've given me warning they will. Duncan's flat is full of my fingerprints, his car is full of my fingerprints and his wife is dead. I was the last person to see her. Nobody else is tied to her at that time.'

Wilkins waved at the little fellow, Charlie, to fetch more beer.

'Yeah, yeah, yeah . . . got the story. Don't give me the television series. Tell me what you want.'

'Okay'. I said. I drew in my breath, '*I* didn't kill her. Perhaps you know who did. But it wasn't me. If the police know now that it wasn't me they're not saying so in public – but they will have to soon. And then everyone's going to go round looking for who else might have done it. And they're going to be looking at her husband, Duncan, and Lenny Grant. In this case "Lenny Grant" means you.'

The new beers came. I hadn't drunk half of the first. Wilkins poured his greedily into the glass. The foam ran over the top.

'Specially imported,' he said. 'I can't drink English beer.'

'Word is, Mr Wilkins, that Lenny Grant is only fronting a gym and a licence for you. Word is he gets venues stitched up easier than any man who ever lived, know what I mean? The word I have is that he has access to your muscle.'

'I haven't got any muscle. I'm a businessman.'

86

I poured some beer into my glass and swirled it around to make some of the fizz go out.

'I really don't have a tape recorder in my leg.' I tapped the shin with my empty beer bottle 'Hollow . . . see? You don't have to make out to be related to the Archbishop of Canterbury to me . . . you don't even have to make out you only own a dry-cleaning business and a porn shop. I don't care. But let me put something to you.'

'Okay, put something to me.' He leaned over near my leg and yelled, 'But that don't mean nothing you've said up till now is true, *right*? And it's not a porn shop. It's a marital aids centre which deals with a growing social need in our society!' He addressed all this to my knee, then sat up again and started chuckling.

I said, 'Alison Duncan is reckoned to be murdered. I'm first on the list but I don't fit for lots of reasons. They'll have to find somebody else. Next on the list is George Duncan, but by all accounts he's playing the part of the widower very nicely. He has a cast-iron alibi for the time when his cuddles is getting her chips . . . right?'

'Go on.'

'And all his carpets have shrunk on account of all the crying and upset poor old George is going through. Next on the list is your friend Leonard Grant, who had a big ruck with George Duncan in the street. Public knowledge. Not-so-public knowledge is the fact that there's a big hole in the front door of Duncan's house where someone shot it with a twelve-bore. Not-so-public knowledge is the fact that he reckons he's had threatening messages of a more explicit kind, like phone calls and a letter telling him to lay off Tommy Lynch.'

'Lynch?'

'A boxer. Don't play dumb.'

He smiled. It wasn't a very friendly smile.

'A boxer you've taken away from Duncan. A boxer who'll have to pay a bit to get the last fight option off Duncan.'

'Balls! Seven thousand quid, the last one's worth on his contract with Duncan. That's pin money compared with what the fight'll gross. We've already paid Duncan his seven thousand quid.'

'Are you receiving me loud and clear?' I tapped my leg

again. I looked Wilkins in the eye. 'Are you sure he's cashed his cheque? Are you sure he's got it? My guess is that he hasn't, and that when the police get fed up with tagging me they're going to try to do it to you. They'll pick up Grant and ask him about the phone calls and the shot-gun blast and the letter. They'll want to know where he was the night Mrs Duncan was murdered and he'd better come up with somewhere better than me, because *he*'s no holder of the Queen's Police Medal. Then they'll show him the contract, which I didn't know the details of until just now but sounds a beaut, and say that he was leaning on Duncan and when Duncan didn't give Lenny Grant did Mrs Duncan in in a very nasty way. The way the story goes after that depends on you, I should think, and your relationship with Lenny Grant. If he loves you and enjoys working for you he'll say "I don't know any Wilkins". Then they'll throw him in the deepest cell in England on his own for a fortnight while they turn you and your entire business upside down. Then they'll drag him out again and ask whether he arranged to have Alison Duncan killed or you did. Again it all depends on your relationship with him. . . .'

'This fairy story is boring. I never killed this woman. I've heard of Duncan but I never even knew he had a wife till today. I'll pay him his seven grand. For all I know I already have. The police won't have anything on me because I didn't do anything. Neither did Len.'

'Well, *somebody* did. It wasn't Santa Claus. And while our friends in the Metropolitan Police are looking for that somebody, business is going to go slack for some people. Some people's faces are going to be in the papers. Some third party is going to get his manager's licence revoked. Somebody's hard-fought-for-and-gained world title prospect fighter is going to go off the boil and all the millions and millions of US dollars that could go with him are going to go off the boil. I think that when the police get fed up with me and start on Lenny Grant you're going to be in a whole pile of trouble, no matter what way they read it.'

'Lenny's all right. He was in here with me and a few others the night that woman was killed.'

'Mr Wilkins.' I stood up. '*That* is not an alibi.'

'So what should I do?'

88

'What should you do? You should listen. You should pay attention to me, then you do what I ask you and I'll do something for you.'

Wilkins stood and pulled his suit straight.

'Show Mister Jenner downstairs, Charlie. He's finished his beer.'

'I haven't,' I said.

'Show him down.'

Charlie took hold of my elbow. I let my beer fall on him, brushed him aside and pointed at the window.

'Down there you'll see a Ford Cortina and further down the road a Bedford van. They're babysitting you, Wilkins.'

'They're always babysitting me. It doesn't mean anything. I'm a legit businessman. I pay my taxes. Someone in the local nick's just got a down on me because I did bird when I was a kid.'

He smiled, waved little Charlie away from my side. I said, 'Those aren't from your local nick and you know it. At the moment they've got a dead woman, a grieving husband with a watertight alibi, me, Lenny Grant and you. I didn't do it and I don't think the police will believe I did it. George Duncan is tucked up tight with a copper who says he was with him, you reckon you never did it and I haven't spoken to your man Grant yet but you reckon he didn't do it too. You two are the best candidates the police will have.'

'Sit down, Jenner. Finish your drink.'

We all three sat.

'It could have been an outsider, some nutter,' Wilkins said.

I shook my head.

'No. It's too much effort to go to. The body was really cut up bad. No one would do that unless it was for a reason.'

'A nutter might.'

'Okay, one might. How'd she get from the Barbican to a railway arch in Shoreditch? If she went out to get fags she wouldn't need to go that far.'

'Maybe someone took her there. Maybe it's some sort of ritual killing . . . how the hell do I know? I'm not a copper. What else could it be if you didn't do it and I didn't do it and Lenny never? Maybe he's fell behind with his freemason's subscription and that's their debt collection department making an example of him . . . maybe anything. It's probably a random killing.' He gulped at his beer, signalled Charlie for another then said, 'London's full of nutters and criminal types and all that. Maybe she was killed by a jealous lover.'

'The police will think you did it', I said. 'They always go for the best prospect and you're it, you and Grant. You had a reason, you've got a rotten alibi and you're quite capable of doing it. All they'll need is one concrete bit of evidence and you'll go in the nick so fast your feet won't touch the ground.'

'Maybe. But they won't find any evidence because I didn't do anything. Nor did Lenny.'

'That won't stop them finding some,' I said. He nodded slowly, squeezing his fat cheeks with his hands so that they nearly reached his eyebrows, then mopping his forehead with the sleeve of his grey suit. I said, 'When I first came in you asked why I needed you. Well I don't. You need me.'

'No I don't. I haven't done nothing.'

'Famous last words, Mister Wilkins. As it happens, I know they're true.'

'How?'

'For several reasons. Some of them I won't go into now. The main one is that I don't see what you have to gain from it. You already had his business.' I held my hand up. 'Okay, okay . . . Lenny Grant did. It doesn't matter. Either way, I don't see why you'd want to put the squeeze on him *if* you were in the squeeze-putting business. There's no profit in it. There's even less profit in killing someone. I'm not sure the police will see it that way, though. They'll just think of you as a good prospect and then they'll go round looking for the evidence. I've no doubt they'll find *something*: a few little things, you getting yourself alibi-ed by known criminal types so it won't stand up in court. . . .'

' . . . *I didn't know I'd need a bloody alibi*!' he yelled. 'If I did I would've been having dinner with a copper or something too . . . a lawyer at least. The first I heard about this is someone phones me this morning.'

He was angry now, pacing the little room. He looked as if he would start throwing things.

'I believe you,' I said.

'Who asked you round here anyway? I haven't done nothing.'

'I believe you. I believe there may be someone else involved here.'

'Who?'

I shrugged. 'Duncan?'

Wilkins went to the wall and leaned his head against it. I went and stood by him.

'Duncan,' he repeated after me. 'Duncan.'

'Or someone doing it for him . . . any idea who that could be?'

'No. George Duncan, eh? What for, insurance money?'

'That's how I see it. I haven't any evidence yet. But I'll find some.'

'What do you want from me?' He turned suddenly and looked into my face.

'Someone did a house in Onslow Gardens, South Ken. Got a lot of gear, two hundred grand's worth of insurance at least, but it's unfencable. It was someone local to here, I know, because a local copper organised an insurance payout. Trouble is, the guy he sent with the money didn't get there. No one knows where he's gone. No one knows where the money's gone either. The copper is understandably getting a little concerned.'

'And?'

'We'd like the gear or the money back. Also the messenger. I believe the copper would prefer the gear to the money. Keeps his street credibility up, know what I mean?'

'Okay. I'll see what I can do.' He waved at Charlie who went outside. Whether for more beer or to make a phone call I never found out. Wilkins sat again.

'What am I getting out of this, Jenner?'

'A cloud of dust,' I said, 'a big one in front of you while I go round leading the men with the big hats towards the real killer. If I keep pointing out that George Duncan may have done it, maybe they'll lay off you and Grant a bit. Maybe you'll still have the fight business. Maybe you won't have to sit on your hands in Brixton nick while they turn you inside out.'

He just turned his back on me, sunk his head down and

began drinking beer again. When I went through to the bar Charlie was nowhere to be seen. Perhaps he was hiding under a table. He wouldn't even have to bend down to do it. It was a bit strange the bar-room was empty, though. Even the oily barman had gone. All there was left was the atmosphere and the furnishings. The atmosphere was stale, old beer, cigarettes and a lavatory smell. The furnishings were nicotine-stained, tacky, well-worn but not too old. The formica had split along the edge of the bar. I don't know what Wilkins spent his money on other than beer, but it certainly wasn't on the trappings of a rich man's life. Apart from a mohair suit and a door entry-phone he seemed to spend his life in slightly more seedy circumstances than me. And that was saying something.

I went downstairs. The door was swinging wide. A light breeze rustled the multi-coloured plastic fly curtain. I pushed the curtain aside and stepped forward. A big hand gripped my throat and I found myself looking at a gun. I made a note to break this new habit as soon as I could.

'Not him. Leave him go.'

The gun dropped, the hand released my throat ever so slowly. I gulped and wiped the tears from my eyes, then stepped fully onto the pavement to find myself confronted by Detective Chief Superintendent Maher.

'Hullo, Jenner. What are you up to, a bit of private enterprise?' He was cocky, dead pleased with himself.

'Someone's got to prove to you I didn't kill that girl,' I said. 'I had ideas that I might as well make a start . . . know what I mean?'

He smiled and took my arm, leading me away from the door and signalling a posse of plainclothes-men up the stairs to Wilkins' drinking club. Wilkins would certainly be in for a surprise when he stepped out for his next beer. I wondered whether he'd get the throat-and-gun treatment too. It concentrates the mind wonderfully.

'How are you, James?'

The street was full of policemen. The staff of the porn shop were all lying on the pavement, including the fat one from behind the porn shop's fly-curtain. He was wearing a red and gold striped shirt and looked like nothing so much as an abandoned sofa at the kerbside. Charlie, Wilkins' miniature minder, and Bill the oily barman were there too, both face down, both handcuffed.

'Is this a raid of some sort?' I asked. Maher was leading me away from the Canary Club's door, away from the porn shop. No doubt he had minions who'd deal with all that. We walked past the prostrate bodies on the pavement. It made me feel like the Pope. Maher held onto my arm, spoke softly to me.

'What did you want from friend Wilkins?'

'I just wanted to know what the score was. I felt pressured by you lot. I wanted to know a bit about him, where he was the night she was killed.'

He nodded thoughtfully and let go of my arm. We walked through the heavy traffic in the High Road, till we were through the little crowd that had gathered around the Canary Club and could look at the incident as outsiders.

It was Thursday. I'd met Duncan in the Bonaventura on Monday. A lot had happened in between. I'd met Maher on Wednesday. Now he was treating me like an old friend, like some old drinking pal he'd tripped over someplace he didn't expect to find him. He waved his hand at the crowd surrounding the Canary Club.

'Ghouls. They want to see blood. They want to see some big criminal. A murderer, eh, Jimmy?'

I didn't answer.

'So, while you were playing private eye, we've got our man. That's what police work is all about, Jimmy. What did you do exactly while you were in the job? Uniform, wasn't it? Unit beat, all that stuff.'

He paused and leaned back against a wall. Maher was enjoying himself. He was telling the long-lost drinking pal about all the things he'd done while he was drunk, all the indiscretions, all the slobbered sentences. Maher would have total recall, of course. He's the type who never gets drunk.

I didn't answer his questions. I didn't want to play his game. A few feet in front of us a truck stopped, waiting to let the traffic in from a side road. The driver looked at the scene outside the Canary Club, then looked at me and laughed and touched his head, as if to say 'stupid'. He leaned forward and let his handbrake off. There was a screech and a puff of air.

'We got our man by detection. First of all we found the gun in the Grand Union Canal,' Maher said.

'The right gun?'

'Looks like it. It's a .32. Preliminary tests say it's our gun. Then the gun appears to have been used in the Manor House bullion job back in 1980. A Hampshire copper went down to Albany Prison and put this to someone – I can't say who of course – who's doing bird for the bullion job.'

I nodded. Of course he couldn't say who. He couldn't say any of it. Why was he doing it? To score a cheap point over me? Didn't seem likely. Maher went on. 'The lag coughed immediately; after all, he's already in custody and a gun he's connected with is used in a murder. He obviously doesn't want to get tangled with it.'

'Good alibi,' I said. He didn't even laugh.

'What the lag coughed was the name of a man, shall we say a third party, he'd passed the gun to. We picked up this third party even before we released you.'

'How long have you had the gun then?'

'Since the morning of the murder; or rather, since the morning we found the corpse. Now, the third party is very frightened, says he's going to cop for it and all that, know what I mean?'

I didn't but I didn't say so. Across the road the crowd was parting to let police vans through. A couple of uniform men were staring at us. A detective, was it Robson? waved at us. The evening sun made the walls of Leytonstone glow yellow and warm. Drivers shielded their eyes. The whole lower deck of a passing bus seemed to burst into laughter spontaneously. I presumed the conductor had been making jokes, but still a busful of laughing Londoners is a strange sight. Maher turned away from the waving detective and watched his own shadow on the sunny yellow wall.

'Well, what good's it getting a man to cop for illegal possession when you've a stiff on your hands. James? No use at all. We stuck him in the cooler for twenty-four hours and he comes out saying a name. The name he's frightened of. The name he'd cop an illegal possession of firearms plea for. Guess what name?'

'Don't tell me – Wilkins.'

Maher nodded at the wall. He said without looking at me, 'You should have stayed in the job, you know. You're good at this.'

'Ha *ha*. Thank you, Mister Maher. I think there are a couple of holes in your story. First of all Wilkins has an alibi.'

'Not one that'll stand up in court.'

'The second is that he has no motive.'

'Oh, come on, James. He's been crowding Duncan out of the fight game for a couple of years.'

'*Grant* has.'

'Grant. Wilkins. It doesn't matter at that point. You know that.'

'I know it,' I said, 'but it doesn't work as a motive. It's useless. He'd already taken Duncan's stuff over – why threaten him? Why kill his *wife* of all people? I'm sorry, Mr Maher, It won't wash. If you've arrested him on that I don't expect your file to get past the Director of Public Prosecutions. Any good defence lawyer would take it to pieces . . . for a start, how did you find the gun?'

'Anonymous tip.' He shrugged.

'It sounds dodgier by the minute.'

He turned and looked into my eyes. His eyes were grey and clear and cool. He wasn't the sort of man to get panicked into showing his hand like that, either for fear or to boast. There had to be something else. Maher provided it.

'Before Alison Duncan was Alison Duncan she was Alison Clark, without an 'e', of Cape Town, South Africa. She came to England and lived here for two years before she met and married Duncan.'

'And?'

'*And* during those two years she appears to have had no visible means of support.'

'On the game?'

'No. Not prostitution. She was supported by *someone*. Didn't you wonder about Wilkins only pressurising Duncan? No other fight managers have been squeezed by him.'

'I'm not an expert at the fight game,' I said. 'I'll take your word for it.'

95

'*Thanks*, James. Now, Leonard Grant's gymnasium only started in business two years ago . . . *two* years. Getting it now?'

'You're saying she was Wilkins' bird before she upped sticks and married dear-old-nearly-legit George Duncan.'

'Yes. There's your real motive, I'd have to say.'

'And what about Duncan going skint? Has he a lot of insurance on his wife? Could he have arranged it?' I said.

'He could. But the case for him isn't as good as the case for Wilkins. With Wilkins I've got motive, opportunity and strong evidence connecting him to the murder weapon. A witness. It would be impossible not to prefer him and his poxy drinking-club alibi as a candidate for arrest when you put him up against George Duncan with his policeman friend as an alibi, his lack of a criminal record and his "all I've done wrong is gone skint . . . since when's that a crime?" I'd be laughed out of court. On the evidence I've got Wilkins is my man. The DPP's office would insist *I'd* have to insist.'

'And his scalp is a nice one to have hanging on your belt next time the Commissioner asks you over for tea and cucumber sandwiches, is that it?'

Robson was waving more urgently from across the road now, yelling something too. Maher waved back. He acted as if he hadn't even heard me.

'You've got a car here, haven't you, James? I must go.'

'Hang on. Has the gun got Wilkins' dabs on it?'

'No. There are none on it at all.'

'And how much insurance does Duncan have?'

'Going on for three hundred grand. It's not unusual in his business, and it costs the same to insure a man and wife as it does the man alone, normally. There's nothing dodgy about the amount of it. It wasn't even taken out recently, nor all at the same time. I don't think that would be an angle. If I were to look somewhere other than Wilkins I wouldn't look in that direction.'

'Where would you look?'

He lit a cigarette, blew the smoke away from me, then looked at his hands. There was nicotine on his fingers.

'I mustn't do this, you know. It's killing me.' He waved the cigarette. 'I don't know where else I'd look. I suppose

96

I'd think the case against Wilkins will be open and shut. I wouldn't look anywhere. I'd end up charging Wilkins and being congratulated for it.'

'I think that stinks. Why are you telling me all this?'

He puffed unhappily at the cigarette again and said, 'Because I think it stinks too.'

He went to walk away, then came back after a few paces.

'uh . . . I don't think my sergeant's that chuffed about the way you parted company with him earlier. I don't think he's pleased at all. I don't think he'd be thrilled to find out you were using his name over the phone to Shoreditch Mortuary, either, James.'

'Me?' I said, all innocence and hands open.

'You. How else could you know she was shot with a pistol? You didn't question it when I told you and the press don't have it yet. Only someone who phoned the mortuary clerk and asked questions making out to be a policeman would know that. It's a crime to impersonate a policeman, James.'

'Hm,' I said. 'It wasn't me. I haven't got a helmet any more.'

'Good. You could also ask your pal O'Keefe to be a bit more subtle than taking a copy of the post-mortem report off a desk in the CID room and making a photocopy. Tell him he's not bloody invisible.'

I laughed.

'You can tell him that.'

Maher shook his head and dogged his filter tip. He'd only taken half a dozen puffs.

'As long as the copy is back on my desk first thing Monday I won't say anything to him. Bye now. I must rush.'

He sounded like a schoolmaster with a class to take. As he crossed back over to Robson he looked like a schoolmaster too, only the class was murder and the students were grown-up men and women.

Twelve

I met Gal in front of the 'old place' as promised at eight. The 'old place' is the Arabian, a boozer on the corner of Cambridge Heath Road and Bishop's Way. It's the 'old place' because my first office was round the corner from it. Gal was leaning on the wall outside when I drove up, hands in pockets, faded-blue-denim, everything. He pushed himself off the wall without taking his hands out of his pockets. I asked him to drive. It wouldn't have surprised me if he'd done that with his hands in his pockets, too.

'That was a manky trick with the Rover, wasn't it?'

He didn't answer.

'Do you know where I've been all day?'

He nodded.

'I know where you've been the last couple of days. Same place as me.' He laughed. 'I'm sorry, Jim, but it's a good laugh us being in nick at the same time.'

'Hysterical. And don't pick me up in any more nicked motors, kid. My credit with the coppers can't stand it.'

We were driving along Hackney Road, towards Old Street.

'Where are we going?'

'To eat first. I was being followed, and I thought I might have to ask you to lose them for me, but they've gone away now.'

'I thought you'd gone off my way of losing tails?'

He was right. Gal was the best loser-of-tails in the business, if there's such a business, but his method is a bit of a strain on the old ticker. Last time he did it for me I was looking for a villain. I only wanted to serve a divorce writ.

Unfortunately some other villains in a Ford Granada wanted him too, and they followed me around like an ambulance waiting for an accident to happen. The accident was going to happen when I (that is, when *they*) found villain number one. I didn't want to serve the writ on a stiff so in all innocence I asked Gal to lose these four mateys in the Granada. I thought he could rush down a side street and turn his lights off, something like that. It would work a treat, I thought. I thought wrong. He did it a couple of times but the Granada stuck with us. Gary decided something a bit more drastic was called for. He drove us all the way to Mortlake, to a level-crossing he knew. Then he waited till the gates were dropping and slammed the old motor through like some sort of demented version of Evil Knievel. I went to sleep for months after with the image of the front of a suburban train etched on my mind. I woke up every morning cut in three. We lost the villains following us. I served the writ for the divorce, which the lady wife got. The husband got ten years in Chelmsford Gaol, but that wasn't just for being a bad husband. The level-crossing keeper got a nervous twitch. I swore I'd never again use Gal as a tail-loser or getaway driver unless it was essential that I lose the tail or get away. My constitution wouldn't stand it.

We drove to Westbourne Grove. I'd had enough of the East End and anyway you have to go to West London if you want to eat half decently. There are a few places in the West End but I didn't fancy them, and there are one or two in the East End but I didn't want to go bumping into any more coppers, guns, villains or what have you. I wanted a big curry and some lager, all that nonsense. I wanted some company that wasn't going to bash me up, point guns at me or put me in a cell. We went to Khan's: a big queue, polite service and good food. I felt as if I'd joined the human race again. Gal sat pushing okra around with his fork and complaining about 'spices'.

'I can't think they're no good for you. They go through me like a dose of salts,' he said. He ate it though, and I told him about my time in the nick and about the dead woman. I told him Wilkins had been arrested for it too.

'Don't surprise me.' He shook his head to emphasise it.

'He's a very dirty specimen. He's got lots of people frightened of him.'

The fans sliced slowly through the thick air above our heads. Plates clattered in some outside room. The waiters glided past, grinning and chattering to each other. They looked happy. People at the tables around us chattered too. They looked happy. Through the plate-glass windows. I could see cars passing, no doubt full of happy, chatting people. I thought of the woman I'd driven from Saffron Walden. Gal was right, of course. Lots of people were frightened of Wilkins and his reputation. That's why he looked such a good prospect for the police. The closer they got to him, the less likely they were to let go. That was even true for Maher. The pressure would be on him not to let go. Wilkins would be a big fish to have on a hook.

I lost my appetite all of a sudden. I paid up and we pushed our way back through the crowd to the street and our car. The weather was breaking, going back to the usual cold way May presents itself. There was quite a breeze out in Westbourne Grove. I still kept all the windows down as Gal drove us down the Euston Road, then over Pentonville Hill. The traffic was heavy again, even though it must have been after ten. People edged their cars forward, creaking their brakes and losing their tempers. Gal hummed to himself and tapped his fingers on the dash. Fumes blew through the open windows. 'You're not saying much. You haven't said why the cops stopped following you,' he said.

'They obviously think Wilkins is their man. They've got him tucked up tight.'

Gal swore and waved his fist at a dark man driving an Alfa with foreign plates. He knows rude signs in all European languages, does Gal. He turned to me again.

'You don't think so though, do you?'

'Drop it for now, Gal,' I said. 'I hope we're going to see something of my Greek friend soon. You worry about turning him up.'

'Are you sure Wilkins won't think you brought the old bill down on him?'

'I'm sure. Leave it. What I want you to do is find Zorba. That's enough for you to think about.'

Gal dropped me and the car both in Stoke Newington,

then set off for the bus. I washed, poured a big scotch, settled in front of a horror movie on the telly and watched all of thirty seconds of it before I was asleep in the chair. Then the phone rang. That's the way it always happens.

Thirteen

I let the phone ring. I didn't want to talk to anyone. I got up and took my untouched whisky into the kitchen. I was still picking my way over cushion covers and books and papers from when the flat had been searched by the police. I knew it wasn't Judy ringing me so I just let the phone ring on. Judy was the only person I wanted to be disturbed for and we have a strict rule that we don't phone each other at home late at night without a very good reason. That way we never find out things about each other we'd rather not know. The phone stopped. If it was Judy she'd give it a couple of minutes then ring again.

I left the whisky on the side and made some cocoa. My kitchen has two stools, a breakfast bar, a fridge, a cooker and two eye-level cupboards. It's so small that if two people go in together getting them out is a surgical matter. It's great if the other person's a girl but if it's a fat man . . . forget it. I crammed myself into this little space and looked down at the street. The window-blind was up and the street looked friendly. There was no Bedford van, no Ford Cortina, none of Wilkins' boys that I could see, just a stepped image of my naked torso reflected in the double glazing. I pulled the blind on that. The phone rang again.

'Hullo.' Pips sounded. A coinbox.

'Jenner?'

'Go on.'

'The matter you discussed with a certain party this evening is solved. You should go to your office.'

It was Wilkins' one-man-submarine, Charlie. I wondered how he reached the phone . . . on a milk crate?

'I thought you went for a ride with the men in blue, Charlie.'

'Not me. It was all a big mistake. I was there for less than an hour when my boss's lawyer got me out.'

'And Wilkins?'

'Not so simple. Someone's stitched him up good and tight. The promise you were made has been kept. Bill and me are both out and rooting for him. We thought you would be rooting for him too.'

'Drop dead, Charlie. I'm tired. Some of us are human. Some of us have to sleep.'

'I think you should go to your office, Jenner. You will need to keep your side of things.'

'Do I look like a fairy godmother?'

'No. I think you should go to your office and I think you should make every effort to help. We would remember it in a very friendly way if you helped.'

'Drop dead.'

I put the phone down, then climbed around the debris of my flat looking for a clean shirt. The ones from my chest of drawers were more crumpled than the one I'd been wearing, but they smelled better. I put on a crumpled shirt, a crumpled rainmac and then I limped my crumpled limp down to my car. Some fairy godmother. Long John Silver was more like it. I bet the little fellow thought of that, too. He didn't say it of course. He wanted something from me.

It was about twelve when I reached Chardray's shop. The door to my office was slightly ajar. I could see that without getting out of the car. Drizzle fell, gathered on my windscreen. I drove on and stopped at a phone box. I rang my number. The tape machine answered. I felt in my pocket for my bleeper. The playback tape only had messages from Bernie-the-barmy-husband. I didn't know what I was going to do about him. If I got the number changed he'd find that. Barmies can be cunning in their obsessive little way. I thought I'd probably write to the wife and ask her, since I'd been kind enough to find her every-loving Bernie-the-barmy, wouldn't she put a little time into dissuading him from phoning me twice a day; I mean half my phone calls are from Bernie-the-barmy. It's getting beyond a joke.

I drove the car back past Chardray's again, parked a hundred yards away and hurried through the drizzle. I gave my door a good wallop with my walking stick, then leaned back tight on the dirty damp concrete wall until a man blundered downstairs. I didn't stop him politely to ask why he was there, was he waiting for me to open up in the morning or something. No. All my politeness was worn out. For all I knew he might have a gun too, like everyone else I seemed to meet nowadays. Maybe he'd be a judo expert and I'd need the aid of a little surprise.

As I heard that man blundering down the darkened stairs I decided to play it dirty. As he came through the doorway I hit him clean in the mouth with the handle of my stick. I heard a nasty crack and it wasn't the stick that got broke. He pitched forward and I heaved it back and gave him a mighty whack on the back of the head too. It is in the hope of such instantaneous retribution for burglars and muggers that Tory ladies live, it is for this kind of justice that they whip themselves into a frenzy at Brighton conferences, peeing on the seats and shrinking the covers. If the hang-'em and fling-'em law-and-order types had been there they'd have loved me. I'd have got a bar to my medal. Unfortunately there was no one to see me do it. The other slight fly in the ointment was the fact that the 'mugger' squirming about on the floor minus his front teeth and in need of a stitched scalp was none other than Bernie-the-barmy-husband. I expected at least a little remonstration from him . . . I mean, he's only slightly barmy. He's enough cogs to know when he's being walloped and whether he's done anything to deserve that treatment.

Bernie said nothing. First of all he sat up and spat into his cupped hands. Under the yellow street lamps it looked like he was spitting black.

'You'll get wet,' I said.

Bernie just pointed up the stairs.

'You'd better get up. It's raining, Bernie.' I was wondering whether you could get caps done overnight, like a tyre change or something. I bet there's an all-night dentist in Earl's Court. I bet he's above an all-night doner-kebab house and I bet he spells it 'All Nite Dentistry. Get Your Caries Clobbered'. I bet he charges two hundred greenies to have it done *per tooth*, too. Oh God, I thought. There's going to be hell to pay when Bernard's ever-loving wifey-poos sees him. She'll sue me, and she'll be right to sue me and what's more she'll win. It was a disappointing thought. No bar to my medal.

'Uh,' said Bernie, pointing up the stairs, 'Uh uh.'

I went upstairs. The stair light was broken, the inner door to my office was open. I pushed it wide. My office has no curtains. Yellow streetlight fell across the room, across the desk. The yellow light fell on my chair and on the man in it. I switched the electric lamp on. He moaned.

'Zorba,' I said. I moved quickly across to him. He looked like he'd fallen off a bus. Face first. His features were bloody and swollen, his lips had ballooned up.

'Sorry,' he whispered through them. 'Sorry, Sjimmy.' His eyes closed for a second and he breathed a long sigh and I thought, 'not another, I can't stand someone else dying on me', but he opened his eyes and he wasn't dead or anything like it, just all beaten up. He looked at the ceiling, and then at the walls. 'I retire,' he said. 'I no play this bishnesh any more.' He closed his eyes again. The effect of talking had exhausted him.

'I'll get an ambulance,' I said.

He kept his eyes closed but shook his head.

'No. I'm gonna be a decorator. You be my first case.' He raised his left hand weakly and waved at the walls. 'This place a mess, Sjimmy. I decorate for you.'

'Okay. You decorate. I'll hire you. Consider yourself hired. Now I'll get the ambulance.'

Zorba raised himself from the chair as well as he could. He grabbed me with the left hand. I looked down, then I realised it had to be the left hand. His right hand was flat on my desk. The fingers were spread wide. The flesh on Zorba's hand looked a little blue. And there was a nail running through the fleshy part of the palm, under his thumb. The nail had been driven into my desk top.

He said, 'No ambulance.'

I nodded. 'I'll be back.'

I went downstairs and started hammering on Chardray's

105

door. He has a little flat at the back of his shop. I hammered and I rang the bell and then I hammered and I rang the bell and I shouted all sorts of rude and vile language that doesn't normally come into my vocabulary. Chardray came down looking all sleepy and asking if I knew it was half-twelve.

'Give me a hammer,' I said.

'A hammer? Why do you want a hammer at this time? Are you gone mad, James? Are you drunk? I have to be up in four hours and you're asking me to fetch you one hammer. Do you want nails too?'

He fetched a nail, to go with the hammer. Then he went inside and bolted the door good and proper and gave me to understand that I shouldn't do it ever again. I threw the nail in the gutter. Bernie-the-barmy had gone. That was one blessing. I went upstairs and fetched the biggest book I could find, then I lay the book next to Zorba's hand, hooked the claw through the nail and pulled, using the book and the hammer head as a fulcrum. I did it quickly. There was no point in hanging about. The nail hadn't hurt him half as much as the beating. I yanked it out and he didn't say a word, just tightened the lids of his closed eyes a little, winced a little.

'Sorry,' he said again.

I tried to lift him. I couldn't do it.

'How do you feel?' I said. It was a stupid question. He smiled. Even that seemed to hurt him. I touched his face. His beard was like a cheese-grater. It's like that every time he leaves off shaving for half an hour.

'I'll get Gal.'

I phoned Gary at home. He didn't complain when I asked him to come out. Gal didn't even complain when I told him not to get in any illegal motors.

'Get a cab,' I said.

'I haven't got any dough . . . what's the time?'

'Quarter to one. Just get one. I'll pay.'

I gave Zorba some gin. I'm sure it's not what you're supposed to give people in his position but I didn't have anything else. He sat back in the chair and sipped the gin and told me what had happened. As I'd figured from what O'Keefe had told me, Zorba hadn't been able to resist a peek in the brown paper bag he'd been given, and when he'd peeked he hadn't been able to resist the packets of used fivers and tenners he'd found inside. It was silly of O'Keefe to trust him with that much money. He'd carried money before but that was when he was doing it for me. Zorba and me are friends . . . so with me it was a question of trust. When O'Keefe dealt with him directly, Zorba felt under no such obligation.

It was partly my fault. I'd cut O'Keefe out when I'd decided not to work with him any more and I should've known he'd try a bit of private enterprise with Gal or Zorba. The trouble was, when Zorba had found out how much money he was carrying, he'd simply taken it straight down the Bank of Nicosia, swapped it for a money draft and sent the draft to his wife with a note saying, 'All is forgiven. Buy a house. I'm following soon.' Or whatever the Greek equivalent is.

Zorba's big mistake was that he didn't take himself with the money. Nobody could've done anything about it. O'Keefe would never have found him. The insurance company O'Keefe had been negotiating for could only have made a fuss about O'Keefe, not about Zorba. He could have spent the rest of his days in peace on some Cypriot balcony, shading his delicate features from the summer heat and quaffing vast amounts of ouzo while he watched his children grow.

I suppose that was his plan in the end, anyway. But he decided first of all to stay around London, 'tidying my affair' as he put it. Tidying his affair took a vital few days, and by that time little Charlie was telling the sellers that, money or no money, they had to get whatever they were selling back to me. Mr Wilkins had said so and Mr Wilkins' word was, in the sellers' world, law.

'How did they find you?'

'They hold blowlamp to my cousin,' he muttered and shook his head slowly. These guys showed a certain style. Their interrogation technique left the likes of O'Keefe and myself asleep at the starting gate. Neither of us had been to the school of blowtorch confessions. O'Keefe had tried to find Zorba and failed, Gal had tried to find him and failed and I've little doubt that if I'd tried I'd have failed too. That's where madmen score . . . they do madder things than the rest of us, things we wouldn't imagine doing.

I poured Zorba some more gin, then went and sat on the stairs. I knew he couldn't answer a load of questions and I felt angry and hurt that someone would treat him so badly, no matter what he'd done. I sat on the stairs and looked down to the doorway, then through the doorway and into the street. The rain kept falling and sometimes a car would pass. I went upstairs again and said, 'Couldn't you get the money back to them? Couldn't you have handed over the cash anyway?'

He shook his head.

'My wife and kids have it.'

I said, 'Damn you,' under my breath and he smiled a little, then Gal came and carted him down to my car. Zorba told us to bring the bag, too, from under my desk. The bag was an old cardboard suitcase with unlikely stickers on the outside (Port Said, Piraeus and New York I saw. There were others) and something more substantial than a spare shirt on the inside. It was because they'd been forced to return the bag the thieves had nailed Zorba to my desk. We drove him down to Bart's Hospital, which has a night casualty ward and is far enough away from Canning Town as to make us feel a little more comfortable about my local police. Gal took him in. I sat in the car and watched. They looked like a couple of drunks staggering across West Smithfield. I turned the radio on and listened to a late-night smooth talker while I waited for Gal. I could hear the articulated meat lorries running up their refrigerator engines. I could see the lights under the market building. I could hear the yells of the night workers, 'all right, all right, back a bit . . . woah!' I left the car and went to a phone box.

'Hullo.'

O'Keefe sounded drowsy, but he'd picked the phone up on the first ring.

'You can stop worrying,' I said. 'I've got something for you.'

He was awake immediately.

'Got it with you?'

'In my car. Can we talk?'

He was silent for a second. I could imagine him looking at the sleeping woman by his side.

'I'll go down to the kitchen.' He put the phone down. I read the names in the phone box. Vera: big, black and willing. Elaine: all requirements catered to. Anne: bottom marks for naughty boys. All the names were followed by phone numbers, all were written in laundry marker. The man from British Telecom with the scrubbing brush was fighting an uphill battle. I wondered if the sleeping woman O'Keefe had just left was really so naïve. Did she think she was married to an upright citizen, a guardian of law, order and morality, or did she think Denis was a bit of a yob . . . did she know where the money for the house in Thorpe Bay and the three weeks a year in Ibiza came from? Not off a copper's salary.

'Go on then,' came O'Keefe's voice again.

'I'm outside Bart's,' I said. 'Zorba's in it. I've got your gear because Wilkins told whoever it was to cough up.'

'*I* told them too. They wouldn't, though,' he said. '*I* told them I'd send them down for five years each. It didn't seem to worry them.'

'Well, Denis, I suppose they knew you weren't serious . . . after all, they could blow the gaff on you. That's one thing. The other is that you don't have the powers of persuasion Wilkins has. Little Charlie probably said "give Denis the gear or I'm going to cut your toes off . . . slowly". I can imagine it, Denis, can't you?'

'Mm.'

'Anyway they got the gear back to me and they found Zorba.'

'How'd they find him? I've been looking for a week.'

'They have the same advantage over you in the persuasion stakes as Wilkins does. That's how. They nearly killed Zorba.'

'Serves the little slag right.'

'Maybe. What are you going to do about them?'

'We'll see.'

'We'll certainly see, Denis. I want a lot of returns on this favour. Know what I mean?'

He didn't answer.

'I'll see you tomorrow night, Denis.'

I could see Gary skipping over the road. O'Keefe still didn't answer so I put the phone down.

'They're keeping him in,' Gal said as we climbed in the car. 'I'm sorry I was a long time. The night clerk got all stroppy when I told him I didn't know where it had happened and I'd found him on the roadside. He got particularly upset when I told him my name was Samuel A. Ritan. It took a while to convince him. He was all for calling the cops.'

I drove round the one-way system in Smithfield.

'There's Duncan's gym,' said Gal, pointing to a Victorian boozer. I stopped. I could just make out the shadows of the equipment in the upper rooms, through the uncurtained windows. Behind us the market men had started work with a vengeance. I left the car and walked back to Grand Avenue, then walked through the painted-iron and glass splendour of the meat market. I don't know what I expected to see. There was sawdust on the floor and men in blood-stained white coats pushed past me. I looked at a lamb, all strung up and hanging from a rail by its hind legs. The salesman ignored me, I obviously didn't look right for a wholesale buyer. I turned and looked from the market back towards George Duncan's gym. I could see straight up to the windows of his gym from here. Another porter pushed past with fresh blood on his coat. He was pushing a big tub full of pigs' heads. Pigs' eyes, past pain now, stared through their blond lashes at me. Some of the blood on the porter's coat had caught my hand as he'd pushed past. I stood under a neon lamp and looked closely at my hand. Blood never seems real. Blood never seems like blood. I thought of the body we'd seen in Shoreditch and a shiver ran down my spine. I went back into the darkness to my car. Gal had re-tuned the radio to a French pop-music station. He was drinking Coke and smoking a cigarette. Gal stood for life and light. Blood and meat meant death and darkness.

I opened the car door. The courtesy light came on. Gal smiled and swigged his Coke. I felt like putting my arms round him but he wouldn't have understood. Instead I said, 'Drive us home, Gal.' And walked round to the passenger side of the car. Gal slid behind the wheel of the car and engaged 'drive'. As we reached the end of Carthusian Street

110

a couple of big red Salvage Corps machines came racing round the corner. Their blue lights were on but the sirens weren't sounding. In the cab we could see the officer pulling on his fireman's jacket: then they were past, all polished paint work headlamps and sliding tyres on the wet street.

'I wouldn't mind driving one of them,' said Gal. ''s a fair old job.'

We crossed the bright lights of Aldersgate Street, then plunged into the darkness of Fann Street and he said it again and I said, angrily and unreasonably. 'Just shut up and drive us home.'

He turned the radio up and did just that.

Fourteen

My auntie used to have a pub in Hadleigh. When I first knew Judy and we were young and innocent we used to go and stay with her for the weekend. It was a nice, unspoilt pub where you could get arrowroot biscuits and a game of darts. Locals would chat politely if you wanted to chat and leave you alone if you wanted to be left alone. On summer Sunday afternoons you could walk down to the castle, which was built for King John or someone and is in such an advanced state of disrepair he wouldn't even be able to raise a mortgage on it nowadays. Judy and I would stand in the ruins of the old castle and look down on the flatlands on the banks of the Thames. Trains would rumble along a track below us, the light would be courtesy of John Constable, with tall black and white cotton wool clouds towering over the Isle of Grain and shafts of sunlight breaking through to us. Judy and I would make big plans for a future that isn't here now and even back then we must've known would never be here. That's half the fun of planning the future . . . unless you're the most boring man on earth it's *never* going to work.

On Friday evening I was driving along the A13 in heavy traffic. Dirt and drizzle lifted off the tarmac before me, making little greasy smuts on the windscreen that the wipers wouldn't shift. By the time I reached Pitsea the rain had stopped and the roads were dry. By the time I reached Hadleigh I was positively bathed in evening sunshine and all the commuters had turned off for someplace else. How kind.

My auntie has long since gone to the great saloon bar in the sky, where there are not only 'afters' but 'befores' (or maybe there are no licensing laws at all), the 'special' is never off, the barman always turns up for work on time and the landlady (i.e. auntie) has a tap of draught champagne conveniently situated next to a tall barstool she favours. I only hope the Guinness in the saloon bar in the sky is good enough for my dad (her brother) to be standing near her tall barstool somewhere reading a celestial *Sporting Life*, backing nags with an endless supply of white fivers and arguing with his mates whether or not B. J. T. Bosanquet really invented the googly. He always swore it was a sporting Abo that invented the googly and he'd read it in a book. He also swore that my auntie's Guinness came up too cold. The idea of the Guinness argument creating (another) rift which would this time last for all eternity is more than I can bear. The Abo would be less of a problem.

The pub's still there and Judy's Metro was in the car park. I went inside and thought I'd got it all wrong at first. It seems as soon as auntie died the brewers sent in a team of interior designers who'd come up with a foolproof plan to make money: '. . . all we need is a leatherette and velour version of Santa's Grotto. They haven't got one of them in Hadleigh.' They certainly have now. The interior walls of auntie's pub had gone. The floor had been raised (or was it the ceiling lowered?) and everything coloured womb-red. The space between the floor and the ceiling was filled with throbbing music and flashing lights.

Judy was at the bar drinking a salad.

'Hullo,' she yelled. 'Pimms?'

'Light and bitter,' I said, shaking my head.

We were the only people in the room apart from the bar staff. It's the kind of pub people don't go to till late. If I'd known in advance I would've been a month late, or a year late, or even never come. By a complicated series of hand gestures the barmaid and I exchanged the information that I wanted a light and bitter and no, I couldn't have one. Would I like a Schlitz instead?

'A *what*?'

113

'*Schlitz!*'

Time was that the only schlitz girls in Hadleigh had were in their schkirtz. I had a Schlitz, then swapped lip-reading lessons with Judy for half an hour.

'*I wanted to meet here because I was being followed,*' I shouted.

'*Oh yes?*'

'*But now I'm not.*'

'*Oh yes?*'

'*No. Did you bring a bag?*'

'*Yes.*' She sipped her fruit salad.

I sipped my Schlitz. I swear I did it. I sipped my Schlitz then I slurped my Schlitz then I swallowed my Schlitz. A certain Stevie Wonder boomed advice on life into my ears and for the first time since one didn't work properly I gave thanks for that fact. Judy insisted I have another beer and I said no but she didn't hear, then we had another of those '*Had a good day at the office?*', 'It's about quarter past seven', '*I didn't ask for the time*', 'What?', '*What?*' conversations. I staggered outside with my head reeling and my eyes seeing everything a green tint. I supervised Judy humping my overnight bag and Zorba's/O'Keefe's cardboard suitcase into the boot of her Metro, then we locked my car good and proper and left it in the pub car park for the weekend while Judy drove us down to Thorpe Bay.

'I'm a bit tired,' I said.

'I'm not surprised.' She drove smoothly and unfussedly. She was always in the right gear and she did all that stuff about never crossing your hands on the steering wheel they teach you at the Police Driving School. I never got the hang of it while I was there – at least not enough to be trusted with more than a Panda car. If you want to drive a big Rover with a red stripe down the side you must *never* cross your hands. You must also remember all the rules in the police driving manual, be able to give a commentary on traffic hazards as you approach them and *never ever* bump into anything while you're driving. I failed on all counts.

Judy drove us beautifully into Southend and then I took over and used my special expertise to find a quiet pub, somewhere to park and a table in the corner where we couldn't be overheard.

'You should have told me what you were going to do,' she said. 'When you saw me outside Scotland Yard you should've told me.'

'I did,' I said. 'I was asked to look after George Duncan's wife and that's what I went off to do. It only became complicated afterwards.'

Judy frowned. She frowns well, even if I say so myself. I kissed her and she frowned more.

'Well it's all over now, Jimmy, and I'm pleased. You can just imagine how I felt when I found out you were in a cell in Peter Street. I never want to go through that again.'

'Nor do I,' I said.

'I felt so helpless.'

'So did I.'

Judy sipped her drink, rum and Coke. I had chosen a pub that didn't do any salad drinks or thumping music. I'm getting too old for that.

'Still it's over now,' she said again.

'You already said that.'

'But you didn't agree. Don't you agree?'

I didn't say anything. It would only lead to an argument.

'Don't you agree?' she insisted. She was getting that 'you'd better agree' look women sometimes go in for.

'No I don't. I don't believe they've got the right man. I don't even believe the woman I took there was George Duncan's wife. That's how I feel about it. The way I feel is that it isn't finished with me and I haven't finished with it . . . all right?'

But it wasn't all right, and she let me know it.

The idea was that we would stay a couple of days with the O'Keefes. The idea was that we'd go there after dinner on Friday night and stay till Sunday afternoon. Mary O'Keefe is a dun-coloured little woman who stays in the posh house in Thorpe Bay and feeds the kids three times a day and gets them off to school in her Ford Escort bang on time. She makes sure Denis has an endless supply of ironed shirts while he makes sure she has an endless supply of money which she doesn't appear either to notice or use. Judy and me had been there before and Mary O'Keefe had immediately bagged her as a fellow female, leading into the kitchen for a fluffy-slippered ladies meeting, a recipe-swapping session. Judy would rather die than buy fluffy slippers and her idea of a recipe is 1) drive to Chinese takeaway, 2) order food, 3) collect food and pay, 4) drive home, 5) eat it. She thinks brownies and flapjacks is a game described in *Scouting for Boys*.

Denis and Mary O'Keefe live on Dunbarton Avenue, Thorpe Bay. It must be the suburban street that out-suburbans all others. There are neat clipped hedges, new double-glazed windows, mock-Georgian doors and bumper-to-bumper Granada Ghias all the way along it. Denis told me once that, when his girls were tiny, he'd had a deputation of middle-aged male neighbours at his door complaining about them peeing in the gutter. That's Thorpe Bay. Nowadays the O'Keefe daughters are neo-pubescents and don't admit to peeing anywhere, ever. They stay in their rooms and listen to pop music while their father rolls his eyes downstairs. The next deputation will be teenage boys.

Judy and me arrived in an icy silence. The girls were in bed and Denis offered me a scotch and the women sherry. Judy didn't even snap at that. She didn't want to hear what Denis had found out and she didn't want to stay in the same room while I listened. Judy went happily into the kitchen to experience the delights of a small glass of sherry and a private viewing of the O'Keefe's new Siemens dishwasher.

Denis threw me the copy of the p-m report.

'Where's the gear?' he said.

'In that cardboard suitcase you took up to our room.'

I read the report while Denis went upstairs and checked the suitcase, then hid it somewhere. I could hear muffled banging about under the roof. The p-m report wasn't very interesting. Female, late twenties, cause of death bullet wound to heart, time of death between midnight and six a.m. (don't stick your neck out, Sir Mark–*I* left her after midnight and she was found not long after six). Under 'Other Comments' he'd written '*scars on arm consistent with healed puncture marks. The marks are of a type that would be caused by the misuse of a hypodermic syringe, though there is no evidence of drug abuse present in the corpse. It would not be unreasonable to infer the subject may be a cured drug abuser of some description.'* There was an empty line and then he'd written *'The subject had seen a pregnancy through to full term within the last five years.'*

Denis came down and gave me another whisky. Sir Mark had bravely hazarded a guess that the missing flesh on the face had been 'cut off with some sharp object, perhaps a butcher's knife'. He noted there were fresh wounds in the gums where the teeth (and he gave the teeth numbers) had been torn out. He wrote that there were marks on the remaining teeth which indicated a pair of pliers may have been used. A hurriedly handwritten addition to the type-written text said: *'In response to your telephone enquiry I can't as yet be positive that the wounds to the face, eyes, teeth and scalp took place after death, though that would at the moment seem likely. You will appreciate this is a preliminary report and . . .'* then it drifted off into bureaucrat-ese and was signed *'Squiggle-squiggle-squiggle'* and then a load of letters to prove he was a medical doctor. Just the unreadable signature would have been enough.

There were some more papers with the report. There was a telex to Officer-in-Charge, CID Cape Town asking for any criminal, medical or dental record available for one Alison May Clark, giving her date of birth as February 3rd 1954, place of birth London, England, a note of the parental address in Cape Town, S.A. and a brief outline of the case in the guarded way that coppers outline things (I don't know for sure the sun'll come up tomorrow, though of course it has come up every morning since the start of time so it *may* do). There was a photostat of the dabs taken off the corpse which I presume would have been transmitted to the South African coppers under separate cover from the telex. They have a special machine that does it at New Scotland Yard. There were some witness statements, including a long and detailed description of me by the cabbie who'd picked me up twice in Saffron Walden. It was a pretty accurate descrip-tion, too, and gave the lie to the idea that people don't see you . . . they just don't say anything. So *English*, that.

'Well,' said Denis, 'enough?'

I slapped the papers with my hand.

'I thought you'd only taken a copy of the p-m report?'

Denis nodded and put his glass on top of a little coaster-shaped lace mat on the coffee table. Everywhere was polished. I could even smell the stuff, smell the lavender they put in it.

'I did,' Denis said. 'Then I had a phone call from DCS Maher's assistant, a Sergeant Robson . . . know him?'

He smiled. So did I.

'A little,' I said, 'Brian Borden's the authority on Maher's assistants. What about it?'

'He was asking me over to see Maher. He said Maher would like some help from me on the Duncan case. He said Maher thought I might have some inside knowledge of the Wilkins organisation . . . what d'yer reckon to that, eh? I said I had a full case-load and he'd better get Maher to speak to my gov'nor about it.'

'And?'

'And quarter of an hour later I was zooming down to join the Murder Squad. On loan. I went and saw Maher and said that I didn't know anything about the "organisation" that wasn't on collators' files in our nick or CIS at the Yard. Then Maher says yeah but he'd like me to lend my mind to it and my guv'nor's agreed so would I mind just doing that? Then he told me to go and see the SOCO and get clued-in from them and he gave me a great stack of statements and stuff to read. He said take it home for the weekend and he said I'd find the top half-dozen – which is the stuff you've got there – the most interesting. Then he asked me a load of questions about you . . . I got the impression, James, that he expected me to see you and he expected, even *wanted* me to show you that stuff.'

He played with his diamond ring, twisting it round and round his finger. I said, 'What did the Scenes of Crime people tell you?'

'Was I right about Maher?' he insisted.

'Yes,' I said. He fetched the whisky and poured us both some. Even the bottle had been polished by his obsessive little Mary. I picked up my glass. I could see clear grease marks where my fingers had been. I saw Denis wiping his glass absently with his handkerchief. He looked through the amber liquid at me. 'I don't think Wilkins did it,' I said. 'Maher has his doubts, too.'

Denis kept squinting through his glass. 'That's hot,' he

said. I could hear his girls arguing upstairs. Mary yelled politely at them that they should go to sleep, then came in to us and pulled the curtains and switched the lamps on. I noticed she touched the curtains lightly as she moved away from them, neatening their hang, evening out the puckers. Judy stayed firmly in the kitchen. I knew she'd be in a hell of a temper, biting her knuckles and learning about strong-flour and cream-cleansers and spray-on-oven-degreasers.

When Denis' wife had gone I said again, 'What did the SOCOs tell you?'

'Nothing. The prints in the Saffron Walden house fit the ones on the body. The prints in the hired Jag fit the ones on the body, the prints in the Barbican flat fit the ones on the body. Boring, isn't it? The only others we could find belong to you and Duncan. Not Wilkins, not Lenny Grant . . . no others.'

'None?' I sat up.

'None. No postman, no gas man, no electricity-board man. None. It seems that Alison Duncan was house-proud.' He waved at the room. 'People *are*, you know.'

The smell of lavender. The polished glass in my hand. A cut glass tumbler with whisky in it. I remembered the scene in Duncan's flat. I remembered the girl not knowing exactly where her own flat was supposed to be. If you wanted to kill someone you'd wipe your fingerprints off, everyone who's ever watched TV knows that. That would mean wiping the surface clean. It would mean wiping *all* the finger-prints off if the scene of the crime was your own home.

'Has everywhere been printed?' I said. 'All over the flat, all over the house in Saffron?'

He nodded. Of course it had. The Scenes of Crime people would go over it with a fine-tooth comb.

'I don't believe it was her, Denis. I don't believe it was his wife.'

'I know. Maher told me you didn't.'

'I think it was a stooge,' I said.

'Then who murdered her and why?'

'The Duncans. For the insurance money. It's obvious.'

'It may be to you, Jimmy, but it's Wilkins that is going to be obvious to everyone else. If you wanted to prove it was someone other than Alison Duncan you'd have to come up with concrete evidence that the body is someone else or you'd have to come up with the real Alison Duncan. One or the other. If Alison Duncan still exists who's in the mortuary? If Alison Duncan still exists then where is *she*? If George Duncan was after getting hold of their insurance money how's he going to share it with his 'dead' wife, and since George was tucked up tight when it happened who *did* do it?'

'I don't know. Have you had an answer from South Africa?'

'Yes. A nice one. Although Mrs Duncan had no parents living she'd a brother called David Clark who's alive and well and living in Cape Town . . . and he's got more form than the Derby winner. Her father had too, but since he's been dead for ten years we can hardly put this down to him.'

'What about medical records and dental records?'

'Unfortunately the doctor who dealt with her had a fire in his office a couple of weeks ago. Very unfortunate, that. He did say that she hadn't had a pregnancy to his knowledge, but that didn't mean she hadn't had a pregnancy. Same goes for the drugs thing. He knew nothing about it, but he says that's probably a habit she'd picked up in Europe, anyway. There's no trace of any dental records as yet.'

'What about immigration?'

'*What* immigration? She's *British*. She comes and goes here as she pleases.'

'And South African immigration?'

He shook his head again.

'She was a kid when she went there. They don't print kids going in. There's no reason. She never committed any crimes either here or there. None we know of. All the evidence is in those houses and in that hired Jag. Both you and Duncan identified the body.'

'Well, he would!' I stood. I felt angry. 'Let me spell out to you what I think, Denis. I think the girl whose body is in the mortuary was duped into being Mrs Duncan for a night. I don't know *how* but I think she was. I think the real Mrs Duncan had hopped off somewhere to lie low while Georgy boy collects the insurance money. She's got this tied up tighter than a duck's backside. I think the flat and the house were cleaned up so that only the new girl's dabs and mine and George's would be in them. Do you see what I'm saying? I think the murderer is the person you think is the victim. Got it? Why on earth else should someone cut off the face on that body?'

'Evidence?' said Denis.

He can be very annoying.

'I haven't got any evidence unless you count a body with a missing face.

'Exactly. Sit down, you'll wake the girls. *Think* about it, Jimmy. Even the missing face isn't evidence. It's exactly what you'd do to terrorise someone.'

I sat on his big velour sofa. The wife popped in again, I presume to find out why I was shouting.

'Having a good time, boys?' she said.

'Fine,' I said.

'Everything all right? Denis has got some beers in the cellar, haven't you, Denis? Why don't you boys try that? I think it's going to be better for you than nasty whisky all evening.'

Denis, to my surprise, dutifully went off to fetch a pack of four fizzy light ales.

'Everything all right?' said Mary when he'd gone.

'Okay. Are you *girls* having a good time?' I said as loudly as I could and as sarcastically as I dared.

'Oh *wonderful*,' she said and clasped her hands together and meant it. 'I get *so* few visitors connected with Denis's work . . . he says he likes to keep it out of the home and I respect that.'

Denis came back. She gave us fresh glasses and took the whisky ones away, smiling at me with her dun-coloured eyes under her dun-coloured soft-set hairdo.

When she'd gone I said, 'If Maher were to broaden his investigation a little he might think along the lines of the body being some poor stooge that would stand for Alison Duncan. He might think the murderer is a murderess. He might want to run those dabs off the cadaver through CRO and he might want to circulate all missing persons agencies with a description of the woman I brought to London . . . who is *not* the woman in the picture they're using in the incident room. He could try drug agencies with the description . . . I mean, if she was some sort of user she'd have to pay somehow. That normally means crime. If there was no crime she'd be registered on a scheme. At least that. Often they're registered and committing crime. There must be a note on her *somewhere*.'

Denis shook his head.

'Done it. He's done all of it. The prints aren't on CRO, but neither were Alison Duncan's. That's a blank – it's a minus to your theory. The description you gave is being circulated now, but Maher says it doesn't differ any from the description of Alison Duncan. Come in on Monday and we'll try a photofit.'

'And what about women of that description who've disappeared?'

'In the last week only two. It's neither of them . . . one's been found and the other has a record and her prints don't fit. In the last month there's probably a dozen who'd fit the description . . . but don't forget if your theory is right they've probably picked someone who's got no ties to anyone.'

'Like who?'

He shrugged and pulled the ring on another can.

I said, 'Like who?' again.

'A whore. A dropout. Something like that. Didn't she talk to you?'

'She talked. But she didn't tell me her prices or something, you know. She might have been, I suppose. I don't know. What about this pregnancy angle?'

'Jimmy, do you know how many women have had babies in Britain and South Africa in the past five years?'

'Okay. Quite a few. What do you think, Denis?'

'I think you're wrong. Wilkins did it. I think it was horrific because it was meant to be. That was his style. He reckoned he'd get away with it because he didn't have to worry about the gun. First of all we wouldn't find it and then we wouldn't tie it to him. Well, we did both and he's well strapped and I'm pleased. We've got him at last.'

Denis's attitude was realistic and mine wasn't, of course. The 'girls' came back in and we played Monopoly till well after midnight, all the time with Judy avoiding talking to me as much as she could so that we built up into one of those huge cold rows that nobody can remember how they started but are ugly enough to hurt everybody. Denis affected to ignore it and his wife bought Mayfair and Park Lane and squealed and squealed when everybody landed on them one after the other and wouldn't let any of us go to bed till she'd won.

I could've sworn she was playing footsie with me under the table . . . at least, something kept rubbing my leg and when I looked up Judy was staring fiercely at her metallic top hat while Denis was counting his money. Mary, meanwhile, smiled and said, 'Your turn.'

Maybe there's more to Mrs Dowdy Thorpe Bay than meets the eye. I certainly hope so . . . for Denis's sake.

Fifteen

We lay awake all night, Judy and me. It's quite a trick to spend five hours in a double bed and never touch. We managed it. After an eternity of lying on my back and staring at the ceiling I felt it must be dawn, so I went and pulled the curtains and looked down at the dark garden, then all around the dark sky. Not a speck of light. I went and sat on the edge of the bed and then Judy rose too, and we dressed together without speaking and without putting the light on. We went out and I left Denis's front door on the latch. There are enough police patrols in Thorpe Bay to protect him in the small hours, I thought. Anyway, the idea he might be burgled amused me.

Judy and me walked down to the front, side by side and still not talking. There was a purple slash across the sky to the east, and a reflection of it in the sea. The houses were black and the road grey. We walked along the promenade, which is merely a seaside road, nothing special, then we stepped down onto the mudflats and began to walk out towards the sea. The purple slash had changed into the edge of a sun now and it rose in a grey sheet of a sky and was striped by black bands of low cloud. We walked through millions of grey worm casts, splashed through tiny flat rivulets of steely sea water and all the time the sun rose slowly and we said nothing. I stopped and rested on a wall which was covered with seaweed. I turned and could see early morning cars moving along the road at the sea's edge – or now the mud's edge. Their lights were on still, even though the dawn had come. I could smell salt in the air and had that metallic, early morning taste in my mouth that comes

124

from seeing a dawn without sleeping first. I had a slight ache in the pit of my stomach and the feeling of my brain being dull and slow. The light fell on us and a sea breeze touched us and the dark bedroom of an hour ago seemed like an eternity away, seemed like someone else. Judy leaned against me and squeezed my arm. Her eyes were closed and there was a slight sheen of light off her smooth pale skin, a faint halo shining through her blond hair.

'I'm sorry I was angry, Jimmy,' she said. 'I was scared for you, and then angry because everyone at work knew about it and you'd embarrassed me. All those stupid things.'

She still hadn't opened her eyes.

I said, 'I know.'

I had no idea what it was supposed to mean. I had to say something. I wasn't thinking of her by now. I was thinking about George Duncan. Why hadn't he told me his Jag was hired? I couldn't think that one out. Perhaps he'd thought it didn't matter. Perhaps it *didn't*. If the flat in the Barbican and the house at Saffron were okay from the point of view of having prints that matched the body, what *wasn't*? Where would I get a load of prints that belonged to someone else? How would I match them to a real Alison Duncan? Where would I find her? It made my head spin just to think about it all.

Past Judy's face I could see two men, hundreds of yards out on the mudflats, digging for bait. They were the shadows of men, not real men. They were matchstick men drawn on a silver grey board. One matchstick man stood and eased his back.

Judy said, 'And so I think it's getting between us. And I think we have to come to some sort of decision. Either we give up our jobs and try something else . . . and probably marry, too . . . or we admit that this thing of ours is coming to an end and we have to part company. That's what I think, Jimmy.'

She opened her eyes and followed my gaze to the bait-diggers.

'You're saying you want to split?' I said.

'*No*! I'm offering to go into an alliterative marriage. I'm saying that I'm willing to put my ticket in on Monday and follow you to the ends of the earth . . . but not if you keep

125

up this private detective fantasy. I'll give it up and you'll give this up too.'

'What'll we do?' I said.

'We're not short of cash between us. We'll sit by a beach in a tumbledown shack and dig worms out of the sand. We'll do anything. Run a pub.'

'I couldn't carry crates.'

'Then I will. Maybe we'll go abroad.'

'There aren't any pubs abroad.'

'Not both!' She laughed. The laugh flew across the mudflats and the bait-diggers stopped and looked towards us. They looked like grave-diggers, suddenly. A shiver ran down my spine. I touched Judy's cheek, for safety and for good luck.

'Sounds good to me, kid,' I said.

We embraced.

'You have three months' notice to work, though, eh?' I said.

She nodded but said nothing.

'Well I'm going to try to sort out this mess in three months. Okay?'

Judy shook her head angrily and walked away, back towards the coast road and reality. A lorry growled over there and clunked its gears. Lights were on in some of the houses overlooking the sea. The real world wanted us back.

Denis was frying bacon when we arrived. Mary and their children were still in bed. A man on the radio was discussing with himself the prospects for a good summer's cricket.

'I've made bacon sandwiches for all of us,' he said. 'And I've got champagne in the fridge for a champagne breakfast.'

'What for?' said Judy suspiciously. Maybe she thought Denis had a mental hook-up with me and knew all about what she'd said on the beach.

'Because your boyfriend here saved my bloody neck this week and I want to celebrate with him, that's why.'

We could hear the girls moving around upstairs.

'What did he do?' Judy said, then immediately, 'No, don't answer. If it's to do with you, Denis, I don't want to know.'

Denis laughed.

126

Judy laughed too, then she said, 'We don't eat bacon.'

Then we all laughed and we told Denis we'd decided to go into the marriage stakes and we all laughed again and he said, 'Well, drink the bloody champagne!'

So we all drank the bloody champagne, even Mary and her daughters Sharon and Cheryl drank bloody champagne, even if it was only a sip for the girls with their mother frowning. Everyone giggled a lot and had a bloody good champagne time, and though we were all doing it for different reasons the good time lasted right through too many bacon sandwiches and a whole lot of cornflakes with yoghurt on top till I went and spoiled it by asking Denis could he get me introduced to the security characters in a couple of the insurance companies that were due to pay out Duncan and also could be discover for me whether Duncan had any car registered to him at DVLC Swansea.

'Any?'

'Absolutely *any*,' I said.

Then I asked couldn't you get fingerprints off paper with some funny trick with powdered graphite the SOCOs had developed and Denis said he thought you could and he'd find out more. Then Judy threw a moody and insisted we had to go home and then Mary O'Keefe threw a moody about that because she'd gone and bought half a cow or something to roast for lunch. Denis took the future bridegroom to his potting shed to explain the facts of life and also plan a campaign for the next seven days. Mary and Judy stayed indoors and I was pleased to see someone else getting the icy silence treatment.

So much for Southend. After picking up my car we diverted and drove home on the more northerly A127. Getting the car meant taking us to auntie's pub again, and I really didn't feel like it. Change is not made without inconvenience, even from worse to better, and auntie's boozer certainly hadn't got any better. As we left auntie's pub's car park I realised I was gritting my teeth so hard it hurt. And I realised I'd been doing it for quite a while.

Sixteen

When I got back to London it seemed dirty, dirtier than usual, and I was tired of it. Any normal man would have taken up Judy's offer like a shot. A normal man would be off planning the wedding and choosing curtains for the new home, wherever that would be. Instead I devoted myself to the task of proving the Metropolitan Police wrong; I devoted myself to freeing a known criminal and gangster from prison on the premise that he was falsely charged, and proving that a dead woman was not dead at all but lurked somewhere in the streets of London, ready to make off with her 'widower' and their ill-gotten cash.

I spent Sunday straightening out my office and my flat. They both looked like a whirlwind had been through them. Though the police are happy to wreck your premises in the course of searching them, they have no real interest in providing a team of cleaning ladies and re-packers to put the joint back into some sort of state.

Judy had agreed that I needed to put things straight, though she made me promise to do it in harness with Maher and O'Keefe and not to take any risks or get involved with Wilkins or any characters like that. When her three months' notice were up we'd pack our bags into a VW camper and spend the rest of the summer finding somewhere sunny where we could put down roots as a married couple. I promised readily, and I kept my promise all through Sunday while I was cleaning my flat, then through most of Sunday evening while I cleaned up my office. It was about nine p.m. my promise went down the tube. I had Chardray upstairs with me, drinking gin. I was explaining that I was getting out of the detective fantasy and getting into the marriage one. He sat on my lumpy sofa and said he thought marriage was a very good idea, which was big of him considering he was losing a regularly-paying tenant and that the reasons we were drinking gin in *my* office was that his wife didn't allow alcohol of any description into their house.

'Is she strict Muslim?' I asked.

He raised his hands and laughed.

'Good heavens no! We're all Christians in my family. No, my wife is just being a strict female . . . I got drunk many years ago and she swore the stuff must never enter the house again.'

'But marriage is good for me?' I said.

Chardray nodded.

'Your Judy is a different cup of tea.'

He giggled at his own joke. There was a light tap at the door and it swung open. Chardray excused himself and little Charlie came in, hiking himself up onto my sofa.

'Hello.'

'Hello, Charlie. What do you want?'

'Uh. . . .' He squeezed his little face with his hands, then dragged them down so that his lower lip pulled clear of his yellow teeth and pink gums for a second. 'There was a misunderstanding here the other day. When I gave orders for you to have that clobber returned I didn't say anything specific about what should happen to your . . . your pal.'

'Zorba?'

'That's right. It was a mistake on my part and I apologise for making it.'

'Don't apologise to me,' I said, 'it wasn't me that ended up nailed to this desk.' I put my finger where the hole in the wood was. Little Charlie inspected the hole, then arched his eyebrows by way of another apology.

'Animals,' he said. He pulled a wad from his jacket and threw it on top of the desk.

'Mr Wilkins, as you know, has been falsely accused. He would like to hire your services to get to the bottom of the matter, since he does not believe the police officers involved will give him a fair crack. He thinks they would like to see him in stir no matter what happens, and that this would be a . . .'

'Shut up, Charlie,' I said. 'I'll get to the bottom of this but it won't be for you or Wilkins. As far as I'm concerned Wilkins could stay in prison for a thousand years. I just want to nail the people that did it.'

'Good.' He leaned back to the sofa. 'Any ideas? Someone who knows him well is stitching the man right up.'

'I've got ideas.' I poured myself another gin and was careful not to offer him one. I picked his wad off my desk and threw it into his lap. 'And they're *my* ideas,' I said loudly. 'They're not for sale to creeps like you.'

He smiled and stuffed the wad back into his jacket. I heard a deep throated cough on my stairs.

'Just my driver,' Charlie said. 'Relax, Alf. Wait down in the motor for me,' he called.

There was the sound of heavy feet descending, then a slam of the outer door.

'Try one of your ideas for who this person might be on me,' Charlie said.

'How about Alison Clark . . . didn't she live with Wilkins?'

Charlie laughed a little strangled laugh, pulled some cigarettes out of his pocket and lit one. He blew smoke through his nostrils, looking like a tiny dragon, laughed again and said, 'No one's going to kill herself just to get at Mr Wilkins. *No one* is that mad.'

I said nothing. Charlie looked at me for a long time.

'Well,' I said, 'you probably know that the shooter was used in a bullion job and that the coppers have drawn a good line on the gun from the robbery to Wilkins.'

'Huh,' he snorted. I gave him the gin. I decided. I wanted to pump him a little.

'It's a good line,' I said. 'Good evidence. So I have to presume that Wilkins was once in possession of this shooter. Then his ex-girlfriend is found shot with it. Either Wilkins shot her or someone close to him got the gun away from him knowing that it would frame him . . . who could that be?'

He shook his head.

'Not you, Charlie?' I said.

He laughed. It was an ugly laugh but he was confident.

'Not me. You can take that for granted.'

130

'Who then?'

He blew smoke through his nostrils again, then hopped down from my sofa and went over to the window. He let the roller blind loose so that it smacked up against itself and the springs rattled. We both watched the lights of cars passing over Canning Town flyover for a while, then Charlie said, 'There's no one close enough who'd have anything to gain by it. There are lots of people who'd do it, given a chance, but none close enough to do it.'

I smiled.

'Except Alison Clark,' I said. 'She could have done it . . . are you with me now?'

Charlie went to the desk, snapped his head back and threw the gin down his throat.

'I'm with you,' he said. 'What about fingerprints and all that? Don't the coppers go into all that?'

'Is it possible about the gun?' I insisted.

He nodded.

'She could have come by that gun, yes . . . she could have known where it was. I'll find out for sure. Er . . . about the Greek. . . .'

'Yes?'

He wrung his hands like a moneylender.

'I've got them round the corner in a car. We've got a hammer and nails down there too, if it'd make you feel any better about being on our side.'

The only reason I didn't bellow, rush at him, pick him up and throw him bodily down the stairs was that I'm not physically capable of it, even with a little worm like Charlie.

'Go away, Charlie, and take your disgusting little mind with you. Let your victims go and tell them they owe me one.'

He shrugged and opened the door.

'I don't suppose your Greek mate would see it like that. He'd probably want to get them back for what they done to him.'

'You're wrong,' I said. 'Zorba's a Christian through and through. He wouldn't *dream* of nailing them too.' Not half he wouldn't. He'd fry them as well.

'You'll keep us in touch with developments, though?'

'Go away, Charlie. Don't call me any more.'

He paused and looked up the stairs at me.
'Go away, Charlie,' I repeated.
He went away.

Seventeen

At seven on Monday I was back at Smithfield. The side entrance of the Dog and Duck was thoroughly bolted and barred and George Duncan's gym above looked deserted. If it was still operating as a gym it should have been full of sweating men by seven a.m. I wasn't very surprised to see it empty.

I walked back into the market. Carcasses hung all around me. Piles of cow flesh were being counted by men in white coats and white straw trilbies. A well-dressed young man rolled up the sleeve of his suit jacket, then poked around the innards of a turkey. When he pulled his hand out again the remains of giblets adhered to his fingers. He shook his head and wiped his hand.

I walked out to the front of the market. To the place where Wallace was executed heaven knows how many years before, and where now cars were queuing to enter the underground car park.

In front of one building stood a line of butchers, facing the street. Half a dozen men. They wore chain mail on one arm and hand. In the other hand they carried sharp, pointed knives about a foot long. Before each man hung a sharpening iron, and right along the row of men, at waist height, was a zinc or dull steel counter about three feet deep. The men worked quickly and smoothly. From behind themselves they picked up a pig's head, cut the ears off (one wipe of the knife on the sharpening iron), cut the cheeks out (another wipe of the knife on the sharpening iron) then the tongue and snout, freeing the flesh with the sharp points of the knife. By the time they'd finished there was a pile of pig flesh ready to swipe into the huge grey bucket behind them and a pink clean skull ready to throw into a grey bin by each man's side. I watched them for a while. One man broke off to greet a girl, an office worker. She was pretty and well-dressed and leaned towards him in an exaggerated way, so as not to brush the bloody apron as she kissed him. The man smiled. He was big and brawny with a freckled, shapeless face and receding ginger hair. He held out a brain-spattered arm to take a polystyrene cup from the girl, then waved her a cheery goodbye as she trotted away. I went over.

'Hello.'

'Can I help you?' he said.

'Maybe. I suppose a lot of people watch you here.'

He nodded and sipped his coffee.

I said, 'Is there anywhere else it's done like this, just facing the street?'

The flabby-faced ginger man shook his head.

'I wouldn't know.' He said. 'This is the only place it's done hereabouts.'

'Buy you another coffee?'

He eyed me suspiciously.

'You a copper?'

'Sort of. I'm a detective. The coffee?'

He muttered no, put his polystyrene cup down and slapped his mailed hand against the other.

'Are the knives special?' I said.

'What do you think?'

I sighed. I was going to get no joy here, I could see.

'Where can you get them?'

'Long Lane . . . what's all this about?'

'Just a few questions. I won't keep you long. Listen, do you remember being watched by a blonde . . . late twenties, very attractive, about five-eight or a bit taller and a little under nine stone? She was probably expensively dressed.'

'No.'

I barred his way back to the counter.

'Will you just think about it?'

He pushed me with a bloody hand.

'If you're a detective where's your warrant card? I don't think you're a detective at all. You're just a chancer . . .

we get all kinds of loonies here, but they normally come after the pubs shut at lunchtime. You're the exception. Now sling your hook, exception.'

'I'm a private detective,' I said, 'and a lot depends on whether you. . . .'

The butcher laughed out loud.

'A *private* detective, eh? Pull the other one, John.'

All his colleagues stopped butchering pigs' heads and laughed too, waggling their knives in their hands as they laughed. A man in a white coat and a straw trilby hat looked out of a door behind the men and scowled, calling, 'Now now, let's be having you.'

I limped off, followed by their jeers. The white-coated man came right out onto the pavement and watched me out of sight, legs apart, hands bunched into fists and the fists leant firmly on his hips. Behind me I could hear the butchers calling.

'Oy-oy-oy! He's a dee-tect-tive!'

Not all my investigations are unalloyed successes.

I went back to Duncan's gym. The locks were undone and I went upstairs, hoping I might find him there. I didn't know what I'd say to him, but I'd have to confront him at some stage. The stairs smelled dank and were dark. I pushed the door open. The equipment lay around, dusty and unused. It doesn't take long for decay to set in. A couple of weeks ago the room would have been bustling at this time in the morning. I'd never been there but I'd been in other gyms and I could imagine it. Now the room looked as if nothing had happened there *ever*. It was eerie. I went through the room to the offices and pushed the frosted glass door of the back office wide with my stick.

A little black man sat behind a desk. I imagine the desk had been Duncan's. There were photos all round it like the photos I'd seen in Duncan's house in Essex. The black man had his feet on the desk and a whisky bottle in his hand.

'Who are you?' he said.

'I was just abut to ask the same question.'

'My name's Leary. Named after the great man.'

'Jimmy Jenner. Named after my dad. D'you work here?'

'Another copper?'

I shook my head.

'Does he owe you money?' asked Leary. He was a neat, handsome man, very poorly dressed. He had slivers of grey in his jet-black woolly hair and fine, even creases around his eyes and mouth. He could have been aged anywhere between thirty-five and sixty, but I guessed he was in the middle of that range somewhere and had just stayed good-looking as he'd become middle-aged.

'No. Not money. How about you?'

Leary tipped the whisky bottle over a glass and held the neck up to me enquiringly.

'No thanks. It's before eight, you know,' I said, then again, 'How about you?'

Leary giggled. The sound echoed round the dusty office and raced round the gym outside, sounding flat and nasty before it came back to me. When I had spoken, my own voice had had the same quality, I'd noticed. I turned and looked back through the doors. Rays of sunlight filtering through the dust in the room outside. In George Duncan's gym the edge seemed to go off things. There was no brightness, no clarity . . . just slowly settling dust.

'I'm the cleaner,' Leary said.

'Does he owe you money?'

He poured himself another scotch and giggled again.

'Yeah. I'm two weeks' wages out. I'm drinking one of them in the boss's whisky right now.' He held the bottle up again. 'Want a day's pay?'

'No thanks. He was mean with you, eh?'

'He was mean with everyone. He was always mean but when that bitch came along he was meaner and she put him up to it.'

'You didn't like her, Leary?'

'She was a bitch. Nothing but the best for them, everybody else gets to eat dust. Even Tommy Lynch she treated like a bum. I was here. I saw it all. You can believe me.'

He slung back the scotch and poured himself another.

'She was a bitch, okay. She was even having George on . . . playing the field. I saw it all. Nobody notices the cleaner, you know? But I was there, even if I was just a nobody. She used to get all the young black boxer boys to squire her round town, and all the rest of it. She was dirty, I'm telling you. She banged like a lavatory door . . . and about as often.'

'Did Duncan know all this?'

He shrugged and sank deeper into his chair. I noticed a hole in the sole of one of his shoes as he crossed one foot over the other on the desk. His right leg, the one that ended up underneath, stayed perfectly still throughout. Leary leaned forward and looked closely into his glass. Then glared at me.

'Who *are* you?'

'Jimmy Jenner, just like I said.'

'Oh yeah . . . that's right. You was a copper once, weren't you?'

He smiled. He wasn't as drunk as he looked.

'That's right,' I said, 'I was.'

'I thought so. I remember faces well and I read the papers a lot. Well, I don't know what you want it for and if anyone asks me I'll swear I never said it, but that girl was the bird of a real villain called Wilkins before he got onto her evil ways and slung her out. Know what I mean?'

'I know.'

'And then she landed on her feet okay when she got tied up with ol' Georgy Porgy here, because he couldn't believe an attractive young bird wanted him and he went all gooey over her and ended up marrying her. I'm glad she's dead; I know you shouldn't speak evil of them but I'm glad she is. He was a mean payer but okay as a bloke before she turned up and then she turned him mean both ways. I hated her.'

He poured another scotch. He'd be a stretcher case by lunchtime if he kept it up.

'She was even going with that other boxing bloke.'

'Which?'

'Grant. Lenny Grant. Young Tommy Lynch told one of the other fighters in the locker room. I was there but they never took no notice of me. Tommy said to the other guy, "I saw her ladyship and Lenny Grant canoodling in a restaurant up west the other night . . . what d'yer think of that?" and they both laughed. It was common knowledge.'

I only didn't whistle because I forced myself not to. Here

137

was a reason for George to bump his wife off. Here was a big problem for my substitute theory. Here was plenty. It confused me.

'What do you want from me, Leary?'

He smiled.

'How about a week's wages?'

'How much is that?'

'A score.'

I put two ten-pound notes on the desk. Did Duncan really only pay twenty pounds per week?

'How do you manage?' I said. 'How do you pay your rent and eat?'

Leary eased his legs off the table. He stood, heavily favouring the right, which was the one with no hole in the shoe.

'I used to be a sailor,' he said, 'many years ago. Then I had an accident and lost my leg, so I've got the old green card and a disability pension.'

I laughed loud and long. We both walked our funny walks through the gymnasium. I was still laughing. I didn't care about any dusty rooms or bad magic and I didn't think any more about there being no edge on things. Leary just made me laugh.

'Listen,' I said, 'where's Long Lane?'

'Two streets over, Jimmy Jenner. I'll see you.'

'You may do that, Leary. You may.'

And I went downstairs chuckling still. I could hear drunken Leary laughing upstairs, too.

Eighteen

That Monday was a busy day for me. By nine thirty I was in Denis O'Keefe's temporary office with the Murder Squad. The operation had been wound down to about half its original size, which wasn't very surprising. There wasn't an infinity of leads and once the original workload of statement-taking was over the job was one of perseverance rather than manpower. It's no good keeping a load of men and women locked up somewhere making passes at each other when they could go back on the street and do a job of work.

I kept the knife I bought in Long Lane hidden till Denis and me were alone together. Denis blanched when I threw it on his desk.

'What's that for?'

'Try it on your forensic people for a comparison with the cuts on that cadaver.'

He picked it up as if it was explosive, between finger and thumb.

'Where d'you get it, Jimmy?'

'From a shop. It's a representative of the genus 'butcher's knife'. As far as I know it's done nothing so far in its life except be wrapped in waxed paper.'

Denis took the knife out of the paper and found a minion to charge with the task of getting it to the forensic lab without chopping any fingers off. Then we settled down with a DC I'd never met before (and whose breath smelled so bad I hope we never meet again) to make up one of those daft identikit pictures that look at once like no member of the human race and all of them – insofar as all members of

139

the human race have eyes and ears and stuff like that. Usually.

It took all morning and about a hundred cups of coffee. We ended up with a picture that, given the circumstances, wasn't unlike the girl I'd driven from Saffron to London. The DC and Denis went out and left me with the identikit for ten minutes and by the time they came back (with yet another cup of coffee each and one for me, too) I'd convinced myself that we'd made a fair likeness.

'What do you think, Denis?'

He shook his head.

'It's the same girl.'

'Nah.' I was sure.

Denis threw a snapshot of Alison Duncan on the desktop. It was a small version of the big picture I'd seen with Maher in the incident room.

'It's the same girl,' he repeated.

I shook my head. The DC with the smelly breath picked up the photograph and my identikit job, looking from one to the other.

'No doubt about it,' he said. 'It's the same girl.'

I slammed my fist on the desk. 'It's not.'

The DC left and Denis came over all fatherly and arm-round-the-shoulders.

'I've got us a lunch-date,' he said. 'You'll enjoy it. It'll do you good.'

'I want to go to Smithfield first and I want you to come with me.'

'We'll be late for the lunch.'

'Phone them, Denis. Display some of that charm of yours. Tell them you hate soup. Anything.'

He shook his head but he phoned our lunch-date anyway. I slipped the snapshot of Alison and the identikit picture into a brown envelope old smelly-breath had left for that purpose, then we went in search of Brian Borden, who was providing the wheels.

By twelve forty-five we were in Smithfield again and I was asking the butcher to look at my pictures. The butcher said something very rude. Brian Borden didn't take kindly to it,

140

and he seemed to think it was a matter of honour not to show the man his warrant card. As if anyone should doubt Brian's word! I was a bit apprehensive about getting heavy with all these wicked-looking knives lying around but Brian would have none of it. He grabbed ginger-bonce's apron and shirt front all in one hand and said, 'We're in a bit of a hurry. Would you please co-operate,' or words to that effect. When the butcher didn't look lively Brian screwed the apron and shirt front up in his hand like you would a paper hanky . . . only the butcher was still inside this paper hanky. His face went red and his freckles stayed the same colour, a sort of ginger brown. He looked as if he had some horrible disease.

'Give me the picture,' said Brian. I gave it to him.

'Do you recognise this person?'

The butcher nodded. Brian let him go. He showed the picture to the other butchers. One other man recognised the photograph of Alison, too. He said. 'She came here and watched us work one day. She asked if she could have a go but old misery-boots in the office was around so I couldn't let her. She was very attractive, though. You'd remember her.'

'Good,' smiled Brian. The man seemed visibly relieved he'd been spared the same treatment as Ginger.

'How about this one?' I pulled my identikit effort from the big brown envelope.

'It's the same girl, sir,' said Ginger. He let the corners of his mouth rise into a smile, then stopped it as he caught Brian Borden's mad eyes.

'Sure?' I said.

He nodded.

'Positive . . . would you gentleman like a nice bit of pork to take away? I'm sure I can fix it with our tally clerk if you want.'

One look along the bloodstained metal counter, one glance at the contents of the grey buckets, convinced the other two they didn't want any free pork, thanks all the same. For myself, I'd come to a decision on the matter before eight o'clock that morning. I was a vegetarian. All I needed was a green 2CV, a shapeless jumper and a 'Nuclear

Power No Thanks' sticker and I could get into just about any party I fancied in Hackney or Islington. Lucky me.

The next stop was carried out with a little less tension on all sides, which was a relief to me at least. We went to the butcher's sundries suppliers where I'd bought my knife. The man there was very polite and very helpful. He just gave all the wrong answers.

'Hello, sir. Anything wrong?'

'No,' I said, 'everything's fine.'

The counter assistant was a narrow, dark-suited man with a dark face and deep-set eyes. He had features about as long as an undertaker's and a nose as sharp as one of his knives. I pulled my photograph out.

'These men are police officers,' I said, 'and we'd like you to take a look at this.'

He picked the picture up.

'Oh *yes* . . . that's poor Mrs Duncan. Her husband is a boxing manager.' He looked at me quickly. 'Is this anything to do with her. . . ?'

'Yes, it's to do with her death. Did she ever buy a knife like the one I bought this morning?'

He pursed his lips.

'I couldn't say, sir. She bought lots of butchery equipment here for her kitchen. We sell the very highest quality. . . .'

'I'm sure you do,' I said, 'but that *particular* knife?'

The same pursing of the lips. If he'd breathed in deeply through his nose he would have got a lungful of his own lip.

'Maybe. I can't say.'

'Don't you keep records?' I said. 'It's important.'

'Not that sort of record, sir, no.'

'Recognise her?'

I'd pulled the identikit picture out too. He smiled.

'It's the same lady, sir.'

'Are you sure? *Look*.'

The counter assistant looked closely at the picture, though I had the impression he did it just to placate me.

'Definite. It's the same lady.'

Nineteen

Our lunch-date had waited for us, which considering who they were was a big deal. We left Brian Borden and the wheels in Smithfield. Denis wanted him to take statements from the counter assistant and the two butchers who'd recognised Alison Duncan. As we walked back to St Bartholomew's Hospital to find a cab I saw a small, perky looking female traffic warden putting a parking ticket on Brian's official Ford Cortina. There'd be some fun when he found that.

We took a cab to the city, then went half a mile in the air to the most luxurious office I've ever been in. We were greeted by two silver haired men in grey suits called Tinner and Lockwood. I never did work out which was which. They were officials of the London and Home Counties General Mutual Insurance Company, which is enough name for three ordinary organisations. Lockwood and Tinner worked in an office which had leather everything, deep-pile carpets and wall-to-wall pretty girl assistants. Panoramic windows looked out over London, and the glass was darkened a little so that nobody got sunstroke or tired eyes or anything. The place was full of phones that rang with a muted, polite burbling sound and they never rang more than once before a pretty girl reached out and answered in hushed tones, 'Mister Tinner's office' or 'Mister Lockwood's office', depending which phone she was answering.

Lockwood or Tinner poured us a couple of drinks while I peered out of one of the windows. It was a long way down. The office seemed like it was the centre of England, at least of London. All roads led to it. Red buses chugged along the streets towards us with the sole purpose of depositing more workers at the foot of the marbled building.

'Good view, eh?' said one of our hosts.

'It's okay.'

He was a blue-eyed dream of a man who would be every-body's perfect Grandaddy at the weekend when he wore his yellow cardy with the leather buttons. I looked across at his companion. The man was a clone of my one.

'Shall we go in?' said my companion. We went through satin-polished oak doors and sat at a table groaning under the weight of a lunch big enough for fifty. Just the four of us ate.

'Denis tells us you're an investigator,' said my companion. I said 'yes' . . . I mean what else is there to call it? The man went on, talking in hushed and reverential tones about the London and the Home Counties General Mutual Insurance Company. Another pretty girl drifted in and out with dishes, empty or full depending on which way she was going. She managed to clear away plenty of unused knives and forks too. I looked over at Denis. Either Tinner or Lockwood was talking to him in reverential tones too, just like my one, and Denis was leaning forward and hanging on the man's every word. It made me sick just to watch him crawling to these creeps.

Suddenly I heard my man saying, 'Directly and through subsidiaries we're exposed to the tune of a hundred and seventy-five.'

'A hundred and seventy-five whats?' I said.

His blue lips tightened and a crumb of cottage cheese stuck to them. A silver-grey eyebrow arched.

'Thousand, Mr Jenner. Directly and through subsidiaries we're exposed in the Duncan affair to the tune of a hundred and seventy-five thousand pounds. Denis says you have a theory on the matter that might save us all of that money. I can assure you we'd be very grateful if you could help us save the money. I'm sure other insurers will feel the same way. We appear to be about a month from having to. . . .'

'Shell out?' I offered. 'Why worry? A hundred and seventy-five grand must be peanuts to an organisation like this.'

He shook his head. The crumb of cottage cheese fell to

144

his deeply cleft chin while he dabbed at the lip where it had been with a linen napkin. I wanted to laugh at him but I couldn't let myself – yet. I wanted to know what he wanted.

'I wouldn't put it like that. We will always pay a legitimate claim. As for the money . . . well, it is a small sum compared with the assets of this organisation. But it wouldn't be a small sum if you save it for us. We'd be *very* grateful. We have shareholders, you know, and they expect us to be frugal with their money and only meet proper claims.'

Just then a pretty waitress cruised in and offered him two bottles of wine that were nearly as old as she was. He didn't even blink.

'We have a lot of work we could offer a trustworthy investigator here, Mister Jenner,' he said.

I shook my head.

'You've got the wrong man. I'm getting out. This is Jenner's last case.'

The blue lips went into a line again and the eyebrow arched again and this time the cottage cheese dropped to his stiff collar. I smiled politely and said, 'You've got lunch on your collar, mate.'

I enjoyed that.

In the lift going down to the street Denis sighed and loosened his collar. 'Well, I've got it but it's no damn thanks to you. . . . "You've got lunch on your collar, mate" indeed. I'm going to have to spend my life working with these blokes, Jim. You should try to be a bit fairer to me if no one else.'

He brandished an envelope very much like the one I was holding.

'So what's that?'

'It's the Duncans' proposal form. And I've got a finger-print officer going there this afternoon to take the dabs of anyone who might have handled it.'

'And then?'

'And then they'll give the proposal form the alcohol and powdered graphite and abracadabras and whatever else they do to them and see what's what by way of prints on the form. And then they'll see if there's a set of female prints that don't fit. And if there is *then* your theory becomes something resembling a runner.'

My stomach settled and the doors opened silently. More light softened by bronze-tinted glass flooded around us and an ancient job's-worth in a commissionaire's uniform took our lapel pins off us and made us sign out.

The street was noisy and boisterous and welcoming and I was glad to be in it: fumes, dust, dirt and all.

'Being a detective means doing lots of long, slow, tedious work,' said Denis. 'You have to engage your brain and those of everyone around you. You have to be intelligent and scientific, all at once.'

He paused to burp, then asked, 'How does your first taster of real detective work feel, then?'

I looked closely into his face to make sure he meant it, then walked away without another word.

Twenty

I spent the afternoon in the bath at home. About four Gal rang and said he was just about to put Zorba on a plane for Cyprus. Zorba was getting out. Who could blame him? He'd got away with a little nest egg and a few contusions. Getting out while he was in front made sense. I could hear all the ding-dong-paging-Mr-Slobberchops-from-Air-France-flight-201 announcements in the background and Zorba came on the line to mutter a fond farewell, hampered only by the fact that his face was still swollen up and his jaw wired so he couldn't actually *say* anything. I said, 'Goodbye, Zorba, hope it works out, give my love to your wife,' and he said, 'Ugh.' I wasn't too upset because it resembled many of our conversations. I said a lot and he said ugh.

About half-four Maher phoned to say that the knife I'd brought in was a 'close mechanical fit' for the weapon that had inflicted the wounds on the body they'd found under the arch. That's forensic-speak for 'the same article'.

'Thanks a lot, James. I'm not sure where it gets us but that's a good piece of detective work by you,' he said.

'What about the stuff O'Keefe brought in?'

'That'll take a couple of days. Come and have a chat with me tomorrow.'

'Okay.'

I made a big pot of tea and tipped it into a Thermos. I wanted to spend an evening thinking and I didn't want to spend it getting up and down to deal with kettles. Then I put on some cotton pyjamas and a terry dressing gown, went into the living room and tipped a huge jigsaw on the table there. The box said it was a view of Hamburg. It could

147

have been anywhere as far as I could see. I suppose I didn't care.

About seven Judy rang.

'Are you busy?'

'A bit. Why?'

'I just wanted to talk, Jimmy, that's all. I've put my papers in and arranged terminal leave – sounds horrible, doesn't it? – and I have to work another five weeks. Then we're fancy free.'

'Great,' I said.

'And I've got the forms.'

'What forms?'

'For the registry office. We said yesterday I'd get them. Are you okay?'

'I'm okay, Judy. I'm a bit preoccupied. That's all.'

'With Duncan?'

'Yes.'

I stared at a jigsaw piece that looked like a crane, only I couldn't work out which way up it should be. What good's a jigsaw you can't do?

'Will it be all done by the time we're ready to pack up and go?'

I crushed the cardboard jigsaw piece in my hand. I could hear that old guardedness in her voice. Then I knew why we'd never done this before. Judy was protecting herself from me.

'Judy, we'll leave as soon as things are ready whether I've finished with this thing or not.'

'Good. Bye, Jimmy.'

'Bye.'

I straightened the jigsaw piece out, then turned the crane round and round in my hand. It still wouldn't go anywhere. If what Leary the cleaner had told me was true George Duncan would have a good motive for killing his wife apart from collecting on the insurance. In fact anyone who had ever met her seemed to have a good motive for killing her. Maybe it was true the way Duncan told it and he hadn't had anything to do with the business. Maybe that was true, but if it was I couldn't account for his strange behaviour in hiring me to protect her and I couldn't account for the weird way they behaved together when he was sending her off.

Also George had a really good motive – he needed the money. The only thing he didn't have was opportunity. Grant, as far as I knew, had an opportunity and I suppose what Leary told me just might have given him a jealousy motive. I wrote a note to myself to check Grant's where-abouts for the night of the murder. His motive didn't look half as strong as George Duncan's though.

I put two bits of sky in my puzzle, then the crane went in. Then I put another bit of sky and looked round for another bit of crane. Outside some kids were arguing shrilly about the ownership of something. A bike, a cart, a pair of roller skates . . . something.

Why cut the face off if not to fool people as to who the body was? It didn't make sense. There were missing pieces.

I rang Denis.

'Hello, prima donna.'

'Don't be like that. How would *you* feel if I lectured *you*?'

He didn't answer.

'Denis,' I went on. 'Did you do that DVLC check to see if Duncan owned any cars?'

'Yes. Nothing there, I'm afraid. He does own a Jag just like the one you drove, but it was nicked a couple of months back. It doesn't have any bearing on this business at all.'

'Jim? . . . Jimmy?' Denis called. My throat tightened.

'Has it been found?'

'No. Why?'

'Because I want a fingerprint from an Alison Duncan who isn't in the mortuary, and I want to confirm it. If I can get a fingerprint from the insurance proposal form and a matching one from somewhere on George Duncan's Jag I've got her.'

'No, James, you haven't got her. You've got a very circumstantial case for the person who signed the insurance form being in George Duncan's motor at some stage. But you won't have another Alison Duncan if such a person exists, until you've got her in your hand or until you can give the body we have a different identity. I'll put the Jag in the Police Gazette as a 'special notice' and we'll hope to turn it up. I'll gee up the forensic lot about the magic they're working on the insurance form, too.'

'I suppose that if I got the fingerprints, even if we didn't have her in custody, your pals Tinner and Lockwood would be saved a payout?'

'I should think that's very likely, Jimmy. You'd be likely to make quite a big of dough.'

'I've already got quite a bit of dough, Denis.'

'Oh yeah.'

I gave up drinking tea and I gave up playing jigsaws. I sat on the sofa drinking scotch and watching people being horrid to each other on TV. It's all they ever seem to do on TV. I couldn't work out where Lenny Grant fitted, if at all.

I rang Lenny Grant's office next morning at nine.

'He can't speak with you, sir. He's in Florida.'

'Give me the number.'

I rang Florida. Eventually I got a tired voice on the end of a hotel switchboard.

'Grant, please,' I said. 'I don't know the room.'

'Hold, please.'

A few seconds later he was on the line. He had a voice that had been trained out of being a cockney, though he still had plenty of cockney inflections. His voice was deep and confident-sounding.

'Grant.'

'Hallo, Mr Grant. My name's Jenner. You don't know me but I know one of your fighters. Tommy Lynch.'

'Yes?'

'Well. I have to talk to you, Mr Grant.'

'Talk.'

'I'd rather not do it over the phone.'

'I'm here for another five weeks, Jenner. Why don't you come round?'

'I'm in England,' I said, 'so coming round won't work, I'm afraid.'

'Then it'll have to be the phone. What about Lynch?'

I cleared my throat.

'Nothing about Lynch. I just said that I knew him by way of introduction. I'm a private detective, Mr Grant, and I was hired to look after a young woman you may know, a woman called Alison May Clark.'

'Don't give me the runaround, Jenner. It's very early here.' He groaned. 'Four thirty a.m. my clock says.'

'Okay. I'll give it to you straight. Alison Clark's married name was Alison Duncan, and I have reason to believe you had an intimate relationship with her before she died. I want to talk to you about that relationship.'

'Not on the phone, you don't. See me when I come back to England.' He hung up. I rang the hotel in Florida again.

'Grant, please.'

'I'm sorry that line's busy. Would you like to hold?'

'No. Do you know where he's calling?'

'I'm sorry sir. That's private information. Would you like to hold?'

This time *I* hung up.

Twenty-One

Grant checked out. The knowledge that he would be covered settled upon me like a great weight even as I did the checking. He'd spent the night 'Alison' was murdered with some immaculately respectable friends . . . in fact the dodgiest thing about the whole business was the way everyone (except Wilkins and myself, of course) had a watertight alibi. As far as I was concerned that meant Wilkins was the only one who definitely hadn't done it – apart from me. Unfortunately the DPP didn't agree and when the file went over to the legal boys Wilkins' arraign-mment was a foregone conclusion. He was left to rot in Brixton Gaol while the legal people got their act together. Alison's body was interred at Kensal Green cemetery, having had all the possible evidence extracted from it and having been released by the coroner. The murder squad was reduced to DS Robson and some uniformed constable while the rest of the circus moved on to a series of race attacks in Camden. *Camden*, for heaven's sake . . . I mean, who's an indigenous Camdener? The race attacks culminated in a murder, all the murder experts went to Camden and the trail on Alison May Duncan's murder went cold.

I shouldn't have been surprised and I shouldn't have been angry but I was both. The days slipped past, became weeks. After Maher did a lot of arm-twisting some Deputy-type character went round to the hotel Grant was staying in in Miami, Fla. and established that the number Lenny Grant had called directly after I called him was his mother's house in Welling, South London. Needless to say, the mother was a little old lady who knew nothing about anything.

I sold my flat and moved in with Judy. We were going to keep her place on as a base after we were married, though the plan was we should buy a VW camper and spend the late summer and autumn wandering around Europe looking for somewhere warm and pleasant to settle. Judy's flat was a sort of backstop, in case all else failed. I gave up the office with Chardray and devoted myself more or less full-time to playing pool with Gal. Then he got a job in a bakery and I was back on the science-fiction novels and jigsaws. I bought a lot of maps and felt like I'd learned them off by heart. Sometimes I played with the idea of having a verbal 'showdown at the okay corral' with George Duncan but I never did it. Denis thought he'd talked me out of it but really I didn't need much talking. There's no point in big dramatic arguments unless you can win them, and I suppose I still dreamed of a day when Maher would slip the cuffs on dear old George.

They did find 'foreign' fingerprints underneath Alison's signature on their joint insurance proposal form, but on its own it didn't count for much. Several other documents were scrutinised but they didn't give up any secrets. No more leads came from South Africa. No women of the right type were reported missing since the night of the murder. George Duncan's stolen Jaguar stayed stolen. Eventually the insurance companies paid him out and he put his big house in Saffron on the market. Robson had his phone tapped and had him followed for a few days at my insistence but we drew a blank. He even had the South African coppers turn over Alison's brother, David, but there was no sign of her there, either. Eventually everyone except me became convinced that Alison May Duncan (née Clark) was in a hole in Kensal Green, albeit minus her mush.

It was the first week of August before we had a break, and even then we had to make it. Duncan's car was dragged out of five fathoms of Loch Rannoch. We were lucky – it was the shallowest part of the Loch. The car had been used months before in a bank hold-up in Glasgow and was carrying false plates. The Scottish police traced it through the engine number, giving the lie to the idea that they're all gamekeepers and traffic wardens. Maher took me up to see it in a boatshed. The car was a mess.

'There's the end of the line for your theory, James,' Maher said.

He was right, too. What wasn't mud was rotten. What wasn't rotten was rusty. It was difficult to believe a car could get into such a state in three months.

'No fingerprint?' I asked hopefully.

Maher shook his head.

'Nothing.'

'Who else has seen it?' I said.

'No one. Just a load of Jock coppers.' He squinted at me. 'Do you have an idea?'

'I was wondering just how quiet we could keep it,' I said.

Outside the rain was belting down, a typical Scottish summer's afternoon. We stood with the boatman, getting soaked while he locked up good and proper, then Maher gave him thirty quid to buy an even better lock for his shed on condition that he kept his mouth shut about the car for a couple of days. Rainwater streamed down our faces as we swore the boatman to silence. He bit his lip and glared at Maher's three damp tenners in his palm for an age before agreeing. Maybe Scottish tenners look different. I've never seen one so I wouldn't know.

'I've never been here before,' I said, trying to be friendly. 'Lovely looking place. Pity about the rain.'

We were squelching back to our car. The boatman said, 'It keeps the midges down.'

We cooked up a good plot driving back to London. The plan was to drop hints at people George Duncan knew. The hints would be to the effect that we'd matched a print from the Jag with a print from their insurance application form. Harry Whitlock would do. Robson was given the job of pulling him in.

Coincidentally, the night Robson collared Harry Whitlock was the night of Tommy Lynch's World Championship fight in Miami. There were plenty of interviews with him and

154

Lenny Grant; plenty of pictures in newspapers and on telly. The fight was on the box live. Maher and me sat in the CID room at Peter Street nick, watching a portable telly while we waited. Lynch got slaughtered. We did a little better.

'Just a few questions, Harry. I think you know Mr Jenner here.'

Harry nodded. His brow was furrowed, his bottom lip stuck out. Harry was telling the world he was unhappy.

'I will help in any way that I am able,' he said in a manner which gave me to believe he had been practising it for half an hour. 'But you must understand, sir, that I know very little about this sad affair. Mister Duncan has left the fight game and I am no longer in his employ.'

'Okay, Harry. Cut the speech,' said Maher. 'I have to ask you a few personal questions about your ex-boss.'

Harry stared at the window before him. Maher presumed that meant he would answer and went on.

'It's to do with the Jaguar car he had stolen . . . you remember that?'

Harry nodded. He remembered the stolen Jaguar.

'Well, we've found it.'

'Good,' said Harry. 'Mister Duncan will be *well* pleased.' Maher smiled.

'But I have a problem with it, Harry. You see, the Jag is covered in a woman's fingerprints. The fingerprints are the same as those we took off an insurance proposal form. They're the same as some prints we took off the inside of the lift to their flat in the Barbican.'

Harry concentrated. The brow and the jutting lower lip nearly met. Harry Whitlock concentrating was a pitiful sight.

'Ye-es.'

'Here's my problem, Harry. It would be reasonable to presume that the fingerprints of the woman who'd had her hands all over George Duncan's car and had put her finger-prints all over their insurance proposal form and had ridden in the lift to their flat was none other than Mrs Alison Duncan. That would be reasonable don't you think?'

'Yes.' Harry was sure about that one.

'But Harry, the prints are *not* those of the woman six feet under in Kensal Green . . . cop my drift? The woman pushing up daisies does not appear to be his wife. I need

155

to know from you whether Duncan had any . . . er, any extra-*marital* relationships.' I do believe Maher was embarrassed.

Harry looked blank.

'Birds. Did he have any birds, Harry?' I said. Maher smiled at me in an indulgent way, but I got the hint. Don't interfere.

'No. He never had no birds. He was always very faithful.'

They went on like this for a while, till DCS Maher had the idea firmly planted in Harry's little mind that we had good forensic evidence that the dead woman wasn't Alison. Then Maher let him go. We didn't think Harry was in on it. We just wanted the message got to Duncan.

'Will you have him followed?' I asked.

'No.' Maher's eyes were gleaming. 'I don't need to. I've got some men on observation outside Duncan's house with cameras. I've got his and Harry's phones both tapped. All we have to do is relax. Would you like to have supper with me?'

'Why not?' I said. Why not indeed . . . we had something to celebrate – nearly. We'd sold thick Harry Whitlock a load of lies . . . clever us.

The next day the papers were full of Tommy Lynch's battered face. He'd been outclassed and outpunched by his American opponent. Tommy said, 'I'll be back,' but according to a little paragraph at the bottom of a story in the *Sun* Lenny Grant wouldn't. He was retiring from the fight game. Wouldn't it be nice to retire before you're forty? I had to laugh at myself, because that's exactly what Judy and me were about to do . . . retire to the sun. I lay abed with Judy reading the papers and feeling clever.

My phone went at eleven.

'Mister Jenner?'

'Yes.'

'Detective Sergeant Robson here. Mister Maher asked me to call you. We have a problem. Duncan's dead.'

'Where's Maher?' I said.

'The Barbican.'

'I'll see him there.'

George Duncan had been waiting outside his bank at nine thirty. He'd emptied his accounts, insurance money, money from the sale of the house in Saffron Walden, the lot. Over four hundred thousand. He'd been covered by police all the way, photographed at every stage. Then he went home, still covered every step of the way by police. No one could work out how he'd managed to shoot himself and no one heard it, but he'd done it. The money had disappeared too.

'The phone?' I asked Maher.

He nodded. A Scenes of Crime Officer was flashing camera lights over the body. The balcony leading into Duncan's house had been taped off, even some parts of the flat were taped off.

'The money?' I asked.

Maher raised an eyebrow. His face was as grey as his hair, pasty. Like a dirty sheet.

'No money anywhere. Harry phoned him from a box ten minutes after he left us last night.'

'Was it Harry?'

'No. He's too dim to be anything other than innocent.' He walked out onto the balcony. I followed. We stood on the spot where I'd thrown Duncan's cut-glass tumbler from all those weeks before. It seemed like a lifetime ago. It was several. 'I'd better come up with a good explanation of this, James,' Maher said.

Well, we didn't think up anything there and then. But I remembered the retiring Lenny Grant in Florida. And I told Maher about my conversation with Leary in Duncan's gym. I can't say he was very happy about me holding out on him, and he simply refused to follow the logic of my argument about how knowing there was another motive for murder would have made him go cold on my substitute woman theory once and for all. He left in bad humour and he wouldn't speak to me, but he had Denis O'Keefe call me in the next day.

Twenty Two

My new wife wasn't too pleased about me disappearing up to Scotland with Maher. She didn't like me closeting myself with Maher when I should have been closeting myself with her. She was *most* displeased about me being involved with the events around George Duncan's death. But she took Denis's phone call the worst of the lot. He rang at a quarter past four.

That's quarter past four in the a.m.

'Huh,' Judy said when the phone rang. She said 'huh' when she answered it, too. Then she said, 'No.'

Then she said, 'No.' Again.

Then there was a silence. Then she said, 'Denis, you pig, I've been married for less than a week. Now get off my sodding phone and leave my husband alone.'

Then she put the phone down. When it rang again I answered.

'Thank God it's you. I was getting my head bitten off there,' Denis said. 'Present yourself in Peter Street nick, as soon as. We've got something to show you, my son.'

Peter Street police station smelled of old cabbage and was full of the sound of billiard cues and the World Service Radio. Neon lights flickered in the public areas. That's how police stations always are at night. Denis was waiting behind the desk for me. He looked like the cat that had got the cream.

'Come in . . . come in.'

I followed him up two flights of stairs and along a corridor painted the vilest green imaginable. Then we went into a darkened room. I could make out the shapes of half a dozen men in chairs.

'Take a seat, James,' came Maher's voice. 'Look at this.'

A beam split the darkness. A bright, blue-white light that burned straight into my eyes. I walked towards it, stumbled against a chair and then turned to look at the wall behind me.

'It's a photo taken by one of our obbo blokes outside the Barbican,' said Maher.

The photograph was of the back of a delivery girl. It was a black-and-white photograph, but from the tone of it the delivery girl seemed to be wearing a green-nylon shopgirl's smock and a green pillbox hat to go with it. She was carrying a large bunch of flowers.

There was a mechanical clatter, then darkness, then a picture of the girl from the front. Her face was a little smudged, but she was young – under thirty – slim, and looked as if she might be attractive once the features were focussed.

'This is the same girl leaving, James. It's the best picture we've got.'

'And?' I said.

'My men spent yesterday afternoon and evening interviewing every person in those flats, establishing exactly who went in and out.'

The mechanical clatter again, and we were back with the first picture.

'No one had any flowers delivered. No one mentioned any flower girl. I sent them back to drag everyone out of bed and ask again . . . but the same. No flowers. Then we turned the rubbish chutes out. You might smell some of my colleagues here.'

There was a polite giggle from Maher's underlings. The boss had made a joke.

'And we found a large bunch of flowers and a cushion with a bullet hole in it.'

Again the mechanical clatter, again the second photo.

'I may be wrong, James, but I think we're looking at a photograph of Alison May Duncan. George is dead, the

159

money's gone, the little bird has flown the nest. I've warned the ports and airports. We'll pick her up.'

'And Wilkins?' I said.

Maher's voice was closer to me now, and I turned and made out his figure in the darkness.

'We'll have him released in a couple of days. Maybe even today. We'll get her, James.'

Then they applauded me and all told me what a loss I'd been to the service. All this was with the lights on. There was hardly a dry eye in the house. Then everyone slapped my back and told me how pleased they were I'd persisted. Then they all assured me they'd catch her.

They didn't, of course.

The last I saw of Alison May Duncan (née Clark) was the headstone above her grave in Kensal Green. She was a lovely girl. I wondered who the hell she was, how they'd ensnared her. I wondered where the real Alison had killed her. And the post-mortem report . . . somewhere should be a young child who was missing her. *Why* did no one miss her?

We went to Kensal Green on what was my way out of London for the last time. I'd sworn privately to myself that I'd never come back. Judy thought it was stupid and morbid to want to go and visit this grave with the wrong body in it, but she didn't resist when I made a fuss about it. She held my arm as we walked down the long tarmacadamed path to the graveside through the thousands of other graves, and she even let me use her handkerchief when we got there. It was a sunny day. I couldn't even pass off my emotions as rain on my face or something. I just had to stand over this grave with the wrong name on it and wonder and regret my own thickheadedness that night in May.

Well, that's how it was that day I left London. We drove back across town and I made a point of going via Archway, which was out of our way. I wanted to say goodbye. I stopped the VW under Suicide Bridge, as the locals call it, and looked over the dusty city. It looked mean and dirty and ugly and I was glad I wouldn't go there any more. That's how I felt.

Twenty Three

'Today is the first of August 1985. Our travels have made us a little wiser but I think that maybe there's more than one type of wise.'

I wrote this in a little journal I keep by my bed. The journal's secret not because I keep it secret but because my wife Judy doesn't pry. I wrote these facts in the journal while sitting on a chair on my balcony drinking beer. It's seven a.m. and I shouldn't be drinking beer. My beer is cold. So's my chair. The sun doesn't hit the balcony until noon because there's an old building opposite that must have been all kinds of things in its time but now is a café and the café has a tall stuccoed front which hides my balcony from morning sunlight, just as the café is in its turn hidden from morning sunlight by a garage behind, and just as my house and bar hide the house behind me from morning sunlight. The sun arrives at noon and by half-twelve everyone wishes it didn't come till three or four in the p.m. But for the morning we all resent the fact that our balconies are looked out over by the next house.

I sit on my balcony and write. Above me, on the lush green hill that overlooks our town, I can see the baking white concrete walls of the rich villas that rich Englishmen and Germans live in. I should write 'rich English and German criminals', for our little town has its share of spectacular north European bankrupts and similar. They live within their white concrete walls and only deign to speak to you over their wallmounted loudspeakers—'Hello, hello, who's calling?'—so that you have to stand in the sun with your straw hat on your head and sweat trickling down your

161

shirt and just wait like the pleb you are until the great man within slips out of his clear-blue-water swimming pool and waves at the maid to let you in. I go to a lot of these houses because I have cooled English beer in the cellar of my bar, Worthington 'E' and Guinness and Bass and several others, and when the guy who normally delivers to the white concrete houses for me gets a breakdown in his van or his mother gets sick or he needs to go to a soccer match or a bullfight, I go. I don't like doing the deliveries because the people in the white concrete houses up the hill treat you as if you're a night-soil carrier or something, just because they've got enormous houses and servants and sun-tanned floozies and Mercedes air-conditioned cars while you, of course, only have a beat-up SEAT and you're delivering their beer. I'd prefer to have my Spanish delivery man go and face all that. That's the economic bargain, that's what it does to you. It gives you the ability to make someone else do the dirty job.

I sit on my balcony and nod my head because I'm tired, and I write in my book when I'm not nodding. Long blue shadows are cast on the roofs around me, then red splashes of pantiles run up the sides of gables. The walls exposed to the sun are an angry, stark white.

I hear a voice singing softly. Below me in the street a kid in a waiter's uniform is wiping marbled table tops. It's him singing some ghastly Spanish pop song. Inside the café early morning workers are taking breakfasts in the yellow of the electric-lit room. Sometimes I can hear their voices raised. I'll never speak Spanish well enough, though, to latch onto their conversations.

I could hear the buzz of a Japanese motor-cycle back in the town somewhere and the burble of the BBC World Service coming from my bedroom, two doors away from this balcony.

I was thinking about my wife, Judy. She's coming here from England today. She doesn't like to fly so she gets the ferry to Santander, then drives. I was thinking that she'd be waking up now in some roadside hotel. When we go away together we make a real trip, finding special places to stay and planning sights to visit. Doing it alone, though, she'll just drive as straight as a die across Spain, through

162

the green and mountainous Basque country, then across the plains of Old Castile, always heading south. If she'd put her foot down she'd have made Madrid last night and stayed there.

We live in Cristo de Limpias, a small town on the southeast coast. If there weren't two headlands in between you'd be able to see Malaga ten miles or so to the north. I don't know why you'd want to see Malaga and neither does anyone else in Cristo, but if you did you'd have to go into the headland flattening business. Due south is the way Judy's heading, or as near due south as dammit. And it's one full day's drive from Madrid.

I was thinking Judy would be getting up about now and having some rock hard cylinder of Spanish bread offered to her for breakfast. She'd wash and go down to our Citröen. She'd throw her bag in the back and wipe the dust off the windscreen. With any luck she'd think about me a little.

I should leave her a note but I just don't know what to say. What should I say? I don't know.

Twenty Four

I've been here in Cristo de Limpias since 1983. I run a bar. The bar's halfway to running me, really. In the two-and-a-bit years I've been here I've gone back to England only twice. I haven't made that many trips in Spain, even. How did I come here? Partly by coincidence, partly by choice.

Judy and me left London in the late summer of 1982. I was mentally exhausted by the Duncan case, far more than I ever thought while I was in London. It was only after a few weeks pottering round France in our VW camper that I started to relax a bit, and it was then I realised what a strain the whole business had been. I blamed myself. I believed that I'd been stupid when I'd parted company with that poor girl in the Barbican. I had *known* something was wrong. I knew from the first moment Duncan asked me to come and see him. I knew from the first time I clapped eyes on that girl in his house in Saffron Walden. I abandoned her because I'd thought she was working some scam with George Duncan and I didn't want to get involved. I never for a moment thought that *she* could be the scam. I never thought people would coldly and brutally kill a young woman just to make some money. *Who* would think that? Maybe some clever people would but I didn't, and I felt stupid and guilty as hell because I hadn't.

The woman, Alison Duncan, never turned up. I had told Maher that I had information (via Tommy Lynch and Leary) she had some sort of involvement with Lenny Grant. The way I saw it, she'd wound George up into believing they could work a number on the insurance, then when we'd dropped word through Harry that we knew what his little game was George must have panicked and phoned her. Alison had gone to the flat in her flower-girl outfit (knowing it would be watched) and shot him. That way she wouldn't have to share the money and she'd be rid of a man she must have considered a ball-and-chain. The way they'd behaved when I'd seen them in the street after the Lynch fight, I had the impression she didn't care much for old George. But then nobody did. He wasn't much of a man. Alison had shot him and wrapped his hand round the gun in a crude attempt to imitate suicide. It never works . . . the finger-prints end up all wrong; the burn marks, if they are present at all, are never in the right place. It simply never works. I suppose Alison would expect the cops to find the whole business an enigma, something they'd never solve. Poli-cemen aren't generally great believers in coincidences and enigmas, though, and I think even if we'd never got that smudgy photograph of her leaving the building the file would have stayed open. Two enigmatic murders in one family are two more than the likes of Maher are able to leave go of lightly. The same must be true of me, in the light of events since then.

Tommy Lynch retired, I know, to a pub in the home counties. All boxers do that, then they get incredibly fat and no one can believe they ever punched their way out of a paper bag. Tommy could've gone on, fighting less good opponents for smaller purses, being interviewed by local radio breakfast programmes instead of Harry Carpenter for *Sportsnight*. He chose not to, and I think he made the right decision. Maher went and interviewed him abut the Lenny Grant/Alison Duncan angle Leary had handed to me that morning in Duncan's dusty, abandoned gym. Tommy said it was true okay, and they should talk to Grant about it. The problem was, where was Grant?

He'd gone to ground in the States after leaving the fight game. There had always been something dodgy about Grant, he was always such an *elusive* figure. Always just off-stage, always the man whose name kept coming up. And yet he was the one with a completely clean record. I'd never met the man but I knew instinctively that there was something very wrong, perhaps that he was the one pulling strings on Alison. Anyway, the Yank coppers managed to follow Lenny Grant's trail of credit card purchases across the United States, then the last anyone saw of him was a suit bought in Las Vegas. The bill for a blue summer-weight men's suit, Maher told me, was the last worldly sighting of one Leonard Grant, wanted for questioning by the British police in the matter of two murders. My feeling was that when they found him Alison May Duncan wouldn't be far away . . . and Grant had to turn up sometime. He had to earn a living. We all do. George's insurance money never would go far, even if Lenny Grant had part of it. No, I was convinced Lenny would turn up. The surprise was *where* he surfaced.

New Year's Day 1983 was when we got a break.

Judy and me were staying in an hotel near Barcelona. You can't spend the winter in a motor-caravan, not even in Spain, and we discovered that if you could put up with being surrounded by 1910 to 1925-vintage English men and women, you could get a real deal on staying in what would be a fairly expensive tourist hotel during the summer. So we checked into the Tempo, a concrete and glass joint ten miles north of Barcelona city. We were on the fifth floor with a concrete balcony overlooking a concrete plaza. After the concrete plaza was a concrete pavement and a concrete road, then sand, then the sea. Raw-boned old men played canasta with fat ladies for hour after hour in the hotel's painted lounge. The most it could lead to was a walk on one of the concrete strips outside, yet the old men and old women flirted remorselessly.

We stayed in our room and plotted which bar we would buy. We planned trips up and down the Spanish coast, visiting properties, judging and weighing prices and facilities. By Christmas we were ready to move on to a little place near Rosas.

On New Year's Day Denis phoned. After passing over the season's greetings and a lot of gossip he said, 'I bumped into your pal Detective Chief Superintendent Maher the other day. He still hasn't given up on that Duncan business, you know.'

'It doesn't surprise me,' I said.

166

'That's right, Jimmy, that's what I told him. I said, 'It won't surprise old Jimmy you're still looking.'

'Well, Denis, you were right,' I said. 'It doesn't surprise me he's still looking for Grant.'

'No, no,' said Denis. 'You've got the wrong end of the stick. He's *found* Grant. Had a good old chat with him. He says Grant seems as clean as a whistle . . . very open, willing to admit he'd had an affair with that bird, Alison. Says he didn't have nothing to do with any murders, though, and he hasn't seen Alison since the night her stand-in was bumped off. Nor for several weeks before that. Maher is still looking for Alison Duncan.'

I lay on my bed and watched storm clouds rolling across the Mediterranean. From a few doors away I could hear the raucous cackle of a couple of old women sharing a joke. Judy was in the bathroom, I could hear the occasional light splash from her bathwater. My hand tensed upon the old-fashioned candlewick bedspread the Spanish hotel supplied.

'Did Maher seem convinced . . . just like that?' I asked.

'Well, he *said* he was, Jimmy. But he said you'd be interested, and to be sure to tell you all of it. It seems like Grant's a building project manager for some American company. He gave the hint that the project was run by the legit end of dirty money.'

'What sort of dirty money, Denis?'

'Yanks' dirty money. I suppose Maher was saying it was crime money . . . you know what he's like, Jimmy. Twenty minutes with Maher and you come out wondering if he's actually said anything at all. You know?'

I knew okay. Maher never said anything without having four other things in his mind as he said it.

'So what did Grant say that convinced Maher?'

'Well, I asked him that question too. He said, "Nothing much." . . . What do you make of the man.'

'He's devious.'

Judy came out of the bathroom. Getting a suntan during the summer had done her lovely legs no harm at all. I wanted the conversation to finish. I had other things in mind.

'He's devious, all right. Anyway, he said to tell you that Grant was a building project manager for a place called the

Juli Complex, a load of time-share villas in some dump down in the south of Spain.'

'*Where*?'

'The south of Spain. Aren't you near there? Maher says the fellow's living in a place called Cristo de Limpias and it's near Malaga and you're especially to know that he hasn't got any girlfriend. That's what Maher said.'

Judy sat beside me on the candlewick, dripping beads of bathwater and dabbing herself with a towel. I made her say 'hullo' to Denis, then when he'd rung off she said, 'What's all that about?'

'He was wishing me Happy New Year,' I said. 'Didn't he wish you?'

'He wished me,' she said. 'What else?'

'Oh, and he said Maher had had a few breaks looking for Lenny Grant.'

'And what's that to do with us? . . . move up a bit.'

'Oh nothing . . .' I said. 'It's nothing.'

'Good.'

We kissed. I said, 'Do you want to go way down south and check it out there? Malaga, that way.'

'No. I would like to buy the place in Rosas we saw.'

'Let's check Malaga. It's only a day's drive each way. Let's check it. We haven't been down there.'

'No.'

She pushed me back on the bed. Who was I to resist? Malaga could wait.

Twenty Five

We spent a week in Malaga on that first occasion. Judy thought we were looking round the seaside villages in the area, *I* was trying to find a way of having a look at Lenny Grant without him having a look at me. I'd had his address from Denis on a second phone call – Maher *really* wanted me to find him – but the problem was Grant's villa was in an exposed position high above the town while the Juli Complex he was meant to be managing was still at the concrete-mixer-and-artist's-impression stage. The only way I could go there without being noticed would be to deliver a load of reinforcing rods. What's the Spanish for 'reinforcing rod'? I didn't have any fears about being spotted on the street by Grant, I'd put on twenty pounds, grown a beard and looked tanned enough to pass for a Spaniard. But I wanted to have a look at him. Really, I'd have liked to observe him for some length of time. I was convinced the woman had to be around somewhere.

Judy, who didn't even know Denis and myself had spoken about the place, came up with the answer.

'I might have found somewhere,' she said. We were eating lunch.

'What somewhere?'

'You know that little place we were in yesterday, Cristo de Limpias? Well, there's a bar there owned by an Englishman. Daniel . . . Daniel . . . oh I can't remember. Anyway Martinez says he's sure this man would sell out. . . .' She paused to crunch at some green salad. 'If he was given the right offer. Martinez says he's fed up with it.'

'Martinez?'

'No.' She laughed. 'This Daniel person. Martinez says Cristo de whatsisname is on the verge of being built up and there's always call for an English bar in a place like that. It could be a good one.'

'Mm.'

'Let's just go there and have a drink,' said Judy. 'Let's go this evening.'

I wiped my mouth with a table-napkin. Suddenly my appetite had gone. I looked through the plate-glass window of the restaurant. A boy was revving a scooter at the kerb-side. One of the waiters went out to remonstrate with him. Great columns of cloud swirled around the sky above us.

Judy said, 'I think we shouldn't keep taking wine with the lunch. You're getting fat, Jimmy.'

'Of course,' I said. I poured myself another glass of wine and drank it anyway. I pulled at my beard, stared at the table . . . did anything rather than look at her for a few seconds. When I did look there was an amused light in her blue eyes. She arched an eyebrow.

'Out with it.'

'I've got something to tell you,' I said. 'Something rather important.'

I won't say she took it well. I won't even say she took it calmly. The meal didn't last much longer, but in the time it did last I think the waiters must have learned enough colloquial English to hold their own on the terraces of Millwall Football Club. Judy was not amused. At first she believed I'd only brought her to Spain because I'd thought I might find Alison there. Then when I finally convinced her I'd only found out from Denis a few days ago that Grant was in Cristo she was all for flying to London and 'having it out' with Maher, the source of the information.

It's a long way from Malaga to Barcelona. We made the entire journey in silence. We spent the next few days in our concrete hotel in silence too. I was reduced to attending the tea-dances with the ancient nut-brown Britons (thank God I can't dance) and watching imported videos. As far as my wife was concerned I was in the doghouse.

170

At the end of the second week in January she finally spoke.

'I've been on the phone to Martinez,' she said. 'I've asked him to make an offer on Bill's Bar.'

'What's Bill's Bar?'

'Don't come the old soldier, Jimmy. Bill's Bar is the one in Cristo de Limpias, you bastard.'

'I thought his name was Daniel,' I said.

'Would you expect the Marquess of Anglesey to be pulling pints in all the pubs with his name?'

I didn't answer. Some days later she made it clear that I was expected to follow up the Alison May Duncan thing one last time and forget it. I didn't know really if Judy had changed her mind because I needed to lay this ghost or if it was because she'd been a policewoman for so long. I never had the nerve to ask, not then nor since. It would be pushing my luck a bit too far. She did say once that she thought Bill's Bar was a very good commercial proposition in an area which was being developed and she didn't see why she should miss out on that because of some crackpot idea I had. 'You're not the Lone Ranger, you know, Jimmy,' she said, which was true. I don't know about the 'commercial proposition' business, though. It sounded like she was looking for a way to let me off the hook. I never asked so I never found out. Marriages are full of things like that.

Twenty Six

I've never needed to change my name or conceal myself. With the peculiar logic common in Spain the owner of Bill's Bar is generally referred to as Bill. Grant didn't use the bar much – he came in once or twice – and I had no fear of being recognised. I'd never met him in England and anyway my appearance had changed considerably since I'd left. The only thing to connect 'Bill' with Jimmy Jenner was the limp. Lots of men have limps. I just settled down and went about my business in the little town. In another part of town Grant went about his. When the Juli Complex was built he began to supervise work on some similar place ten miles away. He kept his house in Cristo, though.

Months went past, then a Christmas, then another Christmas. I'd obviously got it wrong about Mister Grant. He was obviously legit. I met him in the usual course of things; we were, after all, English residents in a small town and I did, after all, sell him his wholesale English beer for his villa. Judy and I just ran our lives and ran our bar and didn't let ourselves be worried by the reason we'd first come here. We treated it as a mistake . . . what the hell. People settle in places for all sorts of reasons. I was just the guy who runs Bill's Bar. Even Judy called me Bill in the bar.

Our lives were *orderly*.

It was nearly two months ago I spotted Grant with the girl. He has a convertible VW Golf and I saw them driving through town. Grant waved 'hullo'. I waved back. The girl next to him was a dark, dark brunette, almost black-haired. As far as I could see her sitting in the car she had a good figure. She was wearing a black cotton dress and it showed

172

her tan to good effect. Her skin was lightly oiled, I saw. She had a red scarf over her shoulders and she was holding it against the wind with her fingertips. As they passed I caught a glint of sunshine from her dark glasses, a flash of a smile aimed at Grant and then they were past me. I pushed through the tourist crowds till I reached the harbour. The Golf was parked there. Grant and his girlfriend in black were taking a table under the sunshade of the most expensive restaurant in Cristo. Blue shade dappled them. The waiter gave them a smarmy smile and bowed. The table had imported English roses on it, blood red and intense against the brilliant white of the starched table cloth. I stepped back into a grocer's doorway and watched them for ten minutes or so. I would have stayed longer but my leg began to hurt. I walked back to my bar and phoned Maher's office. He wasn't there but I spoke to his sergeant (a new one – Robson is now an Inspector).

'My name's Jenner. James Jenner. I want Mister Maher to send me a photograph of a woman called Alison May Clark. He has the address.'

The sergeant had never heard of me and I had to give him the message several times to make sure he'd got it right. I'd made the call from our living room above the bar. Downstairs I could hear the hubbub of my countrymen getting drunk. The day was as hot as hell. Sweat drenched my clothes. I leaned against the wall and felt the cold return of my shirt-back as it pressed against my skin. I felt slightly sick. Judy wasn't around and I wished she was. My heart was beating fast, my forehead was cold and clammy. I went downstairs and pushed myself to the bar. I wanted to drink to obliterate my feelings. I drank but it didn't work. I drank way into the evening when the barman decided enough was enough, even if I was the boss, and he phoned Judy in her friend's house in Malaga and she came home and they both carried me upstairs.

The woman was Alison May Duncan (née Clark) okay. There was no mistaking her from the photograph once it came, dyed hair or no dyed hair, phony American accent or no phony American accent. It was Alison. Grant even

173

brought her to my bar a few times. I stood arm's length away from her and poured them both brandies. I wasn't afraid of being found out. I was Bill MacDonald of Bill's Bar. As far as everyone in Cristo was concerned I was a nice young Englishman with a limp who'd done well in business and come to Spain to half-retire and run a little bar for fun and profit. My wife was just a wife – nearly invisible to outsiders. She was just a young woman with good legs she browned on the balcony above our bar late in the afternoons. If the Spaniards thought of me at all it was as 'the man of the woman with the legs'. So Lenny Grant brought Alison into the bar and introduced me to her as 'Bill' and her to me as 'Susan'. Judy didn't associate Grant's girlfriend with Alison and I didn't encourage her to . . . after all this was two years later and the woman with Grant was a brunette called Susan. I didn't let anyone apart from Maher know of my interest in the woman.

I was biding my time. I wanted her and Lenny Grant. I wanted them for personal reasons. For the poor stupid girl I'd let down. I wanted them for my own pride. I wanted them for justice . . . that's the word. Justice.

At first my plan had been to sit on them until the Spaniards changed their extradition laws. The Spanish would have to before they could join the EEC. The plan was that when the Spanish changed the law I'd pop back to London and lay an information with Maher. It was important not to lay the information too early because the birds would get wind of it and fly . . . to Brazil or Peru or somewhere.

That was the first plan. Then Maher phoned and said he had it from a source in the Home Office that the 'fugitive' legislation in Spain wasn't going to be retrospective.

'He's not sure,' said Maher, 'but that's what he's heard.'

Well, I decided not to take a chance. I began to plan a fishing trip.

Twenty-seven

I have a friend called Jesus.

Don't we all.

My one, though, is called Jesus Maria (fifteen other saints' names) Muela and is a used car dealer in Malaga. I suppose the used car business is doing well in Malaga, because Jesus has an American car with air-conditioning, a big house also with air-conditioning on the green hill above Cristo de Limpias and a fishing boat with no air-conditioning but a pair of Perkins diesels, a marine radio, a cassette player, a lavatory and three bunks. It's a pleasure fishing boat and he keeps it in the marina, not all scruffed up on the beach like real fishermen would. Real fishermen wouldn't have the bunks or the stereo cassette player either. Jesus likes his home comforts.

Jesus is a friend to me indeed. He lets me use his boat to fish with. I know damn all about fishing but I like driving his boat, so I take it out 'fishing' whenever I can get someone to go with me. I need a companion because I find it hard to get around the boat quickly. When I found out how the governments of Britain and Spain were letting me down I planned my fishing trip. I bought a map of the whole coast down to Gib. It looks like it's two hours with the twin Perkins running flat out. Then I waited till my delivery boy was off sick next (it happens about twice a week) and casually dropped a line at Len Grant.

'Here's your Bass. It's cans this time . . . yeah, I'm sorry but the supplier says there's trouble getting the bottled stuff down here. He says we should live in Barcelona . . . ha ha ha. Good joke, eh? By the way, I've got the loan of a little fishing boat, how about a trip out next week with your good lady and mine? The tuna will have started running.'

I wouldn't know a tuna from a mackerel. Jesus wouldn't know either from a '77 Buick, and he *owns* the fishing boat. I do know that when the tuna come into the Med they come through the Straits of Gibraltar, I mean how else would they do it, via Suez? I reckoned I could con my passengers into letting me float them south in a boat with a couple of fishing rods in their hands. I would then go to the heads (I know all the technical terms . . . it's a lavvy on a boat) and come out with a gun and a phrase something like, 'Okay sweetheart, now you get yours. Shaddup and drive this bus to Gib.' American accent non-compulsory.

First of all I sent Judy to London. That wasn't difficult. Her mother is old and broken-down and I know Judy feels guilty about making her sister take all the responsibility. The sister has a life to lead as well. I'm normally pretty negative about Judy disappearing to her mother's house for weeks on end. When I suggested it this time she leaped at the idea.

The next problem was what to do about a boat-hand. At first I thought of asking José, my useless noisy cleaner for my bar. He spent all the time he was in the bar tippling my brandy and boasting about the old days when he'd been a fisherman. I'd no doubt he could handle the boat, but it wasn't fair to let him put himself in danger without volunteering for it. And since I couldn't tell him the story, he couldn't volunteer. Also, I thought the Spanish government wouldn't take too kindly to him abducting foreigners. No, the problem was to find someone who'd do for the job but also it had to be someone who stood to gain from the job. Maher would be perfect, but I couldn't see the Commissioner's Office being very enthusiastic about one of their Detective Chief Superintendents going in for a touch of DIY extradition. That would be taking the spirit of private enterprise a little too far. I couldn't even *tell* Maher, for to tell him would be to compromise him. If I were to be able to pull this trick off, I'd need someone . . . but who?

The day after Judy set out to drive to London I flew there from Malaga. It doesn't take long. I was back the next morning.

Twenty Eight

The first place I went to in London was Northcliffe House, the offices of the *Daily Mail*. The big city was dusty and noisy and confusing, even though I'd once felt it was my own. On this visit I felt like a hick. Red buses boomed past me. Taxis whirled at junctions and raced off in the direction they'd come from. People pushed past me, rude, hurried. The ticket man at the tube station affected not to understand what I was asking for. Eventually I emerged at Chancery Lane Station and made my way down to the *Daily Mail* building feeling like a nervous foreigner.

'He doesn't work for us,' said the polite young man who saw me – even getting as far as him was a triumph of persistence – 'he's a freelancer. He doesn't work for anyone on a regular basis. He just comes up with his own stories.'

'Can't you give me his number? He knows me . . . he's written a couple of pieces on me.'

'I'm sorry.' The young journalist was dressed very formally, the way people would have dressed for his job in the nineteen-fifties. He pulled at the neat knot of his neat red tie and said, 'I'm sorry,' again.

'I've come all the way from Spain,' I said. 'I've come especially to see him and give him a story.'

'Wouldn't one of our staffers do if you just want to sell a story?'

I shook my head.

'Well, I can't help you, Mister . . . Mister. . . .'

'Jenner. I told the bloke in the commissionaire's outfit.'

The neatly dressed young man walked me down to the

door. His adam's apple bobbed as he walked, as if gravity had some effect on it.

'If you'll leave your number I'll have him call if he contacts us,' he said. It was by way of a consolation. I could see now, in the foyer, that they must get nutters in there all day every day asking for someone to sell a scoop to. Who could blame him for rejecting me?

'I haven't booked into an hotel yet,' I said. 'Here's my number in Spain. If he comes give it to him, would you?' He smiled like a young father confessor doling out indulgences, then handed me over to the commissionaires.

I walked a couple of blocks, then headed north to Holborn again, then north again through Gray's Inn. I went into the library in Theobalds Road and began looking through the Brands in the phone book. It was hopeless. Then I picked up the Yellow Pages. There it was . . . *Brand, E. F., Freelance Journalist*. Address and phone number. I went down to the entrance of the library. A young woman was arguing with a porter about whether she was entitled to leave her pram there. I pushed past them and called Brand on the public phone. He answered first time it rang.

My other visit in London was to Leytonstone. I went to see Wilkins. I got little Charlie. He greeted me like a long-lost brother.

'Jimmy, Oh Jimmy. It's good to see you. Well, we were only talking about you a few days ago, weren't we, boys?'

Two men I'd never seen before nodded agreement. We were in Wilkins' shabby plush room behind the bar of the Canary Club. Little Charlie indicated the door and the two men headed for it.

'Beer, Jimmy?'

I shook my head.

'Where's Wilkins?' I said.

'Semi-retired. I'm looking after the front-of-shop part of Mr Wilkins' business operations for him now. Any favours he owes you, consider I owe you.'

'Okay. It's a bit difficult.' I hesitated. Little Charlie hoisted himself onto the sofa and made himself comfortable.

I went on, 'I need a shooter. You know I'm running a club near Malaga now?'

He nodded. Well, I'd promoted my bar to a club . . . what was it to him?

'I have a problem with some heavy old villains moving in on me.' I said. 'So I want to keep a shooter, a pistol, in the place. I don't want anyone shooting at me and me trying to beat them off with a load of bread . . . you know? Even Spanish bread, Charlie. In the ordinary way a bar or club owner would approach the cops for a licence and then go and buy a gun. But I'm a foreigner. It's not allowed.'

He screwed up his tiny face, staring at me.

'If I could come by such an item, how would you get it into Spain?'

'Break it down and put it in my false leg,' I said. 'If I went back by ferry to France and then by train I won't have to go through any of those screening devices they have in airports.'

He thought for a while longer and then stood.

'Have a chair,' he said. 'I've got to make a phone call and there's no way I could do it from here . . . Er, Jimmy?'

'Yes?'

'You won't be reckless with a shooter if I get you one, will you?'

I shook my head.

'Scout's honour, Charlie.'

'Okay. Shout outside if you want a beer or a sandwich or anything. I'm off for about twenty minutes, okay?'

I waited. He was back in ten.

'I've got a geezer coming down from Gerona to give you one. It's a bit old fashioned, a Smith and Wesson. The sort the army used to have. Ever shot one?'

'Yes. I've shot one.'

'Right. Well this guy's doing me a favour. You don't need to pay him for the shooter but it wouldn't hurt anyone if you gave him a good drink for his trouble. He's driving halfway across Spain, he says.'

'Down it.'

'Yeah. That's right. Down it. Did you get your beer? Come on out to the bar then . . . you know Mr Wilkins is going to be *so* choked he's missed you.'

180

I think if he'd been big enough he would've put his arm round my shoulders. As it was Charlie had to content himself with holding the door open with an excess of politeness.

Twenty Nine

I'm on my balcony, trying to compose some note for my wife. I know I won't do it.

It's 7.30 a.m. now. I can hear José crashing about downstairs. Every morning he wakes Judy and me while he breaks the glasses he's supposed to be cleaning and shovels the dirt around from the centre of the bar to less obvious corners. I've never had the heart to sack him. Whenever he cleans Judy and me just lie up here giggling while he crashes around, then he stops and we know he's drinking the cheap brandy I leave out specially rather than have him going behind the counter and beating up my Remy Martin. I sat on my chair on the balcony thinking of the day ahead and thinking of all the things I should write to my wife. Then there was a banging on the shuttered door and an Englishman yelling.

'Jenner . . . hey! Jenner.'

I looked over the balcony and could see Brand standing in front of my shutters, hammering his bare fist on the door part of the shutters. I heard José go and open it.

'I want to speak to Mister Jenner,' Brand said. 'He's expecting me.'

'We no open now. Lunchertime, efen-ing only opening this bar. You go there to café. Good café.'

'I want to speak to Mister Jenner,' Brand repeated patiently.

'No. No Jenner.'

Leaning over the railings I could see José's hand outside the shutter. The finger was waggling back and forth, metronome-style to emphasise the 'no'.

'You go over there.' The hand pointed at the café.

'Let him in!' I yelled. I finished my beer. Beer for breakfast. It was cold, blond Spanish beer and the bottle dribbled it onto my journal. I went downstairs and told José to pull up all the shutters, then to take off home. Brand slid onto a barstool and I pulled the cap off a beer for him. A couple of flies circled lazily over the counter. José heaved the shutters half-up, then eyed the bottle of cheap brandy. I threw him the Remy Martin and said, 'Go home to your wife. I'll see you tomorrow.'

I didn't believe I would though.

Brand smiled.

'An old friend?' he said. It was a stupid question and I ignored it. Brand was nervous. I'd kept him hanging around my bar for three days. When I'd phoned him in London I'd told him he was on to a scoop. A real one. I'd told him Alison May Clark was not dead and buried in Kensal Green but alive and well and living in Malaga. I'd lied about where she was (I mean Malaga versus Cristo) because I hadn't wanted him ferreting around Cristo on his own account.

I didn't like Brand but I could use him. He was a small, tubby Englishman with balding sandy hair and – since he'd been in Spain – a peeling red face. He'd decided when he'd come out that the designer-jeans-and-cheesecloth-shirt was not for him. He was right. He'd have looked like a sweaty cheddar cheese on a denim plinth. Brand went instead for the colonial Africa look: jackets from Alkit with padded triangles clipped in the shoulders, white cotton trousers, heavy, English-leather Jesus-boots. He looked as if he was into Evelyn Waugh in a big way. He stuck out in Cristo like a sore thumb, and I only hoped Lenny and Alison hadn't seen him in my bar.

'Have a beer, Eric. You and me should start the day by drinking some beer. This is going to be a very unconventional day. I'm going fishing. *We*'re going fishing. We're going to be fishers of men.'

Brand grinned and drank his second beer. Shafts of light fell through the half-raised shutters. The area around our feet was flooded with light, but from the waist up we were striped men of darkness.

'Thanks, Jenner.'

183

A trickle of sweat ran down his brow. I could see dampness under the arms of his linen jacket. Sweat adhered to his peeling, unshaven cheeks, then slipped slowly on to his cracked-skin thick lips.

'Today the story happens for you, Eric. Today you have included yourself on a scoop. A real one.'

He nodded. He was pleased. This was why he'd come.

'Good. What's the plan?'

I slapped his shoulder. 'Drink your beer, kid. Leave the planning to me.'

He swigged the beer and stared at me. I must have looked mad.

'Whereabouts in Malaga are they?' he said.

'Nowhere . . . you're sweating. Are you hot?'

Brand nodded that he was hot. I don't think it was the heat which made him sweat, though. I think it was that he was near the lode. He wanted it. He was compulsive, like an old lady on the machines in Las Vegas.

Past Brand, in the street, I saw a kid walk by with his mongrel. Or rather I saw the mongrel and I saw the kid's skinny legs. I walked over to the shuttered door and pushed it wide. I wanted some air. The street was white, then heavy dark shadows fell where the buildings sheltered each other. I was in shadow, brilliantly lit after the darkness of my bar, but still in shadow. The kid with the dog turned and waved but I didn't recognise him. He was standing in the white light by then and I couldn't see him properly. Sweat trickled down my neck, down my back. I could taste the salt on my upper lip. And the day had only just begun. Some men smoked cigarettes down at the corner. Wisps of smoke lifted above them, fat old palms surrounded them, like a crowd. A blue-white sky beat down on us. A couple of black birds strutted up the road, then flapped away as a dusty car passed.

I turned to look across to the café. The waiter nodded to me and I nodded back. A tall man splashed olive oil along a loaf and held it up to eat. He was deep in the darkness of the café and I could only see his head and torso. His face was olive-coloured and pain-featured. All the men in the bar were workers who were breaking-off for breakfast. The tourists came at lunchtime. Since my bar was an English bar I never bothered to open before lunch. The English spent better but they didn't get up in the morning to do it. Right at that moment I felt very warm towards the Spaniards.

I went back in and said to Brand, 'If you want coffee we'll have to go across the way.' I was half hoping he'd say 'yes.'

'I'm okay,' he replied.

'I've got a coffee machine but it takes twenty minutes to start up, so I'm not starting it just for us.'

He didn't answer. I leaned under the bar counter and came up with a plastic bag.

'What do you make of these?' I said.

He smacked his lips and stared at the counter.

'Army issue Smith and Wesson pistol, a bit on the veteran side of vintage. The other one's a sawn-off twelve-bore. Yes?'

He looked tense. I hadn't mentioned guns before. I hadn't even told him exactly *how* Alison Clark and Len Grant were going to be arrested. Brand thought he was just here to watch and then he could sell his world exclusive to the highest bidder. The guns changed all that. He laughed a cracked laugh.

'I thought you'd become just a bar-owner now. What d'you need all the ironmongery for?'

'To go fishing with,' I said. I stood behind the counter with my hand on the guns. 'Don't worry, I'm not going to shoot you.'

Brand made his cracked laugh again.

'So what's it all about? I thought you said they were going to be arrested. Where? What do the guns have to do with it?' he said.

'The police will do the arresting in Gibraltar. The guns are to go fishing with. I'm going fishing and you're coming along to steer the boat.'

Brand smacked his lips and shook his head over his drink. I said nothing. I rang an English number from a wall-phone behind the bar. There was no answer. I rang another.

'Denis? Hi. It's Jimmy here. Listen, Denis, I need you to do something. I want you to wait till about one o'clock your time, that's two ours. Then I want you to give my pal

185

Maher a ring and tell him he needs to have someone standing by at Gibraltar quayside for a fishing boat registered A-alpha A-alpha C-charlie-eight from Malaga, Spain. Tell him it'll have Alison Duncan, Lenny Grant, a journalist called Brand and me on board. No, Brand's just coming for the ride and the story. He's nothing to do with the other two. I don't think Maher will be very surprised when you call him . . . and Denis! Don't call him any earlier, please. Think of this as the last instalment of the favour I did you over the Zorba business.'

Brand put his beer down when I rang off. He closed his eyes and said, 'Are you serious?' Then opened them and stared at me while I put the guns back in the plastic bag and back under the counter. I didn't answer him.

'How do you know I won't tell the Spaniards?' he said. 'How do you know I don't have enough of a story already anyway?'

'I don't,' I said. 'But this is a real cracker, a real scoop. And I think you're not able to pass it up. I reckon you'll want to be on the quay in Gib making notes and snapping away with your Kodak Instamatic. I don't think any journalist could turn it down.'

'Say we're caught?'

'So what? I'm the one with the guns, I'm the one abducting them. You're just a third party. All you have to do is keep your nerve and steer the boat.'

He sighed. He put his beer glass on my counter and I topped another bottle for him. He poured it, sighed and said, 'You're right. I'll do it. You knew I would, eh? Is that why you asked me out here? A staffer couldn't take a chance on being caught, eh?'

I didn't answer. He knew that was why. He looked at his hands and then at me.

'What makes you think I'll keep my nerve?'

I tapped the counter above the guns.

'These. You let me down and I'll shoot you before I shoot them. You'll be more frightened of me than them. I've got the guns.'

Brand eased himself off his stool.

'I think I believe you,' he said. He was right to believe me. By that stage I'd have done anything rather than give

186

up my targets. I was using Brand because I needed a crewman. It was the only way I could think of finding someone who had as much to gain as me by transporting Alison and Lenny. I reckoned his greed for a story that was a real winner would lead him to do almost anything. It was a gamble bringing him in but one I had to take.

Thirty

I went down to the marina at eleven. Row on row of expensive marine hardware seemed to be used only as lilos for pretty girls. 'Here's a daybed, darling. It only cost two hundred and fifty thousand quid and takes four men to run it.' Jesus's boat was down with the more modest ones, though even the modest ones have more in common with a floating motorhome than a trawler. I threw my bag on the deck, then eased myself down off the floating wooden pier. Anyone else would've jumped. I can't. The boat's handrail was burning hot, it stung my fingers. The sky above was clear and the sun was approaching its noon position . . . right over the top of my neck. In half an hour the girls lying on the expensive boats would have to go in or be fried.

I pulled open the door to the saloon. A wave of hot air burst out, beating my face. My shirt was wet with sweat. I could feel salt on my lips. Inside even the soft furnishings were hot to touch. The varnish on the wood felt sticky; maybe it was my imagination. Maybe it was my hand that was sticky. I opened up the hatch to the Perkins, checked their oil, ran my hand along the tappet covers . . . I don't know why. I just needed to touch them. I'd checked the oil only last night. I tucked the sawn-off behind the fire extinguisher, in a corner behind where the hatch opened. A quick look round would never find it, but anything more than that would. Then I went up to the lavatory and stuck the Smith and Wesson under the little wash basin with some gaffer tape. It wasn't very secure and if the sea got rough someone would find themselves with a shooter between their feet while they were having a pony. I didn't expect to be at sea for long enough to let things get rough, weatherwise.

I went back into the little saloon and lay on one of Jesus's bunks. The heat was stifling. I dozed a while. Then I heard someone on deck.

'Jimmy. Hey, Jimmy.'

It was Brand. He sat in the wheelman's chair and oozed sweat and fear.

'You okay?' I said.

He nodded.

'I'm okay. I've brought a friend.' He pulled a bottle of scotch from his bag. 'Want some?'

I said, 'Yes', took the bottle from him and threw it in the drink. He looked as if he was about to cry.

'I'll buy you another in Gibraltar. Have you checked out of your hotel?'

'Yes.'

'Paid?'

'It was a package. I told you. The bloke in the hotel thought I was mad. Haven't you even got some beer?'

'No. There's a kettle down there.' I pointed with my thumb at the saloon. 'Make us some tea.'

'Tea?'

'That's right, *tea*. Then familiarise yourself with the boat. Then come back up here and help me cast off.'

'What about our passengers?' He scratched absently at some peeling skin on his arm.

'We're picking them up at the end of the mole. On the way I have to pick up fuel. I have a gun behind the fire extinguisher in the engine compartment and another taped under the handbasin down there . . . if you should need them.'

Brand's piggy blue eyes narrowed.

'You don't want me to handle a gun do you? I've never done it.'

'No I don't. I want you to know where they are. Then I want you to put the kettle on. Then I want you to come up here and help me put the sun-canopy up before we catch fire or melt, then I want you to cast off the ropes that are tying us to that wooden pier. Got it?'

Brand went below. I turned the key next to the steering

189

wheel so that the plugs would warm in the Perkins, then after a few seconds I turned the key right round so that it spun the self-starter. The engines whined but didn't catch. I left it.

Brand came up and began to pull at one end of the canopy. The blue canvas was bleached by the sun, the metal stays had been pitted by salt, then painted. We heaved at the canopy until it covered the entire after-part of the boat. Then I went and turned the engine key again.

'Trouble?' said Brand.

'No trouble.'

The engines whirred when I turned the key to 'start', then they caught. I revved them for a few seconds, then let the roar die to a throaty burbling sound. Blue diesel smoke drifted lazily across the marina. White light glinted on the little wavelets, then on to my eyes. It was like looking into a glistening white kaleidoscope. Black silhouette figures moved among the tied-up boats. Brand let the ropes go, then jumped back aboard and I gunned the engines and headed for the service pier.

Lenny Grant and Alison Duncan were waiting on the end of the mole, as we had arranged. Alison was wearing a white linen 'sackdress', dark glasses and a white hat tied down with a scarf. Her dyed dark hair peeped from under the hat and scarf. Her lips were full and strong, with red lipstick. I couldn't see her eyes. Grant was sitting on a wicker hamper. He was wearing a short sleeve blue Breton fisherman's shirt and crisp white trousers. He looked as if Harrods or Simpsons had kitted him out for fishing. I never knew Grant in London. I only spoke to him on the phone in Florida the once. Though he was in his late thirties he was tall and dark and well muscled. He looked ten years younger. I don't know how he was in his London days, but the man I picked up on the mole didn't look like a former boxing manager, not if boxing managers were like George Duncan. Leonard Grant looked like he was a retired male model. He had a good tan and a strong jawline and an easy, graceful way of moving. He stood from the hamper and waved to us. I waved back and drew the boat alongside.

We bobbed a little in the swell. Grant handed the hamper to Brand.

'Okay?' He grinned. 'Be careful with that. It has our supper in it.'

Brand helped Alison onto the boat. He stared at her so much I was sure he'd give the game away.

'Be careful with her, too,' Grant said, and leaped aboard. He was very jolly and helped Brand take the hamper down to the saloon.

'No Judy?' Alison said.

'No.' I shook my head and opened up the engines to take us clear of the concrete mole and into open sea. 'She had to go to England for a couple of days.'

'Oh.'

'She'll be there tonight when we get back, I should think.'

Alison nodded. She sat back and clasped her hands on her lap. I looked at them and thought about the girl under the arch in Shoreditch. These were the hands that had done it, I was sure. I'd looked at her hands like that sometimes in my bar. Grant and Brand came out to the deck area again, both carrying bottles of beer and tipping them up to drink.

'I told him you didn't want any,' said Brand.

'Okay.'

'Where's the fishing gear?' said Grant.

'Down the side of the boat in that long box. I can't get it out on my own. . . . I have a bad leg. You know.'

He nodded. A pleasant breeze was running against us and we were having to lift our voices a little to speak clearly. The canvas of the deck canopy flapped above my head. Spray bounced over the bows.

'I'm going out until we get in the stream, about fifteen miles', I called. 'Then we'll get the canopy rolled back and get the fishing gear out. We'll turn towards the Straits and troll upstream for a couple of hours, then downstream until we get back to our starting point. That's what the guy who owns the boat told me to do. He knows all about fish.' Grant nodded agreement, then he climbed forward and leaned over the bow.

'How long?' he called back.

I turned the boat into the swell and set the engines a little faster.

'Three hours this direction. We'll start trolling before four. Then a couple of hours upstream, one back. That's three clear hours fishing. You see the basket of mackerel? That's our bait. We should be all over fishing by seven thirty, then I reckon three hours back to Cristo maximum . . . more like two running with this swell. Should get back for ten.' The finest sea spray flew around Grant's body and he waved and grinned again to show he'd heard.

Oh God, I thought. I hope he doesn't know about fishing, because I don't and Jesus was no good to me on that score at all. He just offered me the use of as many Abba tapes as I wanted and kept bothering me about was I bringing a girl. I bought the mackerel from a fishing smack on the way out to the mole. The fishermen nearly burst a gut laughing when I said '*Tonno*' for the fish we wanted. How long are you staying out there for? they asked, with tears streaming down from their eyes and all their backs red-raw and sore because of all the slapping that had been going on. 'A few hours,' I'd said, and they'd all laughed as if they couldn't bear it, the Englishman was so stupid, and one called out, 'Six weeks is more like it,' and they all laughed again. They sold me the mackerel and they took my money anyway, with that special Spanish philanthropy they often reserve for foreigners . . . especially Englishmen.

Alison settled down to stare at her nails and be beautiful in one of the fishing chairs. I gave Brand the wheel because I thought it would keep him out of trouble, then I went down and lay on a bunk which was both too short and too narrow for me. I wanted to relax. After half an hour Alison came down and sat on the bunk opposite. She took her scarf and hat and sunglasses off and shook her head so that her hair swung. I could have gone to the law and pulled the gun then but I wanted to be out of Spanish waters first.

'Well, Bill,' she said, 'how are you?'

'Not bad,' I said. I was lying on my back as best I could holding a pulp novel above my head as if I were reading it.

'What took our Judy to England?'

'Family stuff, you know. It's boring. Have you been to England, Susan?'

She shook her head.

'I met Len when he was working back home . . . in the States, I mean. And I guess I just,' she laughed nervously, 'well, you know . . . fell in love. So I followed him here.'

'What a nice story,' I said.

She smiled appreciatively. Her American accent was fake, of course, but then so many Americans give themselves fake English accents that she was just bad enough to be accepted by anyone who didn't know. I knew. I hated her. I thought about the guns again. Alison ran her hands down her shins, then caught me watching her.

'Like them?' she said.

I nodded.

'Lenny says they're my best asset. What do you think?' She turned herself a little one way, then a little the other, showing me both profiles.

'I like your face,' I said. 'I've always thought your face is your best asset, Susan. A woman's face is her fortune. Where would she be without it?'

'Where indeed?' she said, and smiled. The hamper was between us, facing her. She flapped the lid open and began to rummage inside.

'Glass of wine? Sandwich? I think Lenny's even put some real caviar in here . . . *doesn't* he know how to live?'

I looked forward. Facing the bow the cabin had two oblong windows made of thick glass. They were screwed into place like portholes, with big brass clips holding them down. I could see Len Grant through one window, at least I could see his feet. I could see the basket of mackerel-bait through the other window. A seagull landed on the basket's edge and peered into it. Suddenly the bird flopped forward into the basket. Len leaned down and grinned at us through the glass. He pulled the dead bird out of the basket and held it against the window. The head had been smashed with a bullet through the eye. The bird's blood smeared the glass. I could see Len was holding a stubby revolver in his other hand. He dropped the bird and slapped his hand against the glass to steady himself. He grinned again and mouthed some words, waving the little gun.

I turned and looked at Alison. She had leaned back from

the hamper and was holding a sandwich in one hand and the brother of Grant's revolver in the other.

'I think he's asking you to put your hands up, Jimmy Jenner,' she said. She bit into her sandwich slowly and voluptuously. Alison had all the time in the world. I was struck by that thought, and the image of my time running out. I'd misjudged them.

'Why?' I said.

'Oh . . . I think he'd like you to do it for lots of reasons.' She brushed a crumb from her lips with the mouth of her gun-barrel. 'But you can put them down. I don't like a lot of drama. Just tell me where your gun is, Jimmy, and that'll be enough for me.'

The American accent had gone completely.

She shook her head slowly and sighed. The bright light from the oblong windows fell across her face, first one side then the other. She fired the pistol into my leg. I cried out and lay back on the bunk.

'Give me your gun or I'll fire it into your real leg,' she said.

'It's tucked behind the fire-extinguisher just in that hatch. I'll fetch it if you want.'

She waved the nose of the little gun.

'You sit right where you are. I just wanted to know where it is.'

I sat right where I was. The room stank from the explosion. I tried to move my ankle a little but it stayed stuck.

'You've shot it through the bloody joint,' I said. I was raising my voice, I knew. I'd been deafened by the pistol shot.

'Bring him out!' Grant yelled.

I climbed the three steps to the deck with difficulty, dragging my false leg like a pirate with one of those stiff wooden things they wear in pantomimes. Grant was at the wheel. He swung the boat from south south east to due east.

'Where are we going?' I said. 'Libya?'

'*We're* going back to Spain,' said Alison. '*You* and your boat are going to sink, way out there at sea.'

'Doesn't that leave a little problem about getting back?'

'Not for us.' Alison said. 'We're being met. You'll have to make your own arrangements.'

Brand was standing in the doorway where Grant had shoved him. His eyes widened in horror.

'You're going to make us swim?'

Alison shook her head.

'No. Of course not. Someone might find you. We're going to shoot you and sink your boat. We'll weight your bodies down, of course.' There was a kindly edge to her voice.

Brand's eyes got even wider. His face twisted, whether in anger or horror I'll never know. He began to lift his hands and take a step forward. Grant shot him twice, once in the chest, once in the head. A big weal of torn flesh appeared, red and glistening above Brand's eye and along his temple. White bone showed through the red tear for a second. Brand clutched his hands to the hole in his shirt front. It was a little hole and it didn't bleed much.

'My God,' he said slowly. 'My God. I'm shot.'

He lifted one hand away from the hole and looked at the smear of his own blood on his palm before using the hand to steady himself on the door jamb.

'I'm shot,' he said again. 'They've bloody shot me.'

He raised his eyes accusingly to mine, then Grant shot him again, high up on the sternum, and this time he did give out a little bow-tie of splashed blood onto his shirt before toppling heavily back into the little cabin. The door swung back and forth, banging lightly on its brass catch with each wave, before one heavier wave made it snap shut on Brand's body.

An hour later we were still heading due east. I was at the wheel. Grant was sitting on the bow drinking from a green glass beer bottle and sweating in the sun. Every now and then he looked out through a pair of binoculars. Alison sat in one of the fishing chairs covering me with a gun.

'Doesn't your hand get tired?'

'You'd better hope it doesn't, Jimmy Jenner, because when I get too tired to hold the gun on you I'll shoot you.'

I looked round at her. She had the sunglasses on again and she looked as if she would shoot me. She was going to eventually, anyway. Her sunglasses were the deepest black. I couldn't see Alison's eyes behind them. I could only see the reflection of the horizon, a flash of sunlight as her head from time to time moved. Waves ran against the dark glass but didn't break. Then my bearded face appeared, and she was about to speak but checked herself.

'How did you recognise me?' I said. 'I've never advertised who I am in Cristo. We'd never even met.'

She shook her head slowly and pointed the gun at me.

'Look where you're going, Jenner. I don't want to bump into anything.'

I looked forward. Apart from the bow, Grant and the horizon there was nothing to see. I kept staring forward though. I didn't want to give her an excuse to shoot me. She'd be doing that soon enough.

Suddenly I was aware of Alison close by my side, almost as an animal presence. She spoke softly.

'George was going broke. That . . . well, Wilkins was driving him out of the business. It was Wilkins' revenge for George taking me. Ha! *Taking* me. I *ran* to him. How could I live with a pig like Wilkins?'

I didn't answer. The steady throb of the diesels ran through us, the sea thudded on the hull. The sun burned my eyes. My head was on the throttles. She was quiet for a long time, then she said, 'We decided one of us had to die, then we could claim the insurance. George had a lot of money for insurance . . . you know about all that of course. What you don't know is that we scoured England for a detective as stupid as you. Then I remembered reading a piece in a newspaper about a bloke with one arm and one leg or something who reckoned he was a detective. When I looked it up I came up with you . . . then George remembered he'd already known you.'

'I've got both arms,' I said, still looking forward. She was touching my shoulder now, and the gun was digging into my side; not hard, just enough to remind me it was there.

'Yes, you have. Well you turned out a bit cleverer than George and I thought, Jenner. Not *much* cleverer, but enough to be a nuisance.'

'But how did you know it was me in Cristo?'

'I *recognised* you. That very first day I saw you here in

196

Cristo, hiding in the shop door while Lenny and I were having lunch . . . what do you think you are, invisible? I thought it was you the minute I saw you. Lenny phoned your wholesaler to check. He asked when Mister Jenner's order was due. The clerk said Mister Jenner's order would be along as usual, but if he wanted to make a supplementary he'd take it now. Simple. One Englishman speaking bad Spanish sounds the same as another.'

I nodded. The wholesaler had my real name because I always paid by cheque. Grant was leaning over the bow now. I didn't know why, then I heard him retch.

'Your friend's not all that well,' I said.

Alison leaned on me, her cotton-covered breast touching my bare arm, her face was close to mine, her gun sticking into my ribs. She said nothing. I could see nothing except the reflection of my own face in her glasses. I saw myself reflected in her. I shivered.

'Who was the girl I drove from Saffron to London?' The words stuck in my throat. I leaned away from her so I was against the safety rail. I could see Lenny-the-bad-sailor chundering over the bow and every now and then a waft of it would come back on the spray. Alison leaned close again and stuck the gun in my ribs again, so hard this time it hurt. She held her face up to mine as if she would be kissed.

'Don't think of jumping overboard, Jenner. I would just as well shoot you in the water as on the boat. I don't care.'

'What about our bodies?' I said. 'Won't you have some explaining to do?'

She laughed. I could feel her breath on my face as she did it. Her spit landed on my lips.

'We're not going back. You two and your boat are going down and you're never going to be found.'

'Don't tell me,' I said, 'someone's waiting ahead with another boat . . . your brother?'

She laughed again.

'A *fast* boat.' She smiled a red-lipsticked smile and ran her tongue over her pearly teeth. 'And yes you're right, my brother's waiting for us.'

'And we get to die, just like before with the girl. Where *was* she from?'

'She was just some prossie. George found her at Kings

Cross. Gave her a story about standing-in as his wife for a couple of days as part of a con he was working. He gave her a few quid.'

'A few quid?'

'A hundred.'

The boat pitched forward and Lenny retched.

'Is that all she was worth? What am *I* worth?'

'A lot of trouble, that's what you're worth. Why all the fuss about some bloody prossie? Did she do a trick for you, Jenner? Is that it?'

This time she stuck the gun even harder into my ribs and leaned up and kissed me on the lips. I wanted to slap her, to spit in her face.

'Did you get the idea for the face job in Smithfield?' I said against her mouth. She kissed me hard again and said, 'How clever you are. How very clever.' She stepped back. 'You've got it all worked out. I killed George too. I hadn't left England at all before then. I didn't for months even after I shot him. Then I went out to Baltimore and set up with Lenny and my brother, but Lenny had to come here. Some very important people he was involved with in America thought he should come. So he came and I've waited till now. I wasn't sure at all about coming back to Europe. . . . Things were pretty good for me as they were.' She laughed again. 'Did you know *he* never knew who you were at all?' she added as an afterthought. 'And all the time you were waiting for me.'

'Not quite. I didn't know you'd turn up. You didn't *need* Lenny. You had George's money, right?'

'*My* money. *I* died for it. What would a good looking woman like me be doing squandering over three hundred thousand on *him*? No, once he told me Harry had phoned to say the police thought he was up to something with me I thought, 'George, my love, you are just going to *have* to go'.

'The suicide wasn't very convincing.'

'I was improvising.' She held the gun up to my head. 'Boom! Like that I went, then I wrapped his hand round the gun. It was the best I could do. He had all the money ready. He thought I was going to run away with him. The suicide was crude but it didn't matter. No one was looking

198

for George's dead wife except you because you were the only one who knew the girl I dumped in Shoreditch wasn't me. We always knew the person we chose for that part might catch on but we reckoned if we used a really rotten, stupid, useless detective it wouldn't matter. No one would take any notice of him.'

Grant retched again, then yelled, 'Boat!' gagging as he did. Alison said, 'So far I've been right,' then turned to look at the boat. 'It's him okay!' she said. 'Looks like the end of the line for you, Jenner.'

She held up the gun and kept it on me for a long time. I could see her finger moving on the trigger. I could hear Lenny retching in the bow. The boat he'd seen was a couple of miles in front of us.

'What will you do about *him*? I said. 'What'll happen when you need to unload him?'

She smiled.

'Why do you think we're all out here?' She said. 'We've realised all our assets, Lenny and me, ready to skip once we'd disposed of you. I don't want to skip with Lenny, though. I've found a nice fellow in Baltimore. An Italian. He'll suit me fine. I thought you and Lenny could die in a shoot-out . . . isn't that a good one?'

'I suppose it is. When will he find out?'

She squeezed the trigger lightly again and said 'Boom!', then she let the gun drop a little.

'He'll find out soon enough.'

She was right. The other boat was coming up fast. Its engines had been started and it was running straight towards us. It was a pleasure fishing boat like ours, only bigger. I could see the dark figure of a man at the wheel as the boat approached. A little closer yet and I could see he was wearing a dark, peaked cap, dark glasses and denim clothes. He swung his boat so that it came to rest beam-on about a hundred yards ahead. Alison stepped back from me and grinned. I knew if I was to try anything it would have to be now. My mouth was dry and my stomach was churning. Alison waved at the dark figure in the other boat and he waved back.

'Come *on*,' she said. 'Get a move on, Jenner.'

I saw a figure move behind the one at the wheel of the

other boat. I couldn't see Grant but I could hear him. I knew that I had to move now but I had no idea what I should do. Alison was too far away for me to jump her. She'd shoot me first. We came closer yet to the other boat. She took her eye off me a second and waved at it again. There was a flash behind the man at the wheel and Alison staggered backwards. She hit the bulkhead and dropped her gun. I bent over her and picked it up. Her neck had been torn open. Blood seeped into the sackdress. Her eyes were open and she was conscious. Air bubbled the tear in her neck every time she breathed. There was a film of sweat on her brow.

I stood up with the gun and shut off the engines. Lenny turned and began to advance. He clearly hadn't heard the shot or seen the flash from the other boat. I pointed my gun at him.

'Stand off, mate. And I bet I'm a better shot than you.'
He kept his gun on me. The other boat approached.
'Jenner! You all right?' a voice called. I didn't recognise it. 'Jenner!'

'Drop the gun now, Lenny,' I said. 'Don't be a hero. You haven't killed anyone.'

Lenny dropped the gun. It slid off the deck and into the sea.

'I'm okay!' I shouted. 'Who are you?'
The boat drew alongside. The man in the denim and the dark glasses threw a rope over. A very small man took his place at the wheel and the man in denim jumped over to me once we'd drawn the boats close together.

Wilkins.
'Is she dead?' he said.
'Not yet.'
He went over and kicked Alison.
'Cow. She soon will be. I won't waste another bullet on her. I'll have him and we'll be on our way.'

I sat heavily in the wheelman's chair.
'Hang on.' I said, 'What are *you* doing here?'
'I wanted that cow more than you did, Jenner. She set me up. And you can't go wandering round London asking for bent shooters without anyone asking themselves "what does he want that for?" With you there could only be one

200

real answer, I reckoned, so little Charlie and me came out here.' Alison groaned and Wilkins scowled. Lenny was sitting on the roof of the cabin, gazing at us in open-mouthed astonishment. Wilkins talked about his trip to Cristo. He was chuckling all the time except when Alison groaned. Then he looked angry. Eventually she groaned one time too many for him and he pulled a little revolver from his pocket and leaned over her and shot her in the head. The bullet went in the middle of the brow and fragments from the back of her skull ricocheted around the steering well like pieces of shrapnel. She didn't lie still though. Her legs and arms flapped on and on, like newly-landed fish. Wilkins had to talk with the soft sound of the flaps and thuds Alison's body made on the deck.

'We followed her brother down to the Marina early this morning, but he spotted us so we had to grab him. He told us about the meeting out here. They'd had you taped for ages, Jimmy. This fishing trip you planned was a godsend. You walked into it.'

Lenny shook his head. He didn't moan or cry or retch or anything now though and I didn't blame him. Wilkins wasn't going to waste much time on them.

'Got a beer, Charlie?' he yelled. Charlie lobbed a can over. 'Open it for us,' said Wilkins. I did and got soaked in foamy beer. He thought it was hilarious.

'Why did the brother tell you?' I asked. 'Why not keep his mouth shut?'

'He did at first. We encouraged him to open it. Now let's get down to business. My plan is we shoot this slag and sink the boat. Then you come back with us and say the boat sank somewhere else. That way everybody's happy . . . eh?'

I shook my head. 'Wait a minute,' I said. I went below and brought up my guns.

'Get in the cabin,' I called to Grant. He climbed past us without a word and went below. I locked the cabin door on him.

'I'm taking him back.'

Wilkins shook his head now and he wasn't laughing any more.

'No.'

'You'll have to shoot me as well, because I have a gun

and I don't intend to see you shoot him and do nothing,' I said. 'If you kill him you'll have to kill me.'

'How do you know I won't?'

I threw the sawn-off and the Smith and Wesson over the side. I pushed Alison's revolver into Wilkins' fat stomach.

'Because I like and trust you,' I said. 'Because you've saved my life. Because I'm going to keep your name out of any reports of what's happened here. Grant won't say anything because life in an English prison wouldn't be too good for him if he did, I guess. *I* won't say anything. All you've done here is to shoot a woman who was about to shoot me. I'm willing to say I had a struggle and overcame her. Don't you think that's better?'

He took my wrist and pulled my gun out of his fat stomach. Wilkins' grey eyes glared at me. His face darkened. I thought he would shoot me and then go on for Grant. I was sure he would. We'd just watched him murder Alison. Wilkins raised his gun to my face and then turned away quickly. He climbed back into his own boat.

'Can you hear me, Grant?' he called.

A muffled 'yes' came from the cabin.

'You do exactly what this man says. Any messing about and I'll be back for you. And I won't bring a shooter. I won't need one.'

I freed the line and little Charlie gunned the big motors. The sea churned behind them.

'No one owes any favours now, Jenner,' Wilkins called. 'We're all square. You just remember that.'

When they'd gone Grant carried Brand's body from the cabin. 'How do you know I won't tell?' He said. 'I saw what he did to her and the cops'll love it. I'll tell all right.'

'You won't have to,' I said. 'I will.' I locked him in the cabin again.

I eased the engines up and set the course to a few degrees west of south west, which I reckoned would take us to Gibraltar. Then I sat back in the wheelman's chair and shivered, even though the sun was high in the sky. I was still shivering when I reached the Rock.